WEDDING

Belles

Other Books by Melanie Jacobson
Perfect Set
Southern Charmed
Painting Kisses
Always Will
Twitterpated
Second Chances
Smart Move
Not My Type
The List

Other Books by Jenny Proctor
The House at Rose Creek
Mountains Between Us
Love at First Note
Wrong For You

Other Books by Becca Wilhite
My Ridiculous Romantic Obsessions
Bright Blue Miracle
Check Me Out

Other Books by Brittany Larsen
Pride and Politics
Sense and Second Chances
The Matchmakers Match

WEDDING *Belles*

A NOVEL IN FOUR PARTS

MELANIE JACOBSON
JENNY PROCTOR
BECCA WILHITE
BRITTANY LARSEN

Part 1: Harper and Zak

By Melanie Jacobson

Chapter One

Harper stared at the sample menu in front of her and dug deep into her etiquette training to find a way to say, "Absolutely not," in a way that would make the caterer in front of her feel complimented, not rejected.

"You certainly have fresh ideas, Mr. Choi." There. That was a diplomatic start. She hoped it didn't sound sarcastic since he looked to be her age, in his late twenties at most.

"Call me Zak." He smiled at her. It was a good smile, toothpaste-ad quality, and with the laugh lines crinkling around his dark brown eyes, it could have been irresistible if Harper was looking for a man. But she wasn't.

"But my clientele is very traditional," she continued. And really, her office should have tipped him off. She'd designed it to look like an elegant Charleston sitting room. "I used a caterer last month for a garden party who put Dijon mustard in the potato salad and it created such a ruckus that it upstaged Beth Martin's hundred-year-old hydrangeas. And that was a tragedy I'm not sure Miss Beth will ever recover from. So this . . ." she waved her hand to encompass the menu, "would push my clients too far. But I wish you good luck finding your client base."

There was no way he was going to find a client base in Charleston with the edgy offerings he'd listed on his menu. At least not with the old money families Harper was targeting on her quest to become Charleston's premiere event planner.

His smile dimmed, and he sat forward and cleared his throat. "I realize that most of this town still considers Julia Child revolutionary for introducing French cooking techniques, but that makes them ripe for the next food revolution. There's a whole world waiting for them if they can evolve past coq au vin."

Harper frowned. She happened to like chicken in wine sauce. The first time she'd had it at a sorority banquet, she'd felt a flush of luxury that was new to her, the little girl from scruffy Goose Creek who got Hamburger Helper on special occasions.

"Sorry." She pushed the menu back across her desk, not sorry at all. "But your information isn't correct. Charleston is full of innovative restaurants who have connected to a customer base that loves what they serve. But I serve a coq au vin crowd and I use caterers who serve coq au vin." Even the name sounded fancy and French, and she liked the way it unfurled on her tongue, unlike . . . what was it? She flicked her eyes over to his menu again. Ah, yes. *Bulgogi.* Her clients wanted a prime rib, reliably sliced and served with mashed potatoes. If they were feeling adventurous, maybe they'd walk on the wild side and make them garlic mashed.

His smile had disappeared, and his sharp cheekbones suddenly stood out without his smile to soften them. She wondered idly what his ancestry was. Based on the Korean influences in the menu he gave her plus his last name, she'd guess a Korean father, but he didn't look full Korean. Maybe a white mother? They'd each done him a favor and passed on their best bits because even his scowl didn't diminish his good looks. She wondered which one of them was to blame for his short temper.

"Thank you for coming in." She pushed back from her desk to indicate that their meeting was at an end, but when he made no move to leave, she hesitated in an awkward half-crouch above her chair before sitting again. "Was there something else?"

"Do you know what foodways are?" he asked.

She blinked at him. "Is that . . . a grocery chain?"

His lips stretched in a quick smile, a mean cousin to the one he'd offered her only a few minutes before. "Foodways is the history of regional dishes. Port cities—like New York, where I'm from—are prime areas for cultural shifts in cuisines." He made a short sound that was maybe supposed to be a laugh, but it wasn't happy. "Usually. Looks like the oldest port in the country has the oldest taste to go with it."

He ignored the menu she'd pushed back toward him and headed for the exit. "Good news," he said as he reached for the handle. "Your branding is on point. No one is going to accuse you of being hip or fresh."

He was halfway out the door before Harper pulled herself together enough to call in her Bridezilla-wrangling voice, "Pleasure not doing business with you!"

His answer was the jangle of the bell hanging over the entrance. Strange. It usually had a cheerful tinkle.

Whatever. Hip and fresh were code words for trendy. She

was all about timeless classics. Who cared what he thought about that? She had enough to handle with her high maintenance clients. The last thing she needed on top of that was a high maintenance caterer.

Speaking of which . . . she glanced down at her watch. Fifteen minutes until the highest maintenance bride of all time appeared.

Harper sighed and pulled out the binder that grew thicker by orders of magnitude after each meeting with the lovely Dahlia Ravenel. It was possible she'd already put in more time planning this wedding than every other event she'd organized since she went solo three years ago. Combined. But Dahlia was a prize, the daughter of one of Charleston's most prominent families, engaged to the son and scion of one of Charleston's other prestigious families. This was the break she'd been working and praying for, the kind of society wedding that *The Post and Courier* would splash on the cover of the local section with her name attached as the wedding planner.

Of all the types of events she did, weddings were her favorite. They were the biggest paycheck, and she had worked out the perfect network from florists to bakers, mostly other rising new vendors who had the same grit and hustle she did. The Ravenel-Calhoun wedding would be a windfall for all of them, a chance to break into the Charleston upper crust and enjoy the fruits of that very rich pie.

Assuming, of course, that she survived Dahlia Ravenel.

And that was by no means certain.

By the time the blushing bride arrived, the groom and maid of honor had already been sitting at Harper's desk for twenty minutes making small talk. At least they were easy with each other. From the conversation, it sounded like the three of them had grown up together. The groom was Deacon Calhoun of the Garden District Calhouns, and Lily, the maid of honor, was Dahlia's cousin, born to the same Charleston caste. If there was anything the silver spooners knew, it was how to keep a sparkling conversation going to gloss over any kind of awkward moment, like the tardiness of the bride who'd demanded their attendance in the first place.

Dahlia finally blew in on a gust of exotic perfume and chatter that burst out of her the second her foot was through the door. "Why didn't anyone tell me that show about the vampires was so good?" she said, scolding her way to Harper's desk, who rose to greet her. "I mean, that show makes Charleston almost seem as interesting and gothic as New Orleans. You'd never know we don't have handsome vampires in every mansion. Speaking of," she said swooping down to drop a kiss on Deacon's lips.

"Did you just call me a vampire?" he asked, and Harper couldn't tell if he was amused or confused by the comparison.

"A handsome vampire," Dahlia corrected. "You know, charming with those dark, brooding good looks and a workaholic night owl. You're a perfect candidate, Deacon."

Deacon shook his head. "Are you telling me that you're almost twenty minutes late for an appointment you made because you got distracted by a TV show?"

She fluttered down to the seat next to him and placed a hand on his knee. "Binge-watching, honey. I know it made me late, and I'm sorry about that, but it's exactly the kind of escapism you need right now. You should try it, Deac."

Lily, the maid of honor, had been watching this all with a

half-smile on her face and now she patted Deacon's other knee. "You're not dark and brooding," she said, which smoothed out the furrow on his forehead. "And Dahlia, if I have to start picking you up for all these appointments, I will. My shift at the hospital starts at two o'clock sharp. We probably better get down to business."

Harper bet she could binge watch a reality show based on these three. She'd met with Dahlia and Lily once before but having the groom in the mix charged the situation with a new energy. Lily was the peacemaker and problem-solver, she could see right away. That meant she'd need to make Lily her primary ally in wrangling Dahlia, who had demonstrated a fierce commitment to the irrational. There was a shorthand in the way they all spoke and touched one another that would have given away their long friendship even if she hadn't already sensed it before Dahlia arrived.

Harper opened her Ravenel-Calhoun binder. Dahlia had chosen her venue and colors at their previous appointment, when Mrs. Ravenel occupied the seat Deacon took now. That had been a bit of tug-of-war between mother and daughter until Mrs. Ravenel had put her foot down and refused to budge on the William-Aiken House. She'd had it reserved since Deacon and Dahlia had announced their engagement the previous year, and Dahlia had only just decided to balk. Harper knew why she wanted it: it was the most prestigious venue in Charleston, a gorgeous historic mansion on King Street with lush grounds and an airy ballroom. Harper, sensing an unconventional streak in her new client, convinced Dahlia that the bright tangerine-painted walls of the dining room added the touch of whimsy she craved.

That victory had seemed to reassure Mrs. Ravenel that the unknown wedding planner Dahlia had chosen was right for the job, but Harper wondered if Mrs. Ravenel even knew that Dahlia had come in to pick the rest of her vendors. If she were a betting woman, she'd put money on Dahlia blindsiding her mother with her next set of choices.

But Harper was not a betting woman because she had no money to lose. Every penny was tied up in the business and the lease she'd signed three months ago for her storefront on George Street to attract wealthier clients. She'd have to use all her considerable skills to direct Dahlia toward choices that would make Mrs. Ravenel happy enough to still sign the check for Harper's services.

She put on her warmest smile and turned to the second tab. "With the venue decided, we need to choose a photographer. I work with the best in Charleston, and—"

She trailed off as Dahlia waved her words away. "My friend Sutton is doing it."

Harper searched her memory but came up blank. "I don't think I've worked with her before."

"You wouldn't have. She gave up shooting weddings a while ago. Very artsy now, but she's my best friend from school, and she agreed to come back to do my wedding."

"That sounds great," Harper said, her smile never slipping. "Artsy" worried her because she didn't think it was a word Mrs. Ravenel would like. But worse, she received a bonus from the vendors she referred, and that meant she could kiss her photographer bonus goodbye. She'd had plans for that money.

Her plans would have to wait, but no hint of her disappointment crept into her voice as she turned to the next tab.

"Let's move right on to food."

At this, Deacon straightened and leaned forward for a better look. Lily grinned. "You're speaking his language."

"I particularly love Burnham's Lowcountry Caterers," Harper said. "Their shrimp and grits are to die for and they do such an elegant presentation with their plating. They elevate our humble food into art." The cranky caterer from the morning flashed through her mind. He might think Charleston needed shaking up, but the city was ripe with restaurants sporting James Beard awards and even a couple of Michelin-starred establishments. There were rising stars who innovated *and* chefs who'd made lucrative careers out of the simple goodness of traditional Charleston cuisine.

"I like shrimp and grits," Deacon said, flipping to the next flier. "But who's your steak specialist?"

Harper turned to the flier for Salthouse Catering. "They're amazing with any cut of cow."

Dahlia's nose wrinkled. "Steak, honey? Really? Why don't we just throw a cookout and serve up some burgers?"

Deacon sat back in his chair. "You took the words right out of my mouth. Why don't we?"

Dahlia rolled her eyes. "Because we're not doing the whole hipster redneck revival thing. So help me, if I see anything in a mason jar or bacon-wrapped anything, I will lose it."

Harper privately agreed with her about the overdone "country living" aesthetic, specifically when it was used by wealthy debutantes who disdained real country living. But now Deacon was frowning.

"If there's no bacon, I walk," he said. He was kidding,

Harper thought. And about the cookout too. Probably.

"Not only do I not want any bacon, I don't love the idea of meat at the wedding either."

Deacon drew a deep breath. "I think it's great that you're exploring vegetarianism, but you know the Calhoun men are going to drink through every bottle of bourbon at the open bar if they have to sit through a vegetarian wedding dinner."

"Pescatarian," Lily said as Dahlia was drawing breath to argue. "That could work as a compromise. What if you have seafood? Seared scallops, shrimp, that kind of thing, maybe even something wrapped in bacon for the carnivores, but no red meat or poultry. Could you live with that?"

Dahlia didn't look thrilled, but she nodded. Deacon shrugged. "I could live with that."

Harper admired Lily's deft handling and jumped on the solution. "I know a couple of perfect catering options." She popped the right menus out of the binder and handed one to each of them.

"Yum," Lily said.

"Looks good to me," Deacon said.

Dahlia only offered a groan.

"Is something wrong?" Harper asked.

Dahlia's whole face scrunched like Harper had handed her raw sewage instead of a catering brochure. It was the first time Harper had ever seen her look anything less than stunningly gorgeous.

Dahlia pushed the menu back. "I've eaten food from all of these caterers at other weddings, and they're all good and totally boring."

Lily winced while Deacon shut his eyes for a few seconds. But Dahlia wasn't finished. "I picked you because you haven't done the weddings for every single one of my friends, but somehow I'm still having this thing in a boring old mansion, and now I'm going to be serving boring old food. I'm not boring," she said, slapping her hand on the open binder. "I'm sorry, but I don't think this is going to work."

Lily was shooting her an apologetic look, Deacon's face had gone blank, and Dahlia had hopped up from her seat and taken a step for the door when Harper panicked. She couldn't let her leave and take her mother's fat checkbook with her.

The words escaped her before she could think better of it. "If you're willing to work with a Gordon Ramsay wannabe who has wild ideas about food, I've got the guy for you."

Dahlia sat back down with a relieved smile. "Tell me more. I think I could be persuaded."

Chapter Two

Perfect. Just perfect.

Zak stood in the back of his food truck scowling at the list taped over the prep counter, at the cross-offs versus the checkmarks. A checkmark was a new client. He had two of those and a whole lot of cross-offs.

Those weren't even two clients. It was two event planners who had promised to keep him in mind if the right opportunity came up.

Most of them were like that Harper this morning. He yanked a slab of short ribs from the cooler. She was the latest in a long string of rejections, but something about hers had gotten to him more, slipping beneath his skin like a thin coating of hot sauce with all of the sting and none of the endorphins.

"You certainly have fresh ideas, Mr. Choi," he mimicked in a shrill voice. He hadn't realized at first that "fresh" could be an insult, but now he could see it was the kiss of death. He slammed the cleaver down to separate the first rib. Diversity had forged the early flavors of Charleston's colonial history. But anything that hadn't been shaken up in three hundred years—no matter how good it was—started to taste a little . . . old. Like three hundred years old.

He hacked at the slab again, working faster. How was he going to break in here? Zak Choi's Epic Plan to Take the Charleston Food Scene By Storm was off to a sputtering start.

He finished up the slab and braced himself against the counter, drawing a calming breath. *Still easier than New York.* At least in Charleston he wasn't facing a million dollar start up hurdle along with everything else.

And he had this food truck. It wasn't the fine dining restaurant he dreamed of in his increasingly distant future, but it was good food—amazing food—and it gave him the grim satisfaction of sticking it to the tradition-worshipping event planners and gatekeepers who spoke of Lowcountry food like it was a religious experience.

Maybe it was, but it was that really boring kind of religion where an old priest said stuff in Latin and everyone repeated it because that's what they'd always done.

"I'll take them to church," he growled, grabbing the braising sauce for the ribs. "But it's going to be one of those whooping and hollering religious experiences." He dipped his finger in and tested it, smiling as the flavor burst on his tongue. "That right there will save your soul."

There wasn't anyone to agree or disagree with him. He hadn't been able to afford an employee yet. It would happen soon, though. He could almost taste it, success as sweet as one of his galbi platters. All it would take was the right person posting about it in the right forum and then the word would get out about the "freshest" taste in town.

He moved down the stainless steel counter to prep the octopus and chili paste for the nakji bokkeum. An hour later he had the windows open, ready for business. He had to keep it simple since he was a one-man operation, but he'd chosen five dishes that only required a little assembly. Today he'd added one new dish he was calling simply Seoul Grits. It was how he imagined the flavor explosion if Korea and South Carolina sailed toward each other at full speed and collided in the middle of the ocean.

Instead of hominy, which is what made southern grits, he used buckwheat boiled in lemon water to give the flat, nutty taste some layers. Then he had skewers of fat prawns marinated in honey garlic ready for flash grilling over the gas range that was already making the truck's interior uncomfortably warm.

Now all he needed was the customers.

The food truck frenzy hadn't taken hold of Charleston's imagination the way it had in other cities, but they were definitely around. He watched through the window as the only other food truck on the block, a sandwich vendor, worked through a line six deep. A couple of people glanced his way, but none of them came over.

Come on, come on, come on.

After fifteen minutes without traffic, he put the skewers back on ice to keep them from spoiling and turned down the heat on the range.

Eventually, a portly middle-aged man who'd stopped by before walked up to the window. Zak gave him a big smile. "Hey, back for more?"

The man nodded, not smiling. "That short rib taco I got last time was something else."

"Glad you liked it. How about today's special? It's a Korean shrimp and grits."

"That's what you are? Korean?" the man asked. "I don't think I know any other Koreans."

"My father's parents are still in Korea, but he grew up here. And my mom is white. From Maine. So I think that just makes me American."

The man gave a small grunt. "Korean. American. Whatever. I'll take the special."

Zak took his money and turned the grill up then dished up the Seoul grits while the shrimp sizzled over the flame. Four minutes later he plated them neatly on top of the buckwheat and garnished it with curls of radish before he handed it to the man.

He took a bite, chewed, and nodded. "Korean shrimp and grits. Good."

"Thanks, man. And if you get a chance, could you post a review on the social media site of your choice? I'm trying to get my name out there."

"I don't fool with that stuff," the man said around a mouthful of grits before he shuffled off in the direction of some office buildings.

"Glad you loved it," Zak called after him loudly, hopeful that some people in the long sandwich line would opt for his shorter wait instead. It worked to the tune of three more satisfied customers who all promised to give him a shout out on their social media. One even took a picture of his food before he ate it, and it made Zak half hope the review would happen. Nothing was better for business than foodie hipsters, and this guy had ugly enough glasses that he might be a hipster.

He only ended up with a dozen customers even though he kept his window open an hour after the sandwich truck drove off. He was pulling out storage containers for the unused food when a lilting voice called through the window, "I'll take the special, please."

He turned with a smile that collapsed as soon as he spotted the owner of the pleasant voice. Harper Day of Great Day Events and coq au vin fame. "Did I leave something in your office?" he asked, turning back to his closing routine before she could answer.

"Yes, actually. A menu. With your Twitter handle, which is how I knew where you'd be right now."

"That was an accident. I didn't mean to leave behind evidence of radical fusion dishes."

"I meant it about ordering the special."

He turned to give her a level stare. "I'm closing."

"What, in the middle of a rush like this?" She glanced both ways down the empty sidewalk. "I can see why you wouldn't need my business."

He shook his head but threw a skewer on the grill. With her purchase, he'd at least cover the cost of the food he'd served today. One more customer and he could have sprung for two whole gallons of gas. Never let it be said that he wasn't living the high life.

He slapped a scoop of buckwheat into the dish and set the shrimp on top.

"Careful, it's spicy." He handed it to her and took the

twenty-dollar bill she withdrew from a leather wallet inside a matching purse. She was annoyingly well put together, he decided, studying the dark blonde, blue-eyed hottie. But that wasn't the right word. She was class, not flash. Harper looked like Charleston somehow, standing there in a flowered dress. It wasn't tight, but it made the point that she had curves. She wore a single pearl on a thin chain drawing attention to her collarbones without ever hinting at her cleavage. Which was a shame.

He scowled again and concentrated on getting her change, but when he handed it to her, she stuck it in his tip jar to join the single dollar at the bottom.

"Thanks," he said.

She nodded but didn't speak as she took another bite. He spun around to finish packing up the kitchen. He did *not* want to finally make the news for causing a food poisoning epidemic because he let shrimp go bad. He scrubbed the grill down and had almost forgotten about Harper when she cleared her throat softly and he turned to find her at the window again, looking up at him.

"I figured you'd left."

"I've been here the whole time."

"Okay. Well." He was suddenly about as good at conversation as his parents' Great Dane. Whatever. It wasn't like small talk had ever been his strong suit. He had a tendency to get uncomfortably intense for people when the conversation strayed to any of the subjects that interested him. And he had a lot of interests.

"I wanted to talk to you about an event," she said.

He couldn't help himself. "What happened to it being a

pleasure *not* doing business with me?"

"Circumstances have changed, and so has my position." He thought he heard her mutter "unfortunately" beneath her breath, but he was curious enough about the "changed circumstances" not to push it. "Could you come by tomorrow morning to talk about it?'

"Sure. But my number was on the menu. You could have called. Why stop by here?"

She held up her empty bowl. "Needed to make sure you were worth the offer."

"I take it I am?" It surprised him how much he wanted to hear her confirm it.

"See you tomorrow, Mr. Foodways."

That shouldn't have warmed him like gamjauk on a New York January day. But it did.

"By the way," she said, stopping and backtracking for a minute. "You should try Shipyard Park around dinner tonight. You might have some luck with the crowds out there for the Little League games."

"Thanks." He doubted it was the kind of crowd that was up for having their classics tampered with, but it wasn't like he'd had great luck at his usual Wednesday night location.

"Just play up the hot pepper factor, give them a scary name and slap it on a sign. The dads will all try to outdo each other to show who can eat the hottest, and you'll rake in the money."

Then she was gone, and he went back to wiping down his counters, but his mind was already summoning and discarding hot sauce possibilities.

He'd been waiting on her doorstep five minutes already when Harper showed up to let herself into her little shop.

"You're early," she said over the tinkling of her ridiculous bell.

"Thanks for the tip about the baseball fields," he said, following her in. He'd made two hundred dollars, and this morning he'd found two more Yelp reviews, both of them raving about his Kimchi Devilbird dish, which was just the fried chicken drummettes and kimchi dish he'd always made, only he'd whipped up a hot sauce with ghost peppers and renamed it. Harper was right. The dads had tried to out-sauce each other all night, and he'd been able to charge a premium for cold bottled water.

"Glad it worked out," she said. "Have a seat."

He did, settling in the white French-style chair across from her matching desk. He liked dark colors and bold lines but had to admit that, though the vibe in her small storefront space was feminine, she'd managed to make her white accents and muted patterns feel calm and welcoming without any fussiness.

She pulled out a binder labeled "Ravenel-Calhoun" and set it in front of him. "I wonder if you might be the right caterer for this wedding. This is a high profile merger between two of Charleston's oldest families. They've been trying to arrange a marriage for three generations, and these two finally fell in love. But they're a case of opposites attract. It's been hard bridging the gap between what everyone else wants and what the bride wants."

"Is she being unreasonable?"

"Most brides are. They want stuff like a carriage drawn by matching dappled grays, or a ceremony on *The Spirit of South Carolina* during hurricane season."

"Those are all real requests?"

"Demands." She waved her hand as if brushing them away. "It's my job to herd them toward more reasonable expectations and make them think the compromise is exactly what they wanted all along while still keeping the check-writer happy. Dahlia is not an unreasonable bride. It's more that she's unconventional."

Understanding dawned. "And I do unconventional food." He smiled, a menu already forming in his mind. "I could do spicy rice cakes with squid—"

She held up her hands in a take-it-easy gesture. "I think it's possible you could be a good fit for this. But."

He crossed his arms. "But?"

"This isn't just about Dahlia. Mrs. Ravenel is going to want to be very involved in all of this, and she's as establishment as it gets in Charleston, unless we're talking about the Calhouns, who are even worse."

"Worse? Why, Miss Day, you sound downright disdainful of the establishment," he teased in what he thought sounded like a perfect imitation of her Charleston drawl.

"Settle down, Scarlett O'Hara," she said. "I love tradition and history. And so does everyone else but Dahlia, so it's my job to make everyone happy when Dahlia wants to rock the boat hard enough to make tidal waves."

"Sounds like a stressful gig," he said. "Why not decline it?"

"Because old Charleston money writes big checks, and I've got big plans. Now, are you interested?"

"Sure." There was no use pretending he couldn't use a cut of a juicy check like that.

"Good. More importantly, are you willing to tone it down for this wedding?"

"I'll keep my tats under wraps."

She glanced over him. "Tats?"

He unbuttoned a cuff and rolled up his sleeve far enough to show her the tattoo of a dragon hiding beneath it. "I'll keep these under wraps."

"It's kind of pretty." She leaned closer to stare at the tattoo. "There's more than one?"

He just smiled.

She shook her head and sat back. "It's about more than hiding your tattoos. You're going to have to cook in a way that pleases Mrs. Ravenel, keep it pescatarian, and still make Dahlia feel like she's getting something . . . what was the word you used? Revolutionary?"

He flushed, hearing how arrogant it sounded when she tossed the word back at him. But then again, it was true. "I think it's a mistake to tone it down. Isn't this supposed to be about making the bride happy?"

"Sure, we could do that. And Dahlia will wear down Mrs. Ravenel until she agrees to it. But based on what I saw when I stopped by for lunch yesterday, you could use the kind of business boost a high-profile wedding will give you, and you won't get it if you freak them out with food they don't know."

He didn't let his expression change, but she'd struck a

nerve as surely as if she'd reached into him and plucked it. That food run at the ballpark last night had meant he could breathe easy for the first time in weeks, but it had only bought him a day or two before he'd be back to pinching his pennies until they hissed like his grill.

"I can do it." He said it quietly. It wasn't something to get excited about, but he couldn't deny the relief. "When is the wedding?"

"Six months." Harper was sorting through papers on her desk as if she'd already forgotten him. He was glad because he hadn't been able to keep a straight face at the disappointment. That was a long time to wait to get paid.

She finally plucked out a bright blue paper and glanced over at him. "Here. I'm organizing the Family Fun Day fundraiser for the children's hospital this Saturday. I've got a slot for another food truck if you want it."

It took as much effort as it had taken to quit smoking cold turkey for him to casually reach out and accept the flier. "Sure. I'll switch around my plans for that day."

A small smile flickered across her lips, as if she knew that his only plan had been to drive around hoping for a good idea for where to park the truck. But all she said was, "Thanks. I appreciate that."

That Southern graciousness. Sometimes he found himself liking it despite his pride in being a straight-talking New Yorker. He gave her a polite nod, like, *No problem, thanks for saving my bacon again, you might be the only reason I can make my credit card minimum this month*, and walked out smiling.

The bell chimed behind him. Maybe it was kind of cute. Maybe.

Chapter Three

Harper glanced over the field, a formerly barren expanse of dead grass. Even the litter had been apathetic, just patches of old chip bags and dusty soda bottles. Someone had made a regular habit of tossing empty Yoohoos when they passed by, but Harper had to wonder where that Yoohoo connoisseur was going. The field was the epitome of the middle of nowhere. It lay at the end of some broken-down businesses at the edge of Charleston on Highway 17 leading toward Walterboro.

Harper would bet most people had forgotten the field was there, even the ones who passed it every day, but there was no mistaking it now. The carnival ride operator had met her at the edge of the field two days before, lifted his eyebrows as he took it all in and said, "I've worked in worse."

By the next morning it had been totally dejunked by a high school club looking for service hours, and by last night it had boasted a half dozen of Harper's favorite carnival rides and a carousel to accommodate any wimps.

She glanced at her watch. It was a little after nine in the morning. Within the hour, the stalls would fill with crafters selling handmade goods, a few churches hawking religion, and a variety of carnival games built by the retired men in the Charleston woodworkers club who had donated their skills *and* the materials, gleeful at having projects to showcase. They'd designed two dozen assorted games to take the money of the good people who cheerfully came to lose it. The money would pay for the new proton accelerator for the children's oncology department.

Also due to arrive soon were the food trucks and Zak Choi. The man cooked some good food. Really good food. And the medical staff was a little more cosmopolitan than much of elite Charleston society because they came from all over the country to work in the hospital. Maybe they'd give his truck a boost.

Not that she cared, really. But it had been a little sad to see him manning that truck by himself the other day, no customers in sight, and Harper had never been able to resist a project.

Just look at the field, after all. It looked as if it had always been meant to host bright, shiny family fun fairs.

Soon the first van arrived to deposit a white-haired woman with a dozen gorgeous quilts that quickly lined the walls of her assigned stall. An apron seller, potter, and sign maker all followed in short order.

After every booth filled, the food trucks rumbled in, pulling into the assigned spots she'd sent them with clearly marked maps. She watched for the lime green paint of Zak's truck. He'd named it Crossroads Cooking. Considering the lecture she'd gotten on foodways, she supposed the name made perfect sense.

Soon it pulled in too, and she made her way over to check in. Not that she wanted to see him or anything. It was just that he was a lesser known quantity, so she might as well start with him as she touched base with all the food vendors.

He hadn't yet opened his windows, which made sense given that the fair didn't officially start for another hour, but she knocked on the door to the kitchen side of it and climbed up.

"Hi," he said, looking up from a refrigerated case. He was unpacking containers of chopped vegetables and herbs.

"Hey. You good to go?" She looked around and frowned. "It's just you today?"

He shrugged. "I got up at four and prepped everything. It'll still be *fresh* and I'll be able to throw things together and run the register. I modified the menu to make sure I could handle a crowd by myself."

"Interesting," she said, impressed that he'd gotten up so early to prep. She realized she'd downgraded her expectations after catching sight of his tattoos, as if they somehow meant he wasn't going to take the gig seriously. But his whole demeanor suggested he took everything *too* seriously, especially himself. Her stereotypes about tattoos was one of the biases she'd carried with her from her childhood neighborhood, where the rough boys and hard girls had inked themselves as a sign of . . . she wasn't sure. It wasn't even rebellion. No one thought twice about tattoos. Except her. Her mother would have killed her three times over if she'd come home with a tattoo.

Hers would have been pretty, though. And small. No flames. Or skulls. Maybe a bluebird, a tiny one somewhere easy to cover.

Not that she'd spent a lot of time thinking about it.

But it definitely would have been a bluebird. Not a cartoony one. A realistic one.

"Was there something else you needed?"

She blinked, mortified to realize she'd been staring at his full dragon tattoo, which was brighter and more beautiful than she'd expected. "Um, no. You know where to find the generator hookups and the bathrooms?"

"Yeah, I saw the fancy toilet rig. Looks like you covered every detail."

She smiled. Given the demographics for the average hospital donor, she'd gone upscale everywhere she could, including renting a bathroom trailer that felt more like an actual restroom than a bunch of wobbly portapotties.

"Good luck today," she said, climbing down from the truck. He was already elbow deep in the cooler again, and she closed the door on what sounded like an absent-minded grunt of thanks.

She headed to the entrance and unhooked the red velvet rope to welcome the small crowd that already waited, beaming as they streamed past and scattered in every direction, each parent pulled by a kid who wanted to look at something different. That's exactly how a successful carnival began.

"Harper!"

She waved at Miriam Tradd, the chairman of the hospital board of trustees, delighted to see her. The woman was as dressed down as Harper had ever seen her in linen pants and a string of small pearls. It was practically sporty for the elegant

Miriam, and it made Harper grin.

"It looks good," Miriam said, surveying the large field again. "I had my doubts when you suggested this location, but it's hard to beat free. And then you worked a miracle on top of that. Is it really possible we're going to make money even with the expense of the ride rentals?"

Harper grinned. "The booth rentals already covered the cost of bringing in the rides, and we'll get another ten percent of their craft sales. We didn't have to pay any food vendors. The trucks will keep whatever they make, but we had no overhead there. It's the games that'll rake in the money."

They both turned to study the nearest one, a horse-racing game Delmar Woodson had built. Players sat on stools in front of Super-Soakers, firing to fill jugs that pulled a small cutout horse forward the faster they filled. Harper didn't quite understand the mechanics of it, but she didn't need to. All she needed to understand was that every stool was occupied, and at least one person waited behind each player for their chance. A racer would have to win three times in a row to pick a prize but still pay each time to play. "We're going to make far more than we give away," she said.

Miriam sniffed the air. "Why, I do believe I smell a proton accelerator in our very near future." She sniffed one more time. "And funnel cake! I love funnel cake."

"Then you should get some. And Miriam? Thanks for giving me the chance," Harper said.

Miriam touched her arm, a gentle, fleeting touch but it warmed Harper straight through. "Are you kidding me? There is nothing we love more than our graduates coming back to work for us."

"You should have let me do this for free," she said.

"Absolutely not," Miriam said. "And if you try to donate your fee, I'll just cut a new check and send it out again until you're tired of playing tag. Besides," she said, winking. "You're half the price of the company we used last year, and so far twice as good."

Harper burst out laughing, strangely mollified to know that she'd been a steal. "It is good, isn't it?"

"It's excellent. Well done."

A steady stream of families flowed through the entrance and filled the grounds. Harper was happiest of all knowing that many of the kids running from booth to booth or screaming with delight from the top of the Zipper were survivors like her, well enough to participate in regular kid things. And while some of them sat in wheelchairs, there were smiles everywhere.

Harper was lucky. She'd had acute leukemia and the doctors caught it early. She'd spent her share of days in the hospital, and she'd always bear some physical scars from her fight. But she'd beaten it, and her good memories of the staff outweighed bad ones of the difficult medical treatment. She had to blink back a rogue tear as she watched dozens of kids and families she knew were fighting similar battles.

There had to be a way she could return her event fee to the hospital without Miriam catching on. She'd figure it out. She pulled out her phone and added it to her to-do list. The to-do list was almighty, and that meant giving that fee back was as good as done.

She scrolled through her event list, pleased at the number of completed items and mentally calculating the most efficient way to get the next items done. Time for another perimeter walk to make sure the crowd flow was good, especially to the money-making games booths.

When she swung past Zak's truck again, her eyes widened at the signs he'd set out. When she'd stopped by his street gig, she'd been impressed with the clean, stylish font of his painted menu board and the simplicity of his offerings. He'd gone the other direction now with a chalkboard menu, each dish offered in a different color. A sinuous chalk dragon wound around the edges. It looked a lot like the tattoo on his arm.

He'd stuck with a few dishes, but he'd changed the name of them. The Korean shrimp and grits she'd enjoyed had become Dragon Tail, and he had another dish called Dragon Meat and yet another named Weeping Warrior. Posters cautioned people to try Weeping Warrior at their own risk. "Extreme Heat Warning. Bold Eaters Only."

She missed the minimalism of his old approach, but he was smart to tailor his offerings to the carnival atmosphere. And it was working. He had a line of men plus one teenaged girl as long as any of the lines at other trucks.

Between the awning and the reflection on his window, she couldn't see Zak clearly, only his hands flashing out now and then to take a customer's money or a few minutes later to hand them their order. But she quickly realized that while he had a line as long as the other trucks, it was partly because it moved more slowly as he ran his one-man show.

She shook herself out of her semi-trance and moved on. That wasn't her problem to solve. She'd gotten him a good gig. It was on him to make the most of it. And yet . . . she didn't like it when systems worked inefficiently. Maybe there was a process she could recommend to help him serve customers faster. But when she positioned herself in front of his truck to study it again an hour later, the line was moving at the same speed as the other trucks. And it was longer.

Huh. Good for him.

When the lunch rush died down in mid-afternoon, she couldn't resist checking in to see what had changed. And also, she had a hankering for his Seoul grits, of all things. Apparently, the cotton candy she'd been snagging wasn't enough to sustain a working woman through a warm spring afternoon.

She stepped up to his window to order, and a teenage girl leaned out.

"What can I get for you?"

Harper spotted the outline of Zak's broad shoulders at the grill. "A word with the chef, please."

"Mr. Choi," the cashier called over her shoulder. "Company."

"Zak," he growled, turning. He sounded like he was tired of issuing the same correction.

The girl just grinned and said, "Sure, Mr. Zak."

He shook his head, but his brow smoothed when he saw Harper. "Hi. Come on back." He pointed toward the truck's rear door, as if Harper should meet him there. He opened it and came down to the last step. Harper had to crane her neck to meet his eyes. He was much taller than her, and she was 5'7, tall for a woman.

"Hey," she said. "I was thinking about trying the Weeping Warrior, but I don't know if I've got the guts."

"I can handle the spice even with my weak white genes."

She had no idea how she was supposed to respond to that,

but he flashed a smile like the one he'd given her his first day in her office. Genuine. She hadn't seen it since and had the odd thought that she'd missed it.

"Kidding," he said. "I have no weak genes. My white genes are awesome too."

She laughed. She couldn't help it. "Which ones helped you get your line running faster?"

"White genes, but they weren't mine." He jerked his thumb over his shoulder at the slight blonde. "That crazy girl was in my line, and when she got to the window she said I was losing business and even a monkey could run the register, so I should let her do it. I said no. She said she'd do it for tips. I decided to let her work for ten minutes so she could see that it's not so easy. Except that was all the time it took for her to get the line humming."

"Those weren't white genes at work. Those were her female genes kicking in. We're smart like that."

"Sexist."

"True."

He nodded. "Yes. True."

"But also, I don't think this arrangement is legal."

"It's definitely not, but her parents popped by looking for her and they're fine with it, so I let her stay. And I got their number if I ever need her for a gig again."

"So it's going well."

He grimaced. "I hate playing up stereotypes to sell food, but it's working."

She touched his arm, the one with the tattoo, and then snatched her hand back. Why had she touched him? Way to be weird. "You do seem to have an honest thing for dragons."

He laughed. "Eighteen-year-old me did. Ten-years-later me is just living with it."

"Which version of Crossroads Catering is going to show up for the Ravenel wedding?"

He ran his hand through his dark hair. "Look, I'm always going to do my food, but I promise to do it in a way that gets the check written. I've got ideas. Let me work on them a little more. But I promise you won't be sorry for choosing me."

Harper didn't tell him she was still questioning her impulsivity. If she'd taken a day or two to do some research, she could have worked out a compromise to keep both Dahlia and her groom happy, and most importantly, Mrs. Ravenel. But she'd panicked when she thought she was about to lose the booking, and now she was committed to the chef standing in front of her, sweaty from the truck kitchen, dragon peeking out from the rolled up sleeves of his chef smock, eyes studying her with a growing warmth that made her realize she was staring. Again.

She pulled her phone from her pocket, pretending she'd gotten a text. "Better go check on the carnival games." That was true, at least. "Good luck for the rest of the day."

He gave her a salute, but he'd barely made it back up the steps when she turned and jogged back to the window, knowing she wore a sheepish expression and unable to help it. "Um, I think I'd like to stick with the grits. I mean," she squinted at the chalkboard, "some dragon tails."

"Ten dollars," said the girl at the window. She'd written "Taylee" on a piece of masking tape and stuck it to her shirt like a nametag.

"She eats free," Zak said, climbing back into the kitchen.

"She's the whole reason we got this job."

Taylee shrugged and cancelled the sale, but Harper stuck the money in the tip jar, which earned her a huge smile when Taylee handed out her food a few minutes later.

She lifted a forkful in a toast of thanks to Zak and took her first bite as she walked away.

The warm burst of flavors stopped her in her tracks and she gave them a minute to wash over her taste buds before she started back up again.

Zak might be vaguely irritating with his irreverent sense of humor and his touchy ego. But dang if he wasn't exactly right about his food genius.

Chapter Four

Zak watched Harper walk away, even leaning out of the window to stare after her until Taylee gave him a strange look that made him realize he was being a creeper.

But this Harper in her jeans and soft blue sweater was a surprise to him. He'd seen her twice in ladylike dresses and perfect hair, but she'd dressed down for the carnival. Even her hair, which she'd pulled into a ponytail. The way she'd fit those dresses hadn't prepared him for the justice she did to a pair of jeans. She had a sweet—

Oh, yeah. He was definitely being a creeper.

He spun back to his grill and prepped the next batch of chicken for the Devilbird Wings, which was the dish that had sold so well at Little League. It was popular here too. He was almost worried he wouldn't have enough food to keep up with the crowd, which was the first time he'd *ever* had that problem since driving his lime green truck down to Charleston.

It was a good problem to have, considering.

They served steadily through the afternoon, but whenever he got a chance, he watched for Harper through the window. She was easy to spot weaving briskly through the crowds, stopping at this booth to check with a vendor, that game to chat with whichever old man was running it.

She often brushed her ponytail back when it fell forward on her shoulder. It was a long rope of . . . what was that color? Caramel? No. Too light. Raw honey. That was it. Her hair was gathered into a rope of raw honey.

Several times he spotted her by an insane-looking ride with death trap cages that flipped and spun while they rotated around a vertical track. It was like a compressed Ferris wheel, only the seats were enclosed so they could spin wildly as they traveled the long, tall loop. He didn't blame her. She was probably checking to make sure it was still safe to operate. He was more of a regular Ferris wheel guy himself. Except he didn't really like those, either. Maybe a carousel. That was more his speed. Literally.

The early dinner crowd heated up, and Taylee's parents checked on her a couple of times. She was happily ringing up the rush. The tip jar filled with every smart remark she made to the customers. They liked their Korean-fusion with a side of sass, it seemed. He shook his head, smiling to himself. He'd felt bad only being able to offer her tips, but she was making out like a bandit.

The evening brought another surprise: lots more women were finding his line and then exclaiming over his food. Word of mouth was spreading. Finally, a little after eight, the crowd thinned as families with worn out children carted them away. Taylee's parents stopped by again, and Zak waved her off.

"Take the money and run," he told her. To her parents he added, "Your daughter is an excellent worker."

Her dad smiled proudly and confirmed that Taylee could work for Zak again any time she was available, but not under the table. Taylee hugged the stuffed tip jar. She looked as if under-the-table payments suited her just fine, but Zak laughed and promised he'd make it legit the next time he got a good opportunity.

And this had been a great one. He hadn't done more than break even since he'd moved to Charleston, and now he was ahead for the first time. Harper might be a micromanager, but he owed her.

He closed the awning on the truck and set to work packing up. When he'd bleached all the food prep surfaces and locked up the coolers, instead of climbing into the cab and driving off, he got out to wander the grounds. The old guys were packing up their games, and a handful of stragglers wandered toward the parked cars with large stuffed animals or balloons in tow.

He wasn't looking for anything in particular, just taking it in. This wasn't the kind of thing he'd had growing up in Brooklyn unless you counted Coney Island, which he didn't. This little enterprise was a sweet Carolina-ed version of that, and even just wandering through, he liked it better than the raucous Coney Island trips of his misspent youth.

The only thing he didn't see—not that he was looking for it—was a honey rope of hair among the booths, not near the quilter folding her blankets into plastic bags or the jewelry-maker stacking trays of handmade earrings. And then he felt a tickle of satisfaction somewhere in his chest when he finally glimpsed a flash of dark blonde as the lights of a ride washed over

Harper. She sat in the back of a booth, bent over a table.

Might as well say hello. So he did.

Her head shot up, and she blinked at him then smiled. He could almost hear the sound of grinding as she switched gears. "Hey," she answered. "Have a good night?"

"Great night." He felt a hundred pounds lighter. Maybe he'd sweated it all out. Maybe he hadn't realized how heavy the burden of scraping by had been until it was lifted.

For the first time he noticed an elderly gentleman sitting next to Harper, his sparse gray hair tufted in a way that put Zak in mind of a startled owl. "What are you guys up to?" He ducked beneath the canvas awning to take a closer look. It had been a game booth, he guessed, based on the painted wooden horse figures and water guns lying on the ground.

The little owl man gave a rueful laugh and waved at the pile of tickets he'd collected. "I was a designer, not an accountant. I lost track of the tickets, so Harper here is saving me from my own stupidity."

"You're a genius, Del. You made us a fortune. Your game will literally save lives." Harper didn't sound prepared to entertain an argument on the subject. "You put us halfway to our goal with this booth alone."

"You said you were a designer?" Zak asked, crouching down to study the painted horses with jockeys atop them. He couldn't quite figure out how the game had operated.

"Industrial design," the old man—Del—said with a touch of pride. "I was at DeVann's for forty years. Made the working man's tools better looking. Not something people think on much, but my redesign made them the bestselling tools in the country."

"Wow," Zak said, studying him with respect. "That's all my dad ever uses. They're really cool-looking."

"I did that," Del said, the pride unmistakable now.

"Will you tell me how this works?" Zak asked, and Del seemed pleased to comply while Harper fiddled with a calculator and a box bursting with tickets.

Del walked him through the entire contraption. It was as genius as Harper had claimed, and Zak kept asking follow-up questions to keep him talking while she worked. And when she finally stood and stretched her back, the tickets all separated into even stacks, Zak decided he had no more questions.

"You heading out?" he asked. May as well walk her to her car.

"Just to the next thing," she said, stopping to drop a quick kiss on Del's cheek. Zak could see him blush even in the shadow of the booth.

Del shooed them out and when Harper headed toward the next game booth, Zak fell into step beside her. "You put this whole thing together?"

"I did," she said, answering a text while still scanning the grounds.

Monitoring, Zak suspected. Assessing, organizing. He knew the look, the focus in her eyes that showed no hint of exhaustion despite having already put in a longer day than his own exhausted self. He'd worn the same look when he'd climbed his way to executive chef at a Brooklyn boutique restaurant, where he'd been solely responsible for making it work. He'd loved the challenge of wrangling the chaos and channeling it into stunning food and a welcoming dining space.

Well. He'd been responsible for making it work all the way until it didn't after a corporate restaurant group had acquired it and machined it into something soulless. But he was full of Seoul. He smiled at his own joke. It had been rough, but it'd opened his eyes to the reality that he was never going to have the capital it took to break out in the ruthless New York restaurant scene. And now he was here, beside Harper, exhausted after a long day of doing food his way. It felt really good.

"What are you smiling about?"

Ah. Yeah. She didn't miss much. "Enjoying the end of a long work day. Is that weird?"

She shook her head. "I get it."

"When do you get to cut out?"

"I don't know. When everyone else is gone. You're last man standing of the food trucks. You can go, you know."

"I know. But I kind of want a break before I climb back into it. Mind if I hang with you for a while?"

"Sure. It won't be interesting though."

It already was, but he just smiled. "Feels good to stretch."

She nodded and they walked. She stopped to thank the vendors who were still there and ask if they needed help, and if a booth was empty she double-checked to make sure nothing had been overlooked, no stray tickets or merchandise, any litter, however small, picked up.

Soon they fell into a routine where he picked up any bits of trash while she examined the rest of the booth. Once she tried to discourage him. "You don't have to do this. Really, go get some sleep."

But he did it anyway, because he understood. He

understood being last man out of the kitchen, not even the mopping of floors beneath his notice when it was his name on the menu.

Several times he noticed her gaze stray to the Zipper, the hellbeast ride that had made him vaguely nauseous each time he saw it spin. But she kept working her way through each booth, sometimes asking him about his customers that day, sometimes working in companionable silence.

When he caught her looking at the Zipper with the same longing he reserved for a perfect filet mignon, he asked, "Do you have to stay until the rides are packed up too?"

She shook her head. "No, they'll load them onto trucks in the morning." And then she gave it the filet mignon look again.

"Do you . . . want to ride that thing?" he asked, finally understanding.

"No. I mean, I would have if I'd had time. But there was always something today."

"But you're almost done. Let me finish, and you can find the ride operator and have him fire it up for you."

Her eyes brightened for a minute then settled back to their usual calm blue. "It's okay. I've still got a dozen booths to check."

"I've watched you. I know how to do it. All the vendors are gone. It's just the cleanup. I'll do it. I want to. Go. Ride."

She chewed at her bottom lip.

"I'm so good at trash pickup. Go."

"Really?"

"A thousand percent really."

She flashed him a grin and darted toward the Zipper. He stepped into the next stall and tidied it up, shaking his head at the idea she'd want to go near that thing but pleased she would get to.

"Come with me."

He spun to find her standing in front of the stall. "It's fine. Enjoy yourself."

"No, I'll only let you keep helping me if you come do this ride with me. It's my favorite. And you've earned it for outlasting all the other food trucks."

"I'll be honest, that feels more like a punishment than a reward." There was no way he was getting on that death trap.

Her eyes widened. "Oh no. You're one of those carousel guys."

That was exactly right, but he didn't like the hint of glee in her accusation.

"No, but I'm not really into flippy rides."

"That's so sweet." She looked at him like he was a clumsy puppy. "It'll be okay. They have to follow a strict safety code for these rides. Come with me."

He opened his mouth to say no, but then she held out her hand. And instead, he took it and said, "Okay."

Her pure giddiness wasn't exactly contagious as they ran to the Zipper, but it was at least enough to distract him until the ride operator closed their cage with a clang and bolted the lock.

"I changed my mind." He grabbed the bars of his safety harness and tugged, but they wouldn't budge. It should have reassured him, but he felt much, much worse. "Hey, I changed my mind!" he yelled again in the direction of the safety operator.

"Ignore him!" Harper called, obviously finding the whole thing funny.

"I mean it, I really want off." But he was too late as the motor rumbled to life and their cage began to rise.

"You'll love it," she yelled over the noise.

He knew with a clarity that grew more horrifying by the minute that he would not love it.

When they reached the top, and the chassis began its first rotation to spin them down, they both screamed, Harper in what sounded like pure joy. But Zak? Zak screamed because he knew he was going to die.

He did not die. It was much, much worse.

The ridiculous bell tinkled as he pushed open the door to Great Day Events. He didn't deserve to step foot in a place with a name like that when he'd singlehandedly ruined what had been a truly excellent day for Harper. And her soft blue sweater.

Until he puked.

And puked some more.

And the spinning, flipping cage had flung the vomit everywhere while Harper screamed, "Stop the ride, stop the ride!" and it took a whole entire revolution for the ride operator to hear her over the motor and shut it down, and Zak had staggered off and collapsed to puke again. He'd been down to bile by that point.

And Harper, in her vomit-splattered sweater, had hovered over him apologizing for making him ride. It was the only thing that could have made him feel worse.

The operator had walked over and said in a bored voice, "Fourth time today." He advised Harper to get Zak water and make him sit with his head between his knees, which she had done until he'd promised nothing was spinning anymore. Then she set to work cleaning off all the cages he'd fouled during his vomitous spiral of shame because the worker had said he was off the clock. The guy at least advanced the cages for her so she wouldn't lose the hospital's security deposit on the attraction.

Attraction.

Ha.

He'd finally admitted to himself that *attraction* had overridden his self-preservation. When she'd held out her hand to him, he'd have taken it and followed her off a cliff.

It might have been better if he had. Instead, he was doing the sorriest walk of shame he'd ever made. He held an apology gift he couldn't afford and yet didn't come close to making things right.

Harper looked up at the sound of the bell. "Zak! How are you feeling?"

Physically, he was fine. But it was humiliating to man up to the woman who'd helped him to his truck then waited until his head was clear enough to drive.

"I'm never going to be able to look you in the face again, but I did want to bring you these." He lifted his elbow a bit to indicate the vase of flowers nestled in its crook.

"They're gorgeous," she said, coming around her desk to accept them. "You didn't have to do this."

"It's nothing." It was both true and not. He'd requested permission from his landlady to cut some of the blossoms that grew beneath the window of the room he rented, then waited until a nearby thrift store had opened to pick out a vintage bottle vase. "They're dahlias. Seemed appropriate."

"It's a gorgeous arrangement." She set them on her desk and leaned down to smell them, which was good because the compliment made his cheeks flush and he didn't need to look like an idiot. Again.

"I'm so sorry about last night," he said. More heat surged to his cheeks.

She whirled to face him. "Oh my gosh, no. That was totally my fault! I should never have made you ride it!"

"You didn't. My ego did. My ego is stupid, but it's dead now. It died in a catastrophic accident last night, and I'll never have to worry about it again. I brought you these too." He handed her a large plastic food bin filled with several smaller tubs. "I made you enough lunches to last you a week."

Her eyes flew to his, and he couldn't meet them. His own gaze slid past her to a framed photograph behind her shoulder of a reception hall decked out pre-gala that looked both luxurious and elegant. It was as fine as anything he'd seen at the weddings he'd cooked for in Manhattan's best hotels. She did good work.

"This is too much," she said. "I want to give it back because you really shouldn't have, but I hate making lunch." And with that, she rounded her desk and set it on the floor beside her chair as if to make sure he couldn't take it back.

"Anyway," he said, fighting the urge to shift from foot to foot, "it's a much better way to say thank you for hooking me up with the carnival yesterday than . . . well. You know."

"I'm glad it worked out for you."

"It definitely did," he said, feeling on more solid ground. "A few of the women requested my card, and I've already booked a sixteenth birthday party next month. And something called a gamecock party?" He let it come out as a question. He'd projected confidence when that call came in an hour ago, but he had no idea what he'd agreed to.

Harper smiled. "University mascot. Sounds like someone wants you to be their tailgate truck before one of the games this fall. You'll just park and serve, and whoever hired you will cover all the food their friends order. I think those are a pretty big deal for food trucks."

Tailgate parties weren't a thing in New York, but he'd run across the idea in his foodways research. They were an excellent example of how local cuisine evolved as home cooks stepped up their game to impress their friends, but he made a mental note to read up more on the subject.

"Sounds like it," he said. He wanted to say more, but he wasn't sure what else there was to say. He rocked on the balls of his feet a couple times. "Well, anyway. I better go."

Harper nodded and turned back to her computer. He was halfway out the door when the little bell jangled sense into him. *Take a shot, Choi. You couldn't possibly come off looking dumber than you already do.*

He walked back to the desk, and Harper smiled at him, an expression of polite interest. This time he found the guts to sit across from her. "So you've decoded more of Charleston for me in three meetings than I've been able to figure out by myself in two months. And worse, I've either been working or getting ready to work the whole time I've been here, so I still don't really know anybody. Would you want to hang out some time?"

Her friendly smile wobbled a bit. "I'm not looking to date right now."

He straightened. "Oh no, sorry. I didn't mean it like that. I meant more like . . . like grab a beer or something, but I don't even know if that's what you guys do here in Charleston."

"Bless your heart," she said, grinning at him.

He narrowed his eyes at her. "I know that means I'm being an idiot."

"Close enough," she said, still grinning. "We do, in fact, drink beer in Charleston. And hang out. But it's not 'you guys.' You're going to have to get comfortable saying 'y'all.' And sorry for jumping to conclusions. I wasn't sure what hanging out means in New York."

"You're cool, that's all," he said. "I don't have much time outside of trying to get my restaurant open, but I think I can promise I wouldn't puke on you again if we went to shoot pool one night. Or whatever, look at rose gardens?" he quickly added when she frowned.

"Maybe not pool," she said. "I take it kind of seriously."

Now that was an interesting new depth. "We're definitely going the next night you have off."

She studied him. "Fine. Wednesday night after you finish at the ballpark. Meet me at Old Bills on Bay Street."

"Loser buys the round," he said, rising and heading to the door with a smirk that lasted until she said, totally unruffled, "I'll have the Guinness."

But by the time he hit the sidewalk he was grinning again. Damn, she was funny.

Chapter Five

It shouldn't have surprised Harper how quickly Old Bill's on Wednesday night became a tradition. Charleston was built on tradition, after all. She expected someday when archaeologists excavated the city, they'd dig down past the old homes and buildings to find a foundation harder than iron. "Tradition," they'd say, studying the mysterious material. "It ran beneath the entire city."

Four Wednesdays later, and here she was nursing her second Guinness of the night. She'd had yet to buy for Zak, although she'd wondered after he made a couple of skilled shots tonight if she might finally need to. But she'd won again, and she smiled at him now as he racked the balls.

"Stripes or solids?" she asked.

"Doesn't matter, does it?"

It didn't. She'd sink both on the break then beat him again.

He grumbled something under his breath. It only made her smile bigger. "Have a sip," she said, sliding from her stool and handing it to him.

"I don't need your pity beer." But when she executed a perfect break, he grumbled again before downing half the drink.

She studied the table for a minute before she looked over at him. "Bad news. I'm going to run it."

He groaned. "I don't want to watch, but I can't look away."

She called every shot before circling back to the eight-ball.

"Bad angle," he said. "I'm going to lose miserably, but at least you didn't run it."

She ignored him and walked around the table once more. "Trick shot, side pocket," she finally said, pointing to the one she meant before leaning against the table and sliding her custom pool cue behind her back.

"No way."

She only looked over her shoulder to double check her alignment, drew back the stick, and hit the cue ball with a sharp, sudden twist. It spun toward the opposite bank, the English she'd put on it causing it to ricochet and bank again before bumping the eight ball hard enough to drop into its pocket, sweet as a kiss. The cue ball rolled to a lazy stop.

"No way!" Zak was on his feet this time, beer forgotten on the table behind him, hands in his hair as his gaze retraced the path her shot had taken.

"Yes way," she said calmly.

"You're amazing. Can you teach me to do that?"

She shrugged.

"I'm serious. That was the coolest thing I've ever seen."

"It's not that hard."

"Bull."

"Okay, it's really hard. I can show you, but it's going to take you years of practice."

"I'm in."

"Come on over then." She cleared his stripes and set up the cue and eight ball. "Study the table, and when you've got it fixed in your brain, lean like I did." She pointed him to the side of the pool table.

He obeyed while she polished off her beer. "Got it," he said, leaning back against the table like she had. "How'd you get so many years of practice?"

"Old Bill is my third stepfather. I barbacked for him through college, and I watched the best come through. I practiced whenever it got slow." She walked up to him and reached around either side of him to position the cue stick.

"You little pool shark. Wait. I guess you never hustled me. You told me you were this good up front."

She nodded. Her words had disappeared suddenly. She hadn't thought through the physical logistics of teaching him this shot. They were almost chest to chest with her arms on either side of him, holding the cue. She tried to peer around him to check the shot. It only caused her to lean against him, the right front half of her body pressed against his. This should not be getting to her.

But this was getting to her.

She made a quick adjustment on his shooting hand and stepped back without meeting his eyes. Instead she scurried to the far end of the pool table and gave him his next instruction.

"You want to hit it hard but twist it right before you strike."

"Like this?"

But she lost focus as she tried to quiet her buzzing nerves, so when the cue ball struck the eight ball instead of shooting past it, she wasn't sure what he'd done wrong.

"Guess not," he said, watching the balls roll away from each other.

She drew a steadying breath. This was *Zak*, her *friend*. These jangly nerves were silly. She just hadn't expected him to smell like a Carolina breeze.

"Try again." She set the balls back in place then perched on a stool to watch.

He set it up. but she could tell before the cue stick struck that he was way off. She shook her head before he even missed the shot.

He sighed. "Guess you're going to have to show me again."

She sent him a quick glance to see if this was an excuse to get her close, but he wasn't even looking at her as he fished out the cue ball.

You're the only one trying to make this a big deal. Settle down, she chided herself as she caught the ball and reset it. And then suddenly he was right there again, slipping past her to lean back against the table and position himself for the shot. "Like this?" he asked, craning around to see over his shoulder.

It made it easier to step into his space—his "frame," her old junior high PE teacher would have called it as she coached awkward middle schoolers on the waltz. Harper could easily believe she'd time warped to seventh grade as she reached around Zak again to correct his cue alignment. She was hyper aware of her own body and filled with sudden regret that she hadn't showered before meeting up with him. Maybe she smelled like stale sweat. Maybe he could feel the weird energy rolling off of her. Maybe—

Maybe this is ZAK and she should relax. She forced herself to release the tension in her shoulders and focus on getting his grip right. "I'm going to shoot for you," she said. "Keep a light hold and pay attention to how it feels."

He made a sound of agreement, so she cocked the cue stick and shot, giving it a sharp twist at the end. She let go and leaned in to watch as the eight-ball dropped right where it should. "See?"

Zak made another sound. She glanced up to find him staring at her instead of the table. She stepped back to give him room. "Did you see how that worked?"

"Maybe?" He turned to look at the table. "But probably not. Show me again?"

This time she was even more suspicious, but his tone had been offhand, and when she tried to read his expression, he was chalking the cue stick, not paying attention to her.

She gestured for him to give her the cue. "Move, dummy."

"I'm a hands-on learner."

She shook her head. "One more time."

Once again, she found herself almost chest to chest with him, but he was even more awkward with his grip this time, and she kept having to make small corrections to his form. "You're set," she said finally. "When I let go, I'll step back and you shoot."

"I'll miss."

"You'll miss a hundred percent of the shots you don't

take."

"That's some Chinese fortune cookie wisdom right there. I'm half-Korean. Don't generalize all Asians, please."

She ignored him. She'd gotten used to his Asian jokes. "Ready?"

There was no answer. Instead she felt a slight ruffling across the top of her hair, like the air had kicked on and stirred it. But this was warm. She glanced up and found Zak's eyes boring into hers.

"Um, hi?" she said.

"Hi," he repeated, softly.

"You ready?"

He took his time to answer. "I think so."

"All right, I'm letting go."

She hadn't even uncurled her fingers from the cue stick totally when he said, "Question."

"Yeah?"

"Tell me again why you're not really looking to date?"

Her fingers froze in a half-claw grip. "Why are you asking me that right now?"

"Curiosity. You know how I am."

She did. He spent half of their billiards nights telling her about all the reading he'd done over the week. He must be the Charleston County Library System's star patron and Google's biggest abuser.

She should step back, but her feet wouldn't move. "I'm too busy to date."

"So you're not already seeing someone?"

Had his head lowered toward hers? "No, I'm not seeing

anyone. I don't have time."

"But we make this work every week."

"This is just pool."

His head had definitely dropped lower, and she stared at his mouth.

"Is it?" he asked quietly.

"Yes?" Why had she put a question mark on that? There was no question mark. She meant to correct it, but somehow her chin had tipped up and speaking felt very hard.

"Huh," Zak said, sounding not in the least befuddled, but Harper could almost hear her own neurons tangling into a knot as they registered the soft puff of his breath against her lips.

"Yes." She said it firmly this time and took a step back. "It's just pool." Zak watched her for a second, a small smile playing over his mouth.

"Okay." He reset and took the shot. Again it went wide. He watched the cue ball roll to a stop before turning back to her, that knowing smile still in place. "Good. Because I'm obviously going to need a lot more lessons."

He could not possibly have suddenly lost the progress he'd made for the last month. He was playing *her*, not pool. This was as bad as the old stretch-and-yawn trick.

"Shut up and rack them." She refused to smile as she retreated back to her stool. She wasn't dumb enough to go down this road. She had no time in her life for a relationship, not when her business was finally getting traction in the right circles. She wouldn't detour for anyone, including a charming New York chef. Not even a really hot one.

Not that she'd noticed.

Chapter Six

Harper definitely noticed the chemistry between them, Zak thought as he toweled his hair dry that night. She had to. It was the first time he'd been sure that he'd finally made some progress in the subtle campaign he'd been waging over the last month. He'd heard it. The hitch in her breathing. He'd felt it. The change in the way even the air had moved around them when she'd leaned in to help him with his shot.

She'd stared at his mouth like maybe instead of muffling it with her hand the way she did to hush up his trash-talking on pool nights, she'd wanted to kiss him instead.

There was no way he'd misread that. She'd totally wanted to.

He hadn't misread her retreat to her stool at the end of the night either. That might have discouraged a different guy, but not him. People only retreated if they sensed a risk. And that meant Harper's feelings were at risk.

Finally.

He balled up his sweaty running clothes and slam dunked them into the hamper.

It had been a long month of slowly coaxing her out of her shell. He'd thought he only wanted her friendship when he left her office that day. But then they'd played their first game of pool and it was game over for him before she even won the first round. She'd been relaxed and funny and smart. So smart.

Also gorgeous. He wasn't blind.

But that all took a backseat to the gem that was Harper Day. He understood her passion and professionalism, her creativity that was obvious the minute you were paying attention. And he was paying attention.

That's why he knew he had to step carefully with her. He wasn't *that* guy, the one who would steamroll over her wishes and nag her into dates or make unwelcome comments on her looks in a quest to win the harassment Olympics. Honestly, he liked her so much at this point that if all she ever wanted from him was friendship, he'd accept it and leave it alone.

But last night . . .

Last night he'd felt it. They'd been resonating at the same frequency, a tension that sizzled in the opinion of an expert on sizzling. And steam.

But also handling things with care.

This was going to be even more delicate than navigating eggshells. Based on her quick withdrawal the second before that almost-kiss—and he was sure that was what it had been—this would be more like making a meringue, whipping up exactly the right amount of interest in her without creating a mess.

He frowned. He didn't love playing games, but she'd shut down if he laid his feelings out plainly. For them to work, she'd have to decide for herself that they were fusion waiting to happen.

All week, he counted down the days until their pool game while devising and discarding different strategies. He had to prove he was her safe place without putting himself any deeper in the friend zone.

By Wednesday, he had no plan. Time to call in an expert. When the lunch rush died down, anyway. Because he had lunch rushes now, sometimes. More and more reviews of Crossroads Cooking had popped up on social media, and people came looking for his truck.

When the lull hit, he pulled out his phone and dialed his sister's number.

"What's up, nerd?"

"Hey to you too, Chloe."

"Heeey," she repeated in a thick drawl. "What do you reckon I can do for you?"

"That's not how they talk down here."

"Meh. That's how everyone not-from-New-York sounds to me. So how's it going?"

"Better. Business is picking up. And I met someone."

His sister squealed, and he held the phone away from his ear, grimacing.

"Tell me," she demanded.

"Her name is Harper, and she's awesome. But she thinks she doesn't want a relationship."

Chloe tsked. "Then she doesn't. You have to respect that."

"I know that, but how would you interpret this?" And he launched into a recap of their last pool night.

"Hmmm. I retract my previous statement. She's into you."

Even though he knew it in his gut, it was good to hear his sister confirm it. She was only eighteen months younger, and she'd dealt with her friends crushing on him all the way through high school. She'd gotten really good at reading these kinds of situations.

He braced himself for some teasing and asked, "How do I help her realize that she does want a relationship?"

"You are hooooooooked," Chloe crowed, and the tops of his ears grew warm, but he didn't contradict her. "Okay, I know what to do. I *told* you that someday you'd be glad I made you watch all the seasons of *Friends* with me. Today is that day, bro."

"I only watched it for the Monica cooking scenes."

"And you need to think 'Monica' now. Harper sounds like a more chill Monica, right?"

"That's a good way to describe her personality." Competitive, detail-oriented, driven, high BS detector. Yep.

"Think about how Monica and Chandler went from friends to more. You're a Ross/Chandler hybrid because you're trying to be her friend. Harper needs a Chandler/Joey. You could use your Chandler sense of humor, but you have to tone down the nerdy Ross focus and not talk about stuff like foodways."

"Hey, she likes hearing about that stuff."

"She *acts* like she does. Only you and your nerd friends actually like it."

"No," he said slowly, thinking back on their conversations. "She asks lots of questions and gives me a truckload of opinions."

"Holy cow," Chloe said with a touch of awe. "If that's true, you may have done it."

"Done what?"

"Found your perfect woman. So don't screw this up."

"Why do you think I called you? Although I'm beginning to regret it."

"No, no, don't. I've got this. You need to dial up your inner Joey. Think effortless cool."

"She's heard me do monologues about foodways. She knows I'm not cool."

"You're all right," she said. "Don't sell yourself short. She's into you. Just be super chill and let her come to you."

"Let her come to me," he repeated. "Super chill. Got it. Bye, nerd."

As he headed out to Old Bill's, he gave himself a mirror check and winked. "How *you* doin'?" And then he grabbed his keys and raced over to meet her, all while rehearsing his new mantra. *Play it cool, play it cool, play it cool.*

It was working.

It was actually working.

Harper had a wary look around her eyes when he walked in, but he just smiled and begged for mercy. "I don't think I can take another ego-beating over my sucky trick shots. Can I get the regular humiliation of losing a normal game?"

She smiled and beat him, but only by two shots. It was enough to loosen her up, and they were right back in their groove. He'd stopped her retreat. Good. Now it was time to change gears.

As they chalked their cues, he stepped closer and leaned in, never taking his eye off the chalk cube. "Don't look, but I think the past president of Sigma Delta Bro-Dude back there is checking you out."

"What?" She started to turn, but he touched her shoulder lightly and dropped his hand.

"I said don't look. Sneak a peek when you're taking a shot from the other side of the pool table. You can't miss him. Polo shirt and Nikes."

"Okay." She gave him a confused look but stepped up to break without saying anything else.

She called stripes, and as she set up for her next shot, she flicked her eyes past Zak before frowning and making a rare miss.

"Were you distracted by his gelled hair?" Zak asked as she passed him.

"Your hair is gelled."

"Sometimes."

"Every time. And there was no one checking me out. Take your shot."

He did, then two more before he missed. "Do you not notice how many guys check you out?"

She lined up her shot. "I used to. Happened when I worked here, especially when I played. They're just surprised to see a woman schooling everyone. I got used to it. Now I don't notice, but I'm sure it still happens."

It did. He caught guys checking her out all the time, and it had nothing to do with her pool-playing. Which was back on point, he noticed, grimacing as she cleared the table before she missed on purpose to avoid a scratch.

He took the only easy shot he had. He'd maybe sink one more before she beat him again. At best he could try to give her a bad setup, but it wasn't likely to slow her down. "I always notice," he said, lining up his cue.

"Notice what?"

"When women check me out. Watch the woman over my left shoulder." It was a blonde a few years older than him. She'd been watching since their game started, probably trying to figure out what was going on between him and Harper.

Harper looked past him and frowned, which caused him to fight a smile of his own. She had no idea how annoyed she looked.

He managed to sink two stripes, but he'd also set up Harper for an easy win which he missed, unfortunately.

"I bet she works in a bank or runs a doctor's office during the day," he said.

"Who?"

"My new girlfriend."

"She's too old for you."

He had to hide another smile.

"And why bank or office?" she asked

"The hair. It's that middle length, practical and businesslike during the day, but then she lets it down to go out at night with friends."

"Wow. You've thought a lot about her."

That was jealousy. It was in the slightly sarcastic way she said it.

"Not everyone gets born with this," he said, picking up her

honey gold ponytail that had slipped in front of her shoulder as she prepared to shoot. He let his hand trail it all the way down as he settled it on her back, not commenting on the fact that she'd frozen. "There. Now it's out of your way."

"Thanks," she said, and missed her easy shot.

He couldn't hide his grin fast enough this time when she turned around to give him room. Her eyes narrowed, but she didn't say anything.

For the rest of the night she paid him back with interest. Anytime he got close to evening the score, she touched his arm and leaned in to make some suddenly urgent comment about the beer nuts or plucked a "piece of lint" from his hair. He knew it was a gimmick, but it only made him work harder to keep the score close so that she'd keep inventing reasons to touch him and throw him off his game.

As she was about to win another game of eight ball, he rested his hand on her lower back. She startled and sunk the eight but sent the cue right after it.

She straightened and stepped away from him in one agitated move.

"I win," he said.

"You're cheating."

"Didn't mean to scare you. I was going to tell you that your boyfriend is leaving."

She didn't even look in Polo guy's direction. "You're cheating," she insisted.

"What? How?"

She leaned her cue stick against the table with careful motions. He recognized the sharp, tight movements. That's how he looked when he was fighting the urge to punch a wall. Maybe he'd overplayed his hand. Maybe he—

Suddenly her fingers were hooked into the front belt loops of his jeans. She hauled him right up to her and stopped him just short of smacking into her.

"You don't think I see it?" she asked, peering up at him from beneath her lashes.

He kept his face blank. "I don't know what you're talking about."

She studied him before her smile broke through. She let go of his belt loops, but he didn't even have a second to regret it because she slid her hands up his chest.

He swallowed. Hard.

"Guess I'm reading you wrong," she said, her hands moving to his shoulders. "Sorry about that." And then she brushed them off and scooped up her pool stick. "See you next week."

And he just stood there gaping after her like a slack-jawed Ross.

The next Wednesday was even worse. Or much, much better, depending on how you wanted to look at it. He honestly wasn't sure he knew.

She played dirty pool, finding ways to touch and distract him no matter how close the score was, but always keeping it just shy of crossing a line where he could call her on it.

He didn't want to. It was the best six games of pool he'd ever lost, and he went home grinning.

The week after that, he began to doubt he was going to survive her. At one point, he scooped her around the waist to move her out of his way for a shot. She slipped right back in front of him and smiled.

Challenge accepted.

He leaned forward to take the shot, and she leaned back but refused to move out of the way. He held the cue on either side of her, an almost embrace as she stayed right where she was, practically in a backbend inside of his shooting frame but still not touching him. "I'm not distracting you, am I?" she asked.

He gritted his teeth and took the shot before stepping back. "Nah."

Not unless she counted making him nearly swallow his tongue as he considered the ab strength that trick had required. He'd like to investigate that further.

When the third week in a row passed with another tortuous, awesome night of cheater pool, he knew it was time to kick it up a notch, as one of his favorite corny TV chefs liked to say. They'd found a good groove, but he couldn't let it turn into a rut. He had to shake things up.

But how?

The answer came in the form of Dahlia Ravenel.

Or a text about her, anyway. He was cleaning up the truck after a good night of vending at Taylee's high school. She'd told him about the bingo fundraiser the marching band boosters ran every Monday night. There were always a couple of dessert-themed food trucks there, but she figured the older crowd needed some protein to fuel their bingo card madness. Then she'd texted her friends about this "lit new truck," and the first night was such a big success that it had become their regular gig.

Not only had he made Taylee a real paycheck employee, but he still let her keep all the Monday tips as a commission for getting him the gig. She had the instincts of a hustler, and it was paying his rent and getting him catering bookings for everything from garden parties to corporate lunches.

Finding employees for those hadn't been tough either. Busboys at high end restaurants were always looking to supplement their cash flow, so he hung out behind Charleston's fanciest dining establishments like a weirdo and recruited them on their smoke breaks.

He'd put away the last of the devilbird marinade when his phone alerted with the tinkling bell effect he'd assigned to Harper. He whipped the phone from his pocket.

Dahlia wants to do a tasting tomorrow. Can you do it?

He texted her right back. **Sure. Midafternoon?**

He'd have to skip a good lunch rush out at a business park in Summerland that Harper had suggested he try, but he knew how important this was to her—to both of them—and he'd need the whole morning to prep the perfect tasting menu.

Instead of texting him back, she called.

"Hey," she said when he answered. Her voice was honey too. "Sorry, I know it's late."

"Don't worry about it. I'm finishing up work."

She groaned. "That makes me feel worse because I'm fixing to make your night longer. I thought we would have another month or two before Dahlia wanted to set the menu. She decides to get on top of things at the worst times. Could we meet tonight to go over your choices?"

He glanced at his watch. "Right now?" It was after nine already.

"Yeah. I'm so sorry. Can I bribe you with ice cream to meet me at my office?"

"I'm one hundred percent corruptible. I'll grab a quick shower and be there in thirty."

He was there to the minute, walking in to find her sitting on the floor facing the door, leaning back against her desk with her eyes half-closed until the bell over the door announced him.

"Thanks for coming." She smiled up at him as he walked toward her. She pushed against the floor like she was going to hoist herself up.

"Here." He hurried to offer a hand. He pulled a little too hard, and she stumbled into him, slightly off balance. "Sorry," he said, catching and steadying her, his hands pressed against her back.

She'd braced her palms against his chest to find her balance, but now they relaxed and simply rested there. "Hi."

"Why were you sitting on the floor?"

"Exhaustion."

His arms tightened around her. She smiled up at him, and he wondered if she was really, truly seeing him. But then her eyes dimmed, and she slipped away from him, gesturing over her shoulder for him to follow. "I promised you ice cream."

She led him to a tiny kitchenette in the back of her store and pulled a pint from the mini-fridge. "I just put it in there, so it should still be cold. I hope."

He realized as she rummaged through a drawer for a spoon that he'd never seen her so dressed down, not even at the pool hall. She was in yoga pants and a zippered hoodie.

"Did you come from the gym?"

She nodded, turning with a spoon in hand. "Dahlia texted me an hour ago, and after I quit freaking out I texted you."

She rested against the counter like she was too tired to stand, and he leaned against the wall opposite, stretching his legs until they met the baseboard next to her. This kitchenette was tiny even by New York standards.

"Don't stress," he said. "At least not about the food. It's handled. But I don't want to talk about it until I get ice cream."

"I only have one spoon." She stared at it sadly.

"I'll share."

She nodded and pried the lid off, scooping a bite and delivering it straight to her own mouth. He struggled not to laugh. So much for sharing.

"My turn," he said, reaching for it.

She scooped another spoonful and extended it to him, sliding it into his mouth. It was soft, even verging on runny, but that barely registered. He watched her carefully, but she didn't seem to feel like feeding another human was one of the most excruciatingly intimate things a person could do. Maybe her exhaustion was eroding her usual defenses.

She repeated the process, serving herself a bite, then him. This time he reached up to wrap his hand around her wrist and hold the spoon steady, but before he touched her a drip of ice cream plopped right in the middle of the dragon on his forearm.

She scooped the drop off with her index finger and popped it into her mouth to lick it off.

What . . . he . . . how . . .

Hell.

No man was that much of a saint.

He pulled the pint from her hand. She gave the tiniest gasp, as if she just realized what signal she'd sent. He believed it. He'd endured her being intentionally sexy when they played cheater pool, but what drove him the craziest was the ways she was effortlessly sexy without realizing it, like standing in her gym clothes eating melted ice cream.

The spoon clattered from her fingers to the floor, but she didn't move to pick it up. Her eyes had lost their tired look.

He straightened and took a short step toward her, giving her no doubt about his intentions so she had a chance to walk away.

"This is a bad idea," she said. But her mouth turned up in a slow smile.

He lowered his head until their lips were almost touching. Almost. She wouldn't be able to say this hadn't been just as much her idea. She hooked her fingers in his belt loops—a move he was really coming to appreciate—and he had to catch himself on the counter behind her as she pulled him in to close the gap.

And then . . .

And then the counter became a necessity as her lips opened beneath his. She tasted like pralines and cream. He couldn't think anymore, and when she made a soft sound as he deepened the kiss, he didn't remember having any thoughts, ever, in his entire life.

There had only been this. Heat and sweetness, and an almost-pain that he would drink deeper if he knew how.

Her hands climbed, exploring his hair and sending an

electric wave over his scalp and down his back.

It was his turn to groan. That pulled another soft whimper from her, and she tangled her fingers in the hair at the nape of his neck. He didn't think it was possible for the kiss to get better until she changed the angle of her head, and it nearly buckled his knees. He had to grab for the counter again.

She pulled away from him, her hands still tangled in his hair, but she opened her eyes to meet his. He watched as they grew from unfocused to clear, and he leaned down to kiss her again before she thought too hard.

She kissed him back for an intense, heady minute before she drew back and rested her forehead against his. "Wait."

"I have been, since the first time you insulted me." He dipped toward her lips again, but she shook her head.

"I mean it."

He stopped and let her collect herself even though it was the last thing he felt like doing. She pressed lightly against his chest, and he backed off immediately.

She took a deep breath then walked out of the kitchenette.

He followed her. "Harper—"

But she held up her hand without turning around, and he stopped talking. She went back to her spot in front of her desk and sat down, drawing her knees up to her chest inside her hoodie.

He sat down cross-legged across from her, careful to give her space.

She finally spoke. "That was stupid."

"It wasn't stupid."

"It was incredibly stupid," she said, plucking at the zipper pull.

"Why?"

"Because even if I was looking for a relationship, which I'm not, you and I are a bad fit."

"That didn't feel like a bad fit." His world had tilted slightly on its axis. That had never happened to him before.

"You can't build a relationship on pheromones."

"Does this only feel like attraction to you? We laugh together. We have long, interesting conversations. I understand who you are. Have I been imagining all of that?"

She dropped her head to her knees. "Did you bring a menu? For tomorrow?"

"Yeah." Was she really going to change the subject just like that?

She held out her hand for it without lifting her head. He fished it out of his backpack and gave it to her. He'd worked hard on it, making sure all the options had some staple of Lowcountry cuisine but dressed up with herbs and seasonings and preparations from global dishes that pushed it to the next level. It may not look like a typical Charleston wedding dinner, but their classic fare was there in the foundations. It was innovative. *Fresh*, he thought with a twist of his lips. It wasn't quite a smile. He was too nervous about her opinion for that.

She studied it slowly, as if she were taking apart and examining each syllable in her mind.

Finally, she handed it back to him. "This is why we don't make sense. When you peel away the chemistry and the funny conversations, underneath you're a restless New Yorker on the cutting edge of everything, and I'm always going to be a Carolina girl who loves tradition. I'm not restless. I don't need change and variety."

"You're saying this menu is a metaphor for why we're a bad fit?"

"It sums it up pretty well."

He dug into his backpack and handed her a new menu.

"What's this?"

"Read it."

She did before glancing up at him in confusion.

He nodded at it. "Isn't that what a classic Charleston wedding menu would look like?"

"It is, but I don't understand why you made this."

"Because I know how important this wedding is to you. I can make all of that and do it as well as anyone in this city. And I will. I had that ready to go because I want you to see that I understand you, and I'll make that food without a single criticism. This wedding will work. *We* will work," he said, pointing between them.

Her mouth had fallen open slightly. Now her eyes warmed, and he felt it spreading through his chest. He knew it. He'd known this would get through to her. He would make three hundred plates of coq au vin with Julia Child's recipe if it made Harper happy.

But she shook her head, and suddenly that warmth felt like a fist instead.

"I think this is the nicest thing anyone's ever done for me. But I would never ask you to be this," she said, handing the menu back to him. "I know it's not you. And it's not going to make Dahlia happy. Neither of those menus is going to work tomorrow because it's not possible to make both sides of that couple happy at the same time. Maybe it's a metaphor for us."

"That's grim."

"It's not a criticism of you," she said quietly. "Her mother and her fiancé want tradition. They want classic. Timeless. She wants edgy and unconventional." She gave him a tired smile and shifted, her knees brushing his. "Or is it hipster and fresh?"

He opened his mouth to object, or maybe apologize for the words he'd thrown at her weeks ago, but she pressed her fingers lightly against his lips to quiet him. "It's okay. Dahlia versus everyone else involved with this wedding is an unsolvable problem, and it wasn't fair to ask you to do it."

He gently tugged her wrist down. "I wanted to," he reminded her. "I still do. Let me figure this out. I'll make it work. I promise."

"It's unsolvable," she repeated. "I need this wedding. And I'm going to lose it."

"Then it's not going to hurt if I give it a shot." He scrubbed his hands over his face and ran through a dozen scenarios in his head, testing them and discarding them before he saw the answer. Then he blinked at her and straightened. "Get them here tomorrow," he said, climbing to his feet and walking to the door. But instead of walking out, he removed the lace-trimmed sash from each of the curtains she'd hung on it to soften the commercial space. "I'm going to need these, plus the location of the nearest twenty-four-hour drugstore."

When Harper stuttered a confused answer, he smiled at her. "Prepare to be amazed," he said and slipped out the door.

Chapter Seven

Amazing.

Harper stared down at the eye masks on her desk. "You made these?"

Zak smiled. "Yeah. I Maria-Von-Trapped those curtains like a glue gun god."

She picked one up and turned it over, delighted by the lacy confection even in the midst of her stress. He'd pulled the lace from her window sashes and attached them to a plain drug store sleep mask in a way that made it look chic and feminine.

"I'm impressed. But what is it for?"

"In food service, we say that half of your appetite is your eyes. But for the Ravenels, it's getting in their way. Dahlia reads the menus that her mother wants, and it's turning her off. Mrs. Ravenel will do the same thing for anything Dahlia wants, mostly because it sounds like this bride doesn't even know what she wants. Just whatever her mother doesn't. So I figured out how to eliminate that bias. Do you trust me?"

It was a simple question. He was asking her if she trusted him to make good food. Yes. Everything she'd tasted of his was incredible. Especially him.

Um. Getting off track here, girl.

And wasn't that always the problem with Zak?

In the same way his food had layers of texture and flavor, so did his questions. Like this one. He was also asking if she trusted him to value her goals.

She sighed. "I have to, don't I?"

"Don't sound so sad about it," he said. "This is going to work. I'm going to set up two tasting stations. One right here for Mrs. Ravenel, and the other over there for Dahlia." He pointed to the table where she displayed different place settings. "You'll work with Dahlia, and I'll work with Mrs. Ravenel. I'll set the dishes up in order, explain them, and then you just make sure it makes into her mouth and not her lap. Are you up for it?"

Harper tried to figure out how this was going to help, but she couldn't see how this was going to solve anything. "I can do that."

"Great. Why do you look worried?"

"I need more details."

"It's not going to make you feel better. Basically, I'm going to have them do a blind taste test so that they can form unbiased opinions."

He was right. She didn't feel better. "That sounds both simple and really complicated."

"It is. Is it okay if I set everything up on your desk and that table?"

She stood, lifting her laptop with her. "Sure. I'll clear them."

As she walked around the desk to set it on a nearby shelf, he stopped her with a hand on her shoulder. He slid it up her neck to run his thumb softly along her jawline. She fought the impulse to press a kiss into his calloused palm. Instead, she stepped back.

"This is going to work," he said.

Layers, again. This food. This relationship.

"I don't see how." She busied herself with clearing the rest of her desk as he brought in a parade of covered dishes from his truck parked behind the shop.

At three o'clock exactly, the other table was set up, and they were ready when the Ravenels walked in.

"Lily and Deacon won't be joining us today?" Harper asked as she opened the door for them.

"Lily picked up a shift at the hospital, and Deacon says he trusts me to choose the food," Dahlia said, brushing past her. She stopped short when she spotted Zak standing by the desk covered in dishes. "Who is this?" she asked, running an eye down the length of his lean frame.

Harper refrained from an eyeroll. Whoo, boy. Deacon was going to have his hands full.

"Ladies, I'd like you to meet Zak Choi, the genius behind Crossroads Cooking. I think you're going to be thrilled with what he's prepared for you today." She prayed that was true.

Curiosity sparkled in Dahlia's eyes, but Mrs. Ravenel looked as if she were refraining from an eyeroll of her own.

"I understand there's a difference of opinion about the

food that should be served," Zak said.

"There shouldn't be." Dahlia's tone held a bitter note. "It's *my* wedding."

"But it's *our* family who's coming to celebrate you, and there are certain expectations for this reception. You've gotten your way with the dress. But the food is about more than just you. You have to compromise." Mrs. Ravenel's reminder had the weary sound of words that had been spoken so many times they'd lost their tread.

Dahlia's face tightened. "You got your way with the venue and music and just about everything else."

"Because Tibetan singing bowls are for California hippie weddings, not walking down the aisle at the William Aiken House."

"They're better than that sleepy quartet you booked. It's supposed to be *my* dream day, not yours. I should *not* have to compromise, not one single thing."

It wasn't even close to the first time Harper had heard the same Bridezilla statement, but she'd never understand it. If you were with the right person, then playing pool at Old Bill's would beat a weekend in the Wentworth Mansion with the wrong person.

Her eyes shot to Zak. Wait . . .

But she had no time to process that because Zak, his warm smile never faltering, was addressing the tense mother and daughter.

"I think you'll both get exactly what you want without any compromise if you're willing to try an experiment. I've tailored a tasting menu for each of you. Harper has told me a lot about your event and your individual preferences. She's the most gifted event planner I've ever worked with, and she understands your priorities well. To let each of you form your own opinion, I'd like to have you try the food separately. Would y'all be willing to do that?"

Harper was proud of his ease with the word y'all. He must have been practicing.

Dahlia and her mother didn't look at each other, but Dahlia shrugged, and Mrs. Ravenel murmured a stiff, "Why not?"

"Thank you for your flexibility. But there's one more thing. I've worked in some of the finest restaurants in New York, and I think turning this into a pure taste experience will be the best way for you to determine what you really want." He held up the blindfolds. "I challenge you to a blind taste test."

Harper kept a straight face, but his wording was a stroke of genius. If he asked or cajoled, Mrs. Ravenel would have turned him down flat, but no Charleston woman would back down from a challenge by a northern boy.

"Fine," Mrs. Ravenel said.

Dahlia liked anything that broke with protocol, Harper was coming to recognize, and she nodded before Zak even finished speaking.

"Excellent," he said. "Dahlia, if you'll follow Harper, and Mrs. Ravenel, why don't you have a seat right here?"

Harper was dying to know what he'd whipped up, but Zak hadn't wanted to risk deregulating any of the food temperatures by removing the covers. When she'd asked to see the menu, he had only tapped his forehead and said, "It's here. And honestly, if you don't think they can both be convinced anyway, does it even matter?"

She guessed not, so now she led Dahlia to her seat and helped her with her blindfold and hoped for the best.

"Let's begin," Zak said. "For your first taste, Mrs. Ravenel will have saffron grits with harbor spices. Dahlia, your dish is called the Spanish Madame, a paella with sensual notes of Berberi spices."

Mrs. Ravenel sputtered at the "Spanish Madame," but when Zak served her bite, she quieted immediately. Dahlia accepted her bite and a slow smile spread across her mouth. "Incredible," she said.

"Not as good as this, I'll bet," her mother said.

Zak smiled. Harper wished she had a better view of the food he was serving Mrs. Ravenel. How was having them fall in love with two different menus going to solve anything? Maybe the goal was to earn Mrs. Ravenel's trust in his cooking.

He worked through each course, naming what each woman was sampling. With each bite, Mrs. Ravenel sounded as pleased as Dahlia looked. When they'd each tasted their last course, he began lifting the covers back into place. "Harper, do you mind doing the same?"

It made no sense, but she did it.

"All right, ladies. Let's have you remove your blindfolds. Then we can sit and see which dishes you're willing to compromise on."

A glance at Mrs. Ravenel's face tempered Harper's mood again. Her expression plainly said she doubted she could like any food that Dahlia loved that much. Dahlia took the empty seat by her mother and Harper moved to stand beside Zak on the other side of the desk.

"The food was excellent," Mrs. Ravenel admitted. "But I've chaired enough galas to know that it's going to be far too complicated to serve two different menus at a sit-down dinner for three hundred."

"That's why we won't," Zak said. "Did you each like the first dish?"

"It was my favorite one," Dahlia said.

Her mother nodded. "Mine too."

He removed the first lid. "Your saffron grits and your Spanish Madame were the same dish," he said, nodding to each woman in turn. "I gave you both the same dishes, but I named them something different and emphasized different elements for each of you. I think I can tell when a woman is enjoying her food. And you both did."

Mrs. Ravenel snorted. Then she chuckled. And soon she was laughing until she had tears in her eyes. Even Dahlia had the giggles before her mother calmed down enough to talk again. "Well, Mr. New York, that's the best Charleston wedding food I've had in my life. If this is what you want, you've got it, Dahlia."

Harper's hand flashed out to grip Zak's. She couldn't believe it. This might work.

"This is what I want," Dahlia confirmed.

"All right, then. We'll check in with you on the decorations next week, Harper. You picked a winner with this chef right here." Her eyes fell to their clasped hands with a knowing smile, but Harper didn't let go. She didn't care if it made her look unprofessional. "Let's go check on your alterations, Dahlia. Should be easy after solving the food crisis. Although we are not calling anything at that wedding the Spanish Madame," she said, and they swept out on the sound of Dahlia's protests.

"It worked," Harper said, turning to Zak, stunned. He leaned down to kiss her, but she pressed her hand against his mouth, trying not to notice how smooth his lips felt against her fingertips. "I'm so thankful I still have that booking, but you had to compromise who you are. I hate that."

He straightened. "I want you to try something."

He held out a tasting spoon with a piece of scallop in a light yellow sauce. She accepted the bite, and she could see from the glint in his eyes that the reversal of their roles from last night wasn't lost on him.

It was such a uniquely Zak flavor, she realized as her taste buds explored it. Delicate and bold, a layer of citrus and then spice but with savory undertones.

"It's perfection."

"I made exactly the food I wanted to, the way I wanted to. I didn't have to compromise anything about the way I cook, and you loved it anyway. Didn't you?"

The hint of uncertainty in that final question undid her. She looked him in the eyes and smiled. "I did. I loved it."

"I adapt, Harper. That's different from compromising. It took me a couple of failed months in Charleston to realize that adapting isn't a failure of creative vision. It's how great chefs survive, as long as they always keep that slight edge and stay hungry for the next new idea. New York doesn't need me, but I've got to save Charleston from itself."

That made her laugh. "I know it's not glamorous like Manhattan, but we've got a pretty good thing going here."

Zak's teasing smiled faded, and her breath grew shallow as his eyes darkened. "We do. You and me. And it doesn't take compromise. It just takes some adapting. If you could—"

But Harper was done listening. She wound her hands around his neck, and he bent to meet her kiss. It was even better than the feast he'd poured his heart into that lay plated so beautifully beside them.

The kiss burned deeper and hotter than his devilbird until she finally leaned back just enough to breathe.

"Have I told you how much I admire your attention to detail?" she asked as he trailed kisses down her neck toward her collarbone.

He paused to rest his forehead against hers, his breath ragged. "Harper . . . I don't want to be just friends anymore. How do you feel about that?"

"Zak," she said, guiding his mouth back to hers, "I'm still not letting you win at pool."

Then he was kissing her again, and she had just enough conscious thought left to be thankful the curtains didn't hang open anymore.

Part 2: Janie and Emmett

By Jenny Proctor

Chapter One

Janie Middleton paced the length of her living room, her emotions a tangled mess. She forced her breathing to slow. In through her nose, out through her mouth just like her therapist had taught her. She was fine. In control. She glanced at her phone, sitting face up on the coffee table. It was still on, the email pulled up on the screen, but she resisted the urge to pick it up and read the message again. She'd already read the stupid thing seventeen times and that was sixteen times too many.

Instead, she flipped the phone over so it lay face down on the table and crossed the room to her cello. Mallory wouldn't be off work for another half hour which meant she couldn't rely on her sister to help her sort out her emotions. After Mallory, music was the next best thing. She pulled her cello out of its case, adjusted the endpin and tuned up before pulling it close to her body. Even just holding it soothed her nerves. She took one more intentional breath and closed her eyes. *Mahler.* She needed to play Mahler.

Forty-five minutes later, Janie looked up and saw her twin sister standing in the living room entry, her arms folded, her head resting against the door jamb.

Janie lifted her bow off the strings. "How long have you been standing there?"

"Long enough," Mallory said. "You're playing Mahler."

It was a statement, not a question. Back in high school, Mallory had referred to Gustav Mahler's compositions as funeral music, which always made Janie roll her eyes. It wasn't funeral music; it just had a darker, more broody sound. Which is exactly why Janie always played it when she was emotional. It was music that really made her *feel* something. Still, even with her amateur understanding of classical music, it hadn't taken long for Mallory to learn that Mahler usually meant Janie would need to talk before too long. Janie watched her sister move to the couch and sit down, her feet propped up on the coffee table. "Okay. Lay it on me."

Janie cracked her neck and shifted, leaning her cello against the wall behind her. For all their physical similarities as identical twins—long straight brown hair, light blue eyes, freckles from head to toe—the sisters were polar opposites in personality. Mallory was outgoing and funny, personable, and friends with everyone. Janie was more reserved and introverted, and lacked Mallory's natural self-confidence. It had taken Janie years, including one of intentional therapy, to feel happy as her own self and not like a shadow of her sister's more sparkly presence. She'd worked hard to accept that different wasn't necessarily better or worse. Sometimes it was just different. Their relationship had weathered a lot over the years, but through it all, one thing never changed. Mallory, more than anyone, was keenly dialed into Janie's emotions and vice versa. They may have had moments of raging jealousy and arguments that rivaled the worst of reality television. But at the core, they were there for each other. No questions asked.

Janie moved to the couch and sat down next to her sister. "I got an email from Emmett Calhoun today."

Mallory's jaw fell open. "*Your* Emmett Calhoun? I mean, not *your* Emmett. I know he was never yours—"

Janie cut her off. "I know what you mean. And yes. Him. High school Emmett Calhoun."

"What for?" Mallory asked.

"My quartet is booked to play his brother's wedding. I guess he wants me to accompany him on some song he wrote for the bride and groom."

"Deacon's getting married?" Mallory propped her elbow up against the back of the couch, her head leaning on her hand. "That's so great."

Janie swallowed her irritation. Mallory had been friends with Emmett. She had a right to be happy that his older brother was getting married. Even if it meant momentarily ignoring her sister's discomfort.

"Right but we're not talking about Deacon right now," Mallory said, likely reading Janie's feelings on her always transparent face. "We're talking about you. And Emmett."

Janie pulled a pillow off the couch and pressed it against her face. "I can't see him again, Mal. You know I can't."

Mallory reached over and smoothed her sister's hair. "Wouldn't you have seen him anyway? At the wedding?"

Janie paused, pulling the pillow away long enough to answer. "Well, yes, I guess. But, that's different. I'll be with my quartet at the wedding, playing the entire time with no expectation of mingling or talking to the wedding party. If I do this, I'll have to see him, practice with him. Spend time with him *alone*." She jammed the pillow back into place.

High school was a long time ago, Janie," Mallory said, her voice endlessly patient. "Almost a decade."

"Seven years is not almost a decade," Janie said into the pillow, her words almost too muffled to hear.

"Sure, it is. Think of all that's happened since then. You graduated from college. You landed your dream job with the symphony. You rented your very own condo with the best roommate ever." Mallory tugged the pillow away. "Emmett Calhoun has nothing on you. You shouldn't feel intimidated."

Except Janie totally did. No way she could spend three years of high school crushing on the same guy and then be all relaxed and happy when he strolled back into her life. Crushing wasn't even an adequate word for what she had felt. Emmett was a musician. A singer/songwriter type who always had his guitar and was constantly playing. In the high school cafeteria. After football games. At prom, at parties, at the beach, literally anywhere he could find an audience. Through it all? Janie had been his most devoted groupie. Had she not been so good at fading into the background, someone probably would have noticed and called her on it. Because if he'd been singing, she'd been listening.

"What are you worried about?" Mallory prompted, when Janie failed to respond. "It's not like he even knew how you felt. You have zero reason to feel uncomfortable around him."

"I'm not worried about him knowing anything," Janie finally said. "It's more like I'm worried that nothing has really changed. That everything I felt back then will resurface and I'll embarrass myself all over again."

"But that's what I'm saying. You didn't embarrass yourself. Emmett never figured out you wrote that note."

Janie cringed. Seven years or not, she could hardly think about the note she'd written senior year, admitting all her feelings for Emmett without wanting to die. She hadn't signed it, but she'd left it in his locker, sure that the clue she'd given him about their shared biology lab sophomore year would be enough to identify her.

It hadn't been. Or at least, if it was, Emmett never sought her out and said anything. After a summer of tears, Janie had left for Vanderbilt University and managed to forget about Emmett altogether. Mostly, anyway.

But now he was back. And somehow, Janie felt like she was in high school all over again, the same queasy feeling she'd had whenever she thought of him then, overtaking her *now*.

"It doesn't matter that he never figured it out," Janie said. "I worked so hard to get over him, Mal. What if he strolls in with his guitar and I just . . ." She couldn't even finish her sentence.

Mallory nudged Janie's thigh with her foot. "Come on. You'll be fine. Besides, he might be married for all you know."

She had a point. They did have a few friends that were already married.

"At the very least, he could have a girlfriend."

Janie leaned back into the couch. A wife *or* a girlfriend? If he still looked anything like he did in high school—all lean and tan with those intense brown eyes—the odds were pretty good. The thought gave her a small measure of comfort. Unavailable was good. Unavailable was safe. But nothing felt safer than not seeing him at all. "I could tell him no," Janie said. "Tell him I'm too busy to rehearse anything outside of our normal repertoire."

Mallory narrowed her gaze like she always did when she thought she knew better than her sister. "Is he willing to pay you?"

Janie chewed her bottom lip. "He didn't name an amount, but his email did say he'd like to hire me to accompany him, so yeah. I'm sure he'd pay me something."

"How much is something?"

"I don't know, really. It's probably up to me what I charge him."

Mallory kept pushing. "Fifty bucks? Five hundred bucks? I'm just trying to figure out how worth it this whole thing might be. Fifty bucks probably isn't worth all the stressing you'll do if you go through with this. But five hundred? I can deal with stressed out Janie if the payout is that much."

Five hundred was too generous. If Janie had to guess, it would be more like one fifty, or two hundred, depending on whether or not she had to transcribe the music. Emmett was obviously talented, but cello music was written on an entirely different clef. She'd be surprised if he showed up with it already transcribed.

"I wouldn't do it for fifty bucks," Janie said. "I'd probably ask one fifty."

"That's a month's worth of groceries." Mallory patted the couch between them for emphasis. "I think you have to go for it."

As a musician, Janie wasn't exactly rolling in extra cash. Her dad had offered more than once to help her out with her bills, but as a point of pride, she'd never taken him up on the offer. He'd been surprised enough when she decided to make music her career. She didn't need to fuel his doubts with her inability to make ends meet. She'd come close a time or two, but somehow another gig always lined up and she'd been able to make it work. Which was the biggest reason why she had to tell Emmett yes.

She turned to her sister. "Thank you for talking me out of my crazy."

Mallory smiled. "You know I got you."

"How are you? How was work?"

Mallory shrugged. "Meh. It's fine I guess. Same old stuff."

Janie wasn't convinced. Her sister had endured a pretty painful break up a few weeks back and was only just starting to emerge from the fog. Mallory didn't have a stellar track record with guys. Admittedly, sometimes she just picked total idiots. But this guy, Preston, had seemed like the real deal. He was one of the dentists in the office where she worked as a hygienist. He was stable, reliable, a little boring, but he'd been good to Mallory. Until all of a sudden, he wasn't. After six months, he'd dumped her and ran off with the office manager, twelve years his senior.

"Stop looking at me like that," Mallory said. "I'm fine. I even flirted with the UPS guy today. That's progress, right?"

Janie forced a smile. She could still see the sadness settled behind Mallory's eyes, but she'd give her sister the victory. She could tell she needed it. "Definitely progress."

Mallory stood. "Are you hungry? I had lunch from this new food truck—Korean fusion something? You would love it, and I would totally be willing to eat it again."

"Korean fusion in Charleston?"

"I know it sounds crazy, but seriously. It'll be your new favorite."

"I believe you," Janie said. "But I had a symphony board meeting this afternoon and they fed us Lewis's Barbecue. I'm still stuffed."

"Fine. But we should go this weekend."

Janie left her sister and headed back to her own room where she could respond to Emmett's email on her laptop. With her track record, she'd fat finger some ridiculous gif if she tried to type a response on her iPhone. She dropped into her desk chair and typed a quick response to Emmett, agreeing to help him and suggesting a few times for them to meet.

There. Done. No turning back.

Before closing her laptop, her fingers hovered over her keyboard, the cursor blinking in the search bar. Back in her high school groupie days, googling Emmett had been a regular occurrence. She'd spent hours searching YouTube, looking for new performances she might have missed. The videos were always homemade and terrible quality, but she hadn't cared.

Before she could think long enough to decide it was a terrible idea, she typed his name, held her breath, and hit enter. The first hit was a reference to the University of South Carolina School of Law Deans List. She clicked on the link and found his name—Emmett Charles Calhoun. He had such a Charleston sounding name. Perfectly proper and Southern. But Emmett had never seemed all that Charleston proper. At least not like the old money his family hailed from. He'd always been more jeans and flannel than khaki shorts and deck shoes. That was part of why she'd liked him so much.

The law school part surprised her. He'd planned to go to Nashville and try to make music work. At least, that's what Mallory had always told her. Crazy that he'd ended up in college instead.

Janie backtracked to the search page. A Facebook profile he probably hadn't updated in years. An obituary for his grandfather that listed him as a survivor. But that was pretty much it. She clicked over to the videos tab to see if there was anything there and finally found her reward. A post, just three weeks old, of Emmett playing at the Tattooed Moose downtown. The caption under the video read, "Emmett Calhoun. Seriously, who is this guy?! I'd def buy his album."

Janie clicked play and leaned forward, scooting to the edge of her seat.

He was good. *So* good. Better than he had been in high school. He looked pretty much the same. A little older, for sure. And broader through the chest and shoulders. But still Emmett.

Just as charming.

Just as adorable.

Janie lowered her head to her desk.

She was in for it. So, so, so in for it.

Chapter Two

Emmett sat in his truck, engine still running, and stared up at the front porch of Janie Middleton's condo. He remembered Mallory more—they'd been in the same circle of friends—but it was hard not to notice identical twins. He did remember that Janie had been quieter, more reserved, and very serious about her music. That level of dedication was the reason he was still sitting in the car and not knocking on her front door, even though it was five minutes past when they were supposed to meet. She was a legit musician. One that had turned her passion into something she got paid to do. She probably read music, wrote music, knew everything there was to know about music.

All he did was play the guitar. Except for a few gigs he'd booked at local bars playing covers, and years of playing for his friends, he didn't have anything even remotely musical on his resume. Three years of law school? Sure. A downtown job waiting tables? Absolutely. But nothing about music. Nothing that qualified him to be here, with a bona fide professional, trying to teach her how to play his song.

Asking her to help had been a bad idea. He could always leave, play the song without the cello part and forget he'd ever asked her. Better yet, he could scrap the idea of playing at the wedding all together.

He groaned and leaned his head on the steering wheel. The horn on his truck honked and he shot up, swearing under his breath. What would she think of him sitting in her driveway honking his horn?

Movement on the porch drew his eyes upward. One of the twins stood in the doorway of the condo, a puzzled expression on her face. His mind registered Mallory at first—she was the one he knew best—but Janie made more sense.

He rolled down his window. "Sorry. I didn't mean to honk."

"Oh. Are you're going to come inside?" She glanced at her watch. "Our meeting was at five, right?"

Yep. For sure Janie. The situation just kept getting better and better.

"Right. Yeah, sorry." Emmett put the window back up. Guess the decision was made, then.

Janie had left the front door open, so Emmett climbed the porch stairs and stepped into the entryway, pulling the door closed behind him. He gripped his guitar case and waited, not sure where to go from there.

"In here," a voice called.

Emmett followed the sound to the left and crossed

through a small eating area before finding Janie in the living room, her cello already out. "Hello," he said. "Sorry about the honk. I was doing some thinking, and I guess my head hit the steering wheel."

Janie pushed her hands into her back pockets. She looked good. Different than he remembered, without all the dark make-up she'd worn in high school.

"No worries," she said. "How have you been?"

"Good, good. You know, just living life." It was a lame answer. But what was he supposed to say? That he'd graduated law school but refused to take the bar because he couldn't face the possibility of becoming a stuffy lawyer in a stuffy town and wind up just like his stuffy father? That in the meantime he was waiting tables at a stuffy restaurant downtown wishing he didn't have to rely on his trust fund to pay the rent? Janie had made something of herself. She played the cello in the freaking Charleston Symphony. Honestly, he was surprised she'd even agreed to accompany him. "What about you?" he asked.

"Yeah. Things are good. Mallory's my roommate."

He nodded. "Tell her I said hello." He shifted his guitar from one hand to the other. He wasn't an expert at reading body language, but Janie seemed . . . uncomfortable? Nervous, maybe? It actually made him feel better to know he wasn't the only one.

"So I guess there's going to be a wedding?" Janie finally said.

"Right, yeah," Emmett answered. "Deacon's marrying Dahlia Ravenel. Do you know her?"

"I don't think so. But, there are a lot of Ravenels in

Charleston." She motioned to the couch. "Um, do you want to sit down? Whenever you're ready we can go over the song."

"Sure. Of course." Emmett moved to the couch and pulled out his guitar. Why was he having such a hard time starting up a conversation? Janie was pretty, yes, but he'd known that coming in. He was never flustered around women. Then again, he'd never had to lay his amateur music at the feet of a professional.

He strummed a chord on his guitar and adjusted the tuning pegs until it sounded right.

"Do you need a tuner?" Janie asked.

Emmett looked up and met her eyes. "Nah, I can hear well enough which way it's off."

She cocked her head. "Right, but one string being tuned to the others is different than being tuned in general. And when I play with you, it's important for our pitches to match."

They would match. He'd been tuning by ear for years and he was always dead on. But she seemed so sincere in the way she'd explained, he wasn't about to contradict her. "I guess I should use the tuner then," he said.

She moved to the music stand sitting beside her cello and picked up the tuner, turning it on before holding it out to his guitar. He plucked a single string, watching as the screen on the digital tuner lit up green, just as he knew it would. He tried not to grin as each following string had the same result.

Janie pursed her lips. "That always happens, doesn't it?"

Emmett smiled, but offered an apologetic shrug. "Yes?"

She laughed. "I guess I should have trusted you. I'm officially jealous now. Perfect pitch is not something I was blessed with."

Hearing her laugh, the way it filled the room around him, eased some of the tension in Emmett's shoulders. He was still nervous—playing for an audience of one felt more intimidating than an entire bar full of people—but there was something about her that put him at ease. He motioned to the open spot next to him. "I think it'll make me less nervous if you sit."

She bit her lip, hesitating just long enough that he expected her to say no and stay where she was. But then she crossed the room and sat down. It wasn't a huge couch, so when they angled inward to face each other, their knees almost touched. He realized in hindsight that might have been why she'd hesitated. Pushing away the thought, he focused on his music, refusing to let the woman beside him unravel his concentration.

With his body curled around his guitar, he played the opening chords of the song. A few measures later, he sang the first line, glancing up to gauge Janie's reaction. To his relief, her eyes weren't on his face, but on his hands. They stayed there, watching him play, making it easier for him to play the love song. If they'd made eye contact, things could have gotten awkward fast. Not that a love song was unexpected; he'd written it for a wedding. But at the wedding he'd be singing to a room full of people, with his brother and Dahlia standing there holding hands. Everyone would know the love he was singing about was theirs. But here, in Janie's living room, with just her listening, it felt . . . different.

When Emmett strummed the last note, the silence settled heavy between them. He looked up and met Janie's gaze, surprised to see tears in her eyes.

She quickly wiped them away. "Sorry." She motioned to

her face. "This is a thing that happens to me. That was a really beautiful song."

"So you think they'll like it?" he asked, not realizing how much he wanted her approval until he'd asked for it.

"They'll love it. Truly. It's perfect."

He soaked up the praise. He knew the song was good. He felt it on a visceral level, deep in his core. But validation wasn't something volunteered all that frequently in his life. At least not from the people that mattered to him most. To hear someone pay him such a specific compliment—someone who hadn't just finished her fourth shot of tequila and was looking for a good time from the night's entertainment—felt good. Really good.

"Thanks. I'm sorry I made you cry."

She smiled. "No you're not. Tears mean you did your job. That's what we want music to do, right? Evoke emotion? Trust me. You nailed it with that one."

"I don't write many love songs," he said. "I guess I'm never really sure how they're going to go."

"It's sweet that you wrote one for your brother."

He stifled a laugh. "Or maybe just sad that I . . . ." He didn't know how to finish the sentence. *That I've never been in love myself, so I write about his life instead?* "I don't know," he finally managed. "It's fine, I guess." The look in Janie's eyes said she wanted more explanation which meant time for a subject change. "Music always makes you cry?"

Janie shrugged. "Not all the time. Just when it's particularly meaningful. I'm not sure why some things resonate and others don't. But when they do, yeah. Tears happen." She tucked her hair behind her ears. "It drives Mallory crazy. That I feel everything so intensely. I think it's a musician thing."

That was something he remembered about high school Janie. Her intensity. From the way she played her cello to the way she looked at people in the hallway. There wasn't anything casual about her at all. She didn't seem the same way now. She had the same presence, but it was more intentional, more in control. "Where'd you end up going to school?" Emmett asked her.

"The Blair School of Music," Janie said. "At Vanderbilt. Over in Nashville? They have a great music program."

Emmett's jaw tightened. They did have a great music program. He'd spent hours researching it, pouring over the school's application process. At one point, he'd even believed he'd be able to convince his father to pay for it. He didn't have to go Nashville just to pursue country music, he could go to Nashville *and* get an education. But his father had been crystal clear on the subject. "You're a Calhoun, son," he had said. "And Calhoun men go to law school. You want to see a penny of your trust fund? You'll stop ranting about music and get yourself to Columbia where you belong."

"I thought about going to Vanderbilt at one point." Emmett plucked at his guitar, strumming a few random chords before looking back at Janie.

Her face lit up. "Yeah? It's a great school. And not just for classical music. I had a lot of classmates studying country music. It would have been perfect for you."

"Yeah, well, my family had different plans." He tried to keep the edge out of his voice, but it was almost impossible.

"That's too bad. I always thought you were going to make

it back in high school. You're so good, Emmett. Truly."

Emmett held her gaze. "I didn't think you knew who I was back in high school."

She scoffed. "Whatever. Everyone knew who you were."

"Maybe. But you weren't exactly like everyone else."

She shook her head, her hands fidgeting with the edge of a throw pillow. "I was a mess in high school."

Emmett didn't know how that could possibly have been true. "You know, I heard you play once?" Emmett said. "It was one of your orchestra concerts. Not at school. It was downtown."

"With the Charleston Youth Symphony?"

He nodded. "I guess, yeah. I had to go for my music appreciation class and write a summary of the piece I enjoyed the most. You played a solo, and it was definitely my favorite."

"Senior year?" Janie asked.

"Yeah, I think so."

"That would have been the Saint-Seans concerto. Man, I worked hard to get that solo."

Emmett propped his guitar against the table and leaned his elbows onto his knees, steepling his fingers. "I think it's really great you turned your music into a career. I wish I had that kind of courage."

She let out a soft laugh. "I wish I had your perfect pitch."

An hour later, Emmett had moved to the piano bench, close to where Janie sat with her cello. He hadn't come with any music written—he didn't know anything about cello music—but Janie was easily able to take the notes he picked out on his guitar, match it on her cello, then transcribe the music onto the staff paper she had on her music stand. It was amazing to watch. Her general musical knowledge was extensive, but her skill on the cello left him almost speechless. When they finally played the song together, with the guitar, vocals and cello all combined, the overall effect had him near jumping out of his chair. On top of his excitement over the song, he could *not* stop staring at Janie. It's possible the music was amplifying his emotions, but she was . . . He didn't even have a word for what she was. Captivating? Stunning? Whatever it was, he couldn't get enough.

Janie reached over and stopped the recording on her iPhone. She'd wanted to have it recorded so she could listen when practicing.

"Will you text that to me?" Emmett asked.

She nodded. "It sounded great, didn't it?"

"Better than I imagined. I'd heard the cello part in my head but hearing it all together like that was awesome."

Janie stood up, heaving her cello over to the large case standing up next to the wall. She placed the cello inside and latched it shut. "You've never had any formal music training, right?" She motioned to him and his guitar. "This is all self-taught?"

"Mostly, I guess," Emmett said. "I mean, I've watched about a million YouTube videos, but that's it."

"Can you read music?"

"Not really. I can tell you what notes I'm playing, but I've never learned how to look at music and tell what's what."

She stared, her mouth slightly open. "That's so annoying."

"What? Why?"

"Because! You're too good to not be able to read music.

104

It's not fair."

He shrugged. "Elvis Presley couldn't read music. I didn't think it was that big a deal."

"Yeah, you wouldn't. But to be as good as you are without any formal training? Most of my classmates at Vanderbilt would hate you."

"That's just it, though. I've been watching you all this time thinking the same thing. How you know the notes and can just write the music out like that."

"I've been studying music since I was 9 years old," Janie argued. "I'm not anything special. I just work really hard. But you have a gift, Emmett."

She'd taken a step toward him as she talked. She was close. Close enough he could reach out and take her hand if he wanted to. And he almost did. Once the thought of touching her had entered his mind, he couldn't stop thinking about what she might feel like. He gripped the neck of his guitar a little tighter. They'd only been together an hour. Holding her hand was probably a little presumptuous. "Hey, will you teach me?" he asked her instead. "How to read music?"

She folded her arms across her chest and studied him. She was debating something in her mind, he could tell, her eyes flicking this way and that. "What like, right now?" she finally asked.

Emmett glanced at his watch. "Actually, I have best man duties with Deacon and Dahlia tonight. Some sort of cake tasting thing. But another time. Maybe we could grab dinner somewhere and then come back here?" He realized after the words were out of his mouth he'd just asked Janie out on a date. He didn't mind the thought. He hadn't been on a real date in months. And Janie was the most impressive woman he'd been around in twice that long. He held his breath, waiting for her response.

"I would really like that," she said.

He didn't even try to contain his smile. "Good. Me too."

She walked him to the door a few minutes later. "Hey, can I have your phone?" she asked.

He pulled it out of his pocket and unlocked it before handing it over. Her fingers brushed against his as she took it. Had they lingered for a second before she pulled away? Did he make that up? He watched as she pulled up his texts and sent a message.

"There." She handed it back. "I just sent myself a text. So I can send you the recording, and so now you have my number." She looked up at him through her lashes, her teeth holding onto her bottom lip in a way that made his nerves tingle and his breath hitch.

"Thanks," he said. "I'll definitely text you."

"This is, um . . ." She tucked a strand of hair behind her ears and shook her head. "This is not what I expected."

Emmett opened the front door. "No, me neither." He stepped onto the porch, looking back with a grin. "But I'm not disappointed."

Chapter Three

Janie paced around her living room. "No way, no way, no way." She sat down on the couch, then got up again, moved to the piano bench, then sat down one more time. She couldn't focus. Couldn't sit.

Having never really experienced Emmett up close and in person back in high school, save their short stint in biology as lab partners, Janie didn't have a ton to go on. But this. Today. The hour they'd spent together was better than anything she might have imagined in high school.

With his biceps and his dimples and his calloused finger tips and the way his words melted from his lips when he sang. Had she not had her cello to hold onto, she might have fallen out of her chair.

A wave of envy washed over her. Janie was talented and she knew it, but she was no prodigy. She'd told Emmett she wasn't anything special, and she'd meant it. She'd gotten as far as she had because of her work ethic and her commitment to her music, but she'd never go on tour as an acclaimed soloist. Not in her wildest dreams. That required a measure of raw talent she simply didn't have. But Emmett had it, that intangible something that just made him *more*. She'd seen it back in high school. But she'd forgotten how powerful his presence was. He was magnetic. Constantly tugging on every part of her, inside and out.

And he'd asked her to dinner.

Emmett Calhoun had asked *her* to dinner.

Hours upon hours of her teenage life had been spent fantasizing about that very thing, and now *It. Was. Happening.*

Forty-five minutes later, Janie still sat in the living room listening to the recording she'd made of Emmett's song. For possibly the sixty seventh time.

"Is that him?"

Janie jumped and turned around.

Mallory stood in the doorway, still wearing her pale pink scrubs form work. Janie scrambled to turn off her phone. "Where have you been? I must have texted you a billion times!"

Mallory sat down beside her. "Sorry. A procedure went late so I stayed to assist."

Janie had been waiting for this very moment, when she could finally launch into a detailed accounting of her afternoon with Emmett, explaining every minute in thorough detail and ending with a drumroll opening to the song they'd recorded. But Mallory looked awful, her face drawn, her eyes watery and sad.

"Mal, what's wrong?" Janie asked. "You look awful."

Mallory shrugged. "It's dumb, really."

"It's not dumb. Not if it made you feel like this."

Mallory wiped her eyes with the back of her hand. "Tasha sent pictures to one of the other hygienists today."

Janie narrowed her eyes. Office manager Tasha? "Pictures of what?"

"Of them. The happy couple. Lounging next to the ocean somewhere."

"Dude. Doesn't she have kids?" Janie said. "How can she have left her family like that?"

"I don't think she has kids," Mallory said. "A cat, maybe."

"Seriously, I think you need to look for another job. There are dentists everywhere. Get a fresh start. Where there won't be reminders of what he did every time you turn around."

Mallory sighed and dropped her head into her sister's lap. "Maybe you're right."

Janie brushed a hand over her sister's hair. Preston was an idiot and didn't deserve one more of Mallory's tears. "Come on," Janie said. "We're going out tonight."

"No," Mallory grumbled. "I just got home. I don't want to go back out."

"But there's nothing to eat here and it's time for dinner. We can go to that Korean food truck you mentioned."

Mallory didn't respond.

"Or, go get fried green tomatoes at Blossom?"

Mallory shifted, turning her head toward Janie in interest.

"And then go to Jeni's for ice cream?"

That did the trick. "Okay," Mallory said, sitting up. "You

win. Let me go change my clothes."

Ha. Every time. Fried green tomatoes and Jeni's ice cream worked magic when it came to Mallory.

Janie watched from the far side of the bar while a Citadel cadet chatted up her sister. He was cute, but didn't look older than nineteen, maybe twenty. Still, he was making Mallory laugh which was exactly the kind of thing she needed. When her cell phone buzzed from her bag, she pulled it out, instantly hoping it was Emmett.

She smiled when she saw his name lighting up her screen.

Today was a really, really good day, he had texted.

She typed out a response. ***Yes. Yes it was***.

I realized after I left we never talked about payment. What do you normally charge for this kind of thing?

She considered his question. She'd never really *done* this kind of thing. It's not like she had a point of reference. But then, it almost felt wrong to get paid for the hour she'd spent with Emmett. It felt a lot more like hanging out with a friend than a business arrangement, and with the promise of dinner? If things were going to get personal, she'd rather it *all* be personal. She typed out her response. ***How about you buy me dinner and we call it even?***

Mallory would hate that she'd given up the extra cash, but that hardly mattered to Janie. Not anymore.

Deal. Are you busy tomorrow night?

Mallory dropped onto a barstool beside her. "What's making you all smiley and happy?" She craned her neck, trying to look at Janie's phone.

"It's nothing," Janie said, turning off her phone and laying it face down on the bar. It wasn't so much that she wanted to keep Emmett a secret from her sister. It was more she didn't want to rub her own sudden happiness in her sister's face. She'd tell her later. When she wasn't feeling so down. "Tell me about your new friend." Janie looked pointedly over Mallory's shoulder. The cadet raised his glass and smiled when Janie made eye contact.

"Please," Mallory said. "He's adorable, but he graduated from high school, like, twenty minutes ago."

"He's in a bar, Mal. He can't be that young."

"Twenty-one? Eighteen? What's the difference? They're both too young for me," Mallory said.

"Maybe long term, but for a quick rebound? Why not?"

Mallory's expression tightened. "Janie, please don't push me. I'm not ready, okay? You got me out of the house, you fed me, I flirted. I think that's enough for one night."

Janie pulled her sister into a hug. "Of course it is. You did good." They stood up and gathered their belongings. "Ice cream on the way home?"

Mallory nodded. "Absolutely."

The line outside of Jeni's Splendid Ice Cream was longer than usual, winding half a block down King Street. Rather than deal with trying to find a parking space, Mallory agreed to circle the block while Janie waited in line. Jeni's was that kind of ice cream. It was always worth the wait. Janie didn't need to study the menu—she always ordered the exact same thing and so did her sister—so she pulled out her phone to respond to Emmett's text.

Sorry it took so long to respond, she typed. *I'm out with Mallory.*

Anywhere fun? His response came through almost immediately.

Getting ice cream at Jeni's. But then home for pajamas and Netflix. We are nothing if not party animals.

You're at Jeni's right now? I'm two blocks away.

Janie immediately looked over her shoulder, which was dumb. Two blocks away was not right outside Jeni's storefront. Still, her pulse quickened at the thought of possibly seeing him again.

Still cake tasting? she asked. *You're a good brother/best man.*

Dahlia has changed her mind no less than fifty times. I like the chocolate, but I think it would taste better with some ice cream. He finished the text with a little winking emoji.

Janie stared at her phone and resisted the urge to run laps around the inside of the ice cream shop, yelling to anyone who would listen that Emmett Calhoun was flirting with her.

Hopefully you'll get out of there before Jeni's closes, Janie texted back. *A reward for your endless patience!*

Will you still be there? he asked.

Janie had half a mind to call Mallory and tell her to find a parking space. She'd happily wait at Jeni's for Emmett to show up. But it was already a miracle Mallory had agreed to a night out in the first place. And she'd been clear when they left the bar. She was ready to go home.

I wish, Janie responded. ***Mallory doesn't feel great. She's getting over a bad break up and can only take so much of the social scene. I promised her an early night in. Pajamas and Netflix, remember?*** She typed out another message before he could respond. ***But I am free for dinner tomorrow night.***

It was her turn to order so she slipped her phone into the back pocket of her jeans, only semi-distracted when it buzzed, and then buzzed again with incoming messages. With an ice cream cone in each hand, she had no choice but to leave it there until she was back in the car. She handed Mallory her cone, then yanked out her phone, dropping it in her lap before buckling her seatbelt.

"Oh, this was a good idea," Mallory said, taking her first bite. "Any new flavors on the board?"

"Just the usual."

Janie's phone buzzed again, this time with a text from her dad. Janie forced herself to ignore the unread messages from Emmett, opening only the newest one.

"Dad wants to know how you're holding up," she said, through a mouth full of her brown butter almond brittle.

"Uggh, will you answer him for me? He just wants me to talk about stuff, and I'm all talked out. Rehashing with him will make me cry and I'm kinda enjoying being numb right now. It's way easier."

"You know he means well," Janie said.

"Maybe. But he could also just be bored." Mallory turned on her blinker and turned off of King Street, heading toward the battery. It wasn't the fastest way home, but the detour had become routine for the sisters. Whenever they were downtown and had time to kill, they always picked routes that drove them past St. Phillips Episcopal on Church Street—it had the best graveyard—or took them past all the old mansions that lined Battery Park.

"I never get tired of these houses," Janie said, through another bite of her ice cream. "And Dad's not bored. He cares, Mallory. You have to call him and tell him you're okay."

She rolled her eyes. "Fine. I'll call him tomorrow. But he needs to start dating again. He's been divorced five years. Enough with the single life. Get a girlfriend already and leave your daughters alone."

Janie tried not to laugh. "You don't really mean that."

Mallory shot her a quick glance before easing into an empty parking space on the far side of the park, looking out across the Cooper River toward the open ocean. A light blinked steadily out on Fort Sumter, guiding ships into the harbor. Mallory rolled down the windows, letting in a steady breeze blowing off the water. It smelled like fish and salt and home and instantly made Janie happy.

"I do mean it," Mallory said. "I don't want him to be as bad as Mom. But a little distraction would be good for him." Their mother, presently sailing the Caribbean with her newest love, Jacques, had dated more men since her divorce was final than Janie and Mallory had their entire lives. *Combined.* Their father, on the other hand, had spent at least two years nursing his broken heart before picking himself up, drying off his tears, and pouring all of his emotional energy into his twin daughters. His *fully-grown* twin daughters. Not that their age mattered to him.

Janie finished the last bite of her ice cream and picked up her phone. "I'm responding on your behalf this time," she said. "But you have to call him back. Before the week is out."

"Fine," Mallory said. "But just remember how much I ran interference when you broke up with Ben."

Janie sighed. "Ohhh, I adored Ben." It was more a wistful thought than a painful one. Ben was Janie's only serious boyfriend, a violinist she had worshipped passionately until he took his musical genius self and moved to New York to play with the Philharmonic. She couldn't fault him that, but it was still a crushing blow to lose him. And a big reason Mallory had decided that Janie didn't need to ever date other artists. She needed someone more stable, reliable. Like an accountant. Or a podiatrist.

"Wait," Mallory said. "I can't believe I forgot to ask. How was your thing with Emmett this afternoon?"

Janie hesitated. She still wasn't sure Mallory was up for the whole story. But no matter how hard she tired, she couldn't suppress her grin. "Are you sure you don't mind talking about it?" she asked.

Mallory scrunched up her eyebrows. "Why would I mind? Come on. Spill it."

Janie bit her lip. "We're having dinner tomorrow night."

Her sister froze. "Shut. Up."

"I've been dying to tell you all night, but then you were feeling all sad and I didn't want to make it worse. But seriously,

Mallory, if you could have been there this afternoon. It was so incredibly amazing." Janie launched into a minute-by-minute explanation of the hour she spent with Emmett from the way he smelled, to the lopsided lift of his smile and the hints of copper in his deep brown eyes. "And he wants me to help him learn how to read music," she finished. "We're getting together tomorrow night. For dinner and music lessons."

Mallory hadn't moved the entire time Janie talked. She just stared, her expression frozen somewhere between shock and annoyance.

"You look annoyed. Why do you look annoyed?" Janie asked.

"I'm not," Mallory said carefully, her face shifting to a more neutral expression. "Is tomorrow, like, a date? Is that how he made it sound?"

Janie paused and thought. He hadn't called it a date, but it had definitely felt like that was his meaning, from the way he'd looked at her, to the comment he made on his way out the door about not being disappointed. "It's a date," she finally said. "I'm sure of it."

"Wow," Mallory said. She leaned back in her seat.

"What do you mean, wow? Why don't you sound happy for me?" Janie's mood had been soaring all night. To have Mallory stomp on her excitement was annoying. And unexpected.

"I'm happy for you," she said. "I guess I'm just . . . surprised."

"Why?" Janie asked, her voice defensive. "That he acted interested in me?"

"No, of course not," Mallory said. "Of course he's interested in you. You're fabulous. It just happened kind of fast, you know? I mean, you were only together an hour."

"But it's not like we've only known each other an hour. We went to school together for years. A little bit of shared history can go a long way."

Mallory reached out and motioned for Janie to take her hand.

Janie hesitated, tension growing in her shoulders. The look on Mallory's face said a lecture was coming, and she didn't want a lecture. She wanted to be happy that a great guy seemed into her and was going to buy her dinner. At least, she hoped. If she could ever respond to his texts. Finally, she pushed out a breath and grabbed her sister's fingers with her own.

Mallory squeezed gently. "Just be careful, okay? After one hour, you sound as far gone as you did after three years. Don't lose your head to this guy, okay? You said yourself how hard you worked to get over him."

Janie softened, squeezing her sister's hand in return. At the very least, she could understand where her sister was coming from. "I know. You're right. And I promise I'll be careful."

"I don't want to see you get hurt, Janie."

Janie nodded. "That's because you always love me best. But if you could see him again, you'd understand. It's different this time. He's different."

"You can't know that this soon, Janie."

Janie bit her lip. She wouldn't argue with Mallory about it. She understood her sister's caution. But she also couldn't explain what the afternoon with Emmett had felt like, with the music and the shared looks between them. It had been incredible, plain and simple.

And she wasn't about to let her twin sister's skepticism dim the magic.

Chapter Four

Emmett took extra care getting ready for his date with Janie. He tried on three different shirts before settling on a soft plaid with button snaps, the sleeves rolled up to his elbow. It was a shirt his brother hated. It wasn't near preppy enough for a Calhoun, but that made him want to wear it more. Deacon could keep his pretty pink shirts and pressed khakis. He could keep all of it. Downtown society, the yacht club, the pew down at Second Presbyterian where his family had been sitting every Sunday for five generations. He was tired of it all.

One hour with Janie had reignited his desire to find his career in music and leave his old life behind. She'd made her dreams work, why couldn't he? But as soon as he'd allowed the thought to take form, doubt came close behind.

He was too old.

Too unoriginal.

His family would never support him.

He glanced in the mirror one last time before picking up his keys. That last part was what rankled the most. His father didn't go so far as to fund his bank account. But the only reason his part-time job waiting tables was enough to cover all his expenses was because his housing and transportation were taken care of. His apartment on East Bay Street was owned by his family, and his truck had been a high school graduation gift.

How much longer the money would last, Emmett didn't know. Every day he wasn't studying for the South Carolina bar was a day counted against him. He half expected his father to show up any day and turn him out.

And maybe that's what he needed. It would make him man up, at least.

He and Janie had agreed to meet downtown at Butcher and Bee for dinner. It was one of Charleston's more eclectic eateries that seemed a little too green for Emmett's liking, but Janie had assured him there was a secret menu item he would love, as long as he was a fan of cheese and burgers. That had been enough to convince him.

He parked his truck and found Janie standing in front of the restaurant. She wore a simple black dress just short enough to make her legs look miles long and her hair was down, loose waves hanging over her shoulders. When their eyes met and she smiled—a full genuine smile—it felt like the world tipped and then righted again. It was a smile he couldn't un-see. And now that he'd seen that joy on her face, he craved it.

He stopped in front of her. "Hello."

"Hi." She leaned forward and took his hand, squeezing it

for a moment before kissing him on the cheek.

Well, that had to be a good sign.

She kept hold of his hand. "Ready?"

"I'm following you," he said. "You're sure I'm going to like this place?"

"You're going to think you won't when you read the menu. But trust me. You won't be disappointed."

He let Janie take the lead on ordering and grinned when he realized the secret menu item she ordered for him was an actual cheeseburger. He thought she'd been exaggerating just to get him there. "It's not just any cheeseburger," she said. "But I still think you'll like it. Seriously though, if you're not willing to at least try the whipped feta and honey, we can't be friends."

"You're passionate about your food, I see," Emmett said.

She took a sip of her water. "Among other things, yes."

"It's not so much that I mind fancy food. I just generally like it with a side of beef."

She rolled her eyes. "You and every other Charlestonian."

They talked all the way through dinner. About nothing, really, but that's what made it so easy. They laughed the most when they reminisced about high school. Teachers they'd both had, the actual real tears Janie had cried when they'd dissected a fetal pig in biology lab. And Mallory's endless string of bad boyfriends.

"Do you remember when she dated that freshman?" Emmett asked. "Was that our senior year?"

"We were juniors," Janie corrected him. "And to be fair, he did *not* look like a freshman."

Emmett laughed. "Seriously, that girl had the weirdest taste in guys."

Janie shook her head. "Not much has changed. It makes me sad. I just want her to be happy and she keeps ending up with these guys that stomp all over her heart."

It felt like a good opening, so Emmett amped up the conversation game. "What about you?" he asked. "Any broken hearts in your history?"

She didn't hesitate to respond, which felt like a good thing. No emotions too close to the surface. "Lots of stupid dating, but only one serious boyfriend. Another musician who left me for the New York Philharmonic."

"Ouch."

"Not at all," Janie said. "*I* would leave me for the New York Phil, and I think I'm pretty great. What about you?"

He shrugged. "There's not much to tell."

"Come on. We're twenty-five. And you're—" she motioned to him, waving her hand up and down, "—all of that. Surely there's been someone."

He stifled a laugh. "Sure. I dated a few girls in college. But nothing that ever really went anywhere."

She nodded, considering. "Okay. I like a man without baggage."

And he liked a woman with her confidence. In one sense it was weird, because that confidence reminded him a lot of high school Mallory. But Janie seemed more grounded, more at peace with herself than Mallory had ever been. Like she knew exactly who she was meant to be. Man, he envied that.

After dinner, he followed her back to her condo. He

carried his guitar up the steps behind her, careful to keep his gaze from lingering too long on the curve of her—

"Mallory might be home," Janie said, pulling his focus to her face. "I hope that's okay." She unlocked the door and led him inside.

"Sure. It'd be nice to see her again."

Instead, they found an empty house, a note from Mallory stuck to the fridge.

"Gone to Dad's to reassure him of my well-being. HAPPY NOW?" the note read.

"What's that all about?" Emmett asked as Janie poured them each a drink.

Janie handed his over, then kicked her shoes off, leading him to the living room in her bare feet. There was something so casual about the gesture, it almost felt . . . intimate. Like she was letting him see the at-home and personal version of herself. "My Dad," she said over her shoulder, "is a kind and lovely man who is devoted wholeheartedly to the happiness of his daughters. If we disappear for too long, he's been known to serial text."

"Sounds rough," Emmett said. He set his drink on the coffee table and pulled out his guitar.

"Except, it really isn't. He's so sweet about it. And he's pretty good at respecting our boundaries. I mean, we joke, but honestly, we feel lucky to have someone so completely on our team, you know?"

Emmett wondered what that might feel like. His family was definitely on his team. But only if he played the game exactly the way they wanted.

"Ready to learn?" Janie asked.

Emmett nodded. He was nearly drunk on Janie's presence. Two days, and he was so far gone, he'd have agreed to study the Cyrillic alphabet if Janie were his teacher. He ran a hand through his hair. When was the last time he'd ever felt something so fast? Maybe never.

Janie started in with a basic explanation of how to read music. Talking about staffs and clefs, whole notes and half notes. Her instruction mostly made sense. Music was a language that already felt pretty intuitive. She was only giving what he knew more structure than it had inside his brain. But it still took him twice as much energy to focus. Every time she moved and he caught a whiff of her scent—vanilla, maybe, and something like oranges—he had to will himself to zero in on her words and not just her lips.

"Are you even listening to what I'm saying?" Janie asked.

Emmett snapped to attention. "I'm listening to everything you're saying."

She cocked her head. "Then why do you look like you're on a completely different planet? I swear I'm not trying to be boring."

"You're not boring."

"Then what is it?"

"Honestly?"

She nodded.

"I can't stop thinking about whether or not I'm going to get to kiss you at the end of the night."

Her face flooded with color, and her eyes dropped to the floor. For a speck of a second, her confidence was gone, and she looked like she wanted to crawl inside herself and disappear. But then she looked up, meeting his gaze head on, her eyes lit with a fire he'd never seen before. She stood from where she sat on the piano bench, closing the distance between them in two short strides. When her lips met his, he was ready.

Her lips were warm and soft and electric. The kiss was hesitant at first, but then she turned her face, deepening their connection and nearly undoing him. He surrendered to her lead, wrapping his arms around her, his fingers tracing the exposed skin on her back. Her hands moved to his neck, then slid forward, cradling either side of his face. She broke the kiss but kept her forehead close. "There," she said softly. "You don't have to wonder anymore. Maybe now you'll pay better attention."

His shoulders lifted in silent laughter and he shook his head. "Not likely."

An hour later, they sat on the couch, as many parts of them touching as he could manage while still holding his guitar. It was Janie that made him pick it up again. Emmett would have traded it for Janie in his arms in a second, but when she asked him to sing to her, he couldn't say no.

He sang the last words of his favorite Blake Shelton song and strummed the final chord.

Janie smiled. "You sing it better than he does."

"Ha," Emmett said. "I wish."

"Have you ever made a demo?" she asked.

The question made him feel exposed, like she'd ripped off a bandage and exposed the raw skin underneath. Making a demo implied he was ready to attempt a career. No doubt he wanted it; but wanting something and feeling ready for something were two different things. He'd been swimming upriver his whole life when it came to his music. Having someone express genuine interest, without any judgement felt revolutionary. "Nah. I've thought about it a few times. But what would I do with it? It's not like you can just mail a demo to Nashville."

"Why not?"

Emmett nudged her with his shoulder. "Listen, Miss Vanderbilt University. Not all of us are as fortunate as you. Record labels don't take unsolicited submissions." He'd done enough research to know that much. "You gotta know somebody. And I don't know anybody."

"You're a Calhoun. Your family is one of the oldest and richest in Charleston. Surely somebody knows *somebody*."

"Nope. Not unless you're trying to get into law school or launch your first political campaign."

"Is that why you went to law school? Because of your family?" Janie leaned her head against his shoulder, her fingers tracing lines up and down his forearm. Somehow, her touch made it easier to answer. Like she'd already accepted him regardless of what he had to say.

"Yep," he said softly. "Went to SC Law just like Deacon. Just like my dad. Just like his dad. I graduated and everything."

Janie pushed herself up, a hand pressed against his chest. "Are you practicing law? I guess I thought . . ." Her words trailed off. "I don't know what I thought. I know you went to law school. Google told me that much. But, I've been thinking about you as a musician. How have we not talked about your day job?"

"Chill, Janie. This is our first date," Emmett joked.

She scrunched up her face. "No, I'm calling yesterday a date too. That makes this number two. Besides, 'What do you do?' is like a starter question. How did we skip over that one?"

"Honestly, I try and avoid talking about college and work. Most people don't understand why I'm not practicing law and don't hesitate to share their opinions. Nobody understands."

"Try me," Janie said.

He took a long breath, slow and deep. "I graduated from law school, but I don't practice law."

"Okay. Why not?"

"Well, first, I can't. I still haven't taken the bar, so I'm licensed to practice exactly nowhere. Second, I don't want to. I don't want to be a lawyer."

She hugged her arms around a pillow, like she was creating a barrier between them. A wall she'd keep building with every new thing she learned about his lack of progress, his lack of . . . everything. "Have you always known you didn't want to do it?" she asked. "Be a lawyer?"

Emmett took a deep breath and leaned forward, propping his elbows on his knees. "I don't know. I think I thought law would grow on me. The pressure from my family was pretty intense, but that last year it got really bad. The closer I got to graduation, the more Dad talked about bringing me into the practice. I knew I couldn't do it."

"So what are you doing?"

"Waiting tables downtown. Playing gigs whenever I can get 'em. Waiting for something to happen, I guess."

Janie flung the pillow from her lap with a huff. "Well, that's not going to work."

Emmett shot her a look. "What's that supposed to mean?"

"You can't just sit around and wait for something to happen. You gotta make it happen. Make a demo." Her eyes lit up. "We'll do one together. We'll do your new song. It's so perfect, Emmett. Oh! And I have a friend who has a recording studio downtown. I'm sure he'll let us use it for close to nothing."

Emmett appreciated her enthusiasm, but she was talking like he actually had the ability to make it in a very competitive music industry. "I'm just some guy with a guitar, Janie. I'm not anything special."

She stared. "Emmett, I've seen you play enough times to know that isn't true. I'm admittedly not a connoisseur of country, but I do know music. You are something special."

Why was it so hard for him to believe her words? "So then what?" he said. "We make a demo. What do I do with it?"

"I don't know. We send it to all the bars around Charleston and try and get you more gigs. Maybe we send it to the local radio station." She chewed on her lip, her eyes darting this way and that. He could almost hear the gears turning in her head. "Maybe I could send it to a few of my professors at Vanderbilt. They all live right there in Nashville. I'm sure the university has connections in the recording industry. It can't hurt to check, right?"

Emmett stared. She'd said *we*. Like she was on his team and willing to help him. Even though she knew about his law degree. About his last name. His family money. With all that, she still thought he could make *music* work.

He wasn't going to lie. Singing country music was a quick way to impress women. But in his experience, it wasn't a gig that earned him trips home to meet the parents. He was the fling. The exciting weekend. But long term? If given the choice, most women wanted the lawyer. But Janie wasn't most women. He'd been saying that from the start. "You'd help me with all that?" he finally asked.

"Of course I would. Why wouldn't I?"

What could he say to that? Nothing, that's what. Instead, he leaned forward and kissed her again.

Chapter Five

One week turned into two weeks, then into three, then six, then eight. But the weeks hardly mattered. Monday, Tuesday, Saturday, whatever. Janie was so far gone on Emmett, if she didn't have reminders going off on her phone telling her where she was supposed to be and when she was supposed to be there, her life might have fallen apart. Not that she cared. Emmett was enough.

They texted every day.

Saw each other every weekend.

And a couple times during the week as well.

He'd been to one of her symphony concerts. She'd gone to see him play a set at the Tattooed Moose. From the front row, this time. No more hiding in the shadows.

The one downside? The closer she grew to Emmett, the more strain she felt on her relationship with Mallory. Her sister was distant. More withdrawn. And not at all interested in hearing anything about Janie's new relationship. Janie suspected it was jealousy. Not of Emmett, specifically, but definitely of her happiness in general. Janie shrugged it off. She'd spent her entire high school experience jealous of her sister. What did it matter if the tables were turned for once?

A little more than a week before Deacon's wedding, Janie lounged in her living room waiting for Mallory to get home. They were supposed to have met for hot yoga earlier in the evening, but Mal never showed. She'd responded to Janie's text—at least she knew she wasn't dead—but she hadn't offered any explanation as to where she was or why she'd stood Janie up.

Her phone chimed with a text and Janie reached for it, picking it up off the coffee table.

Do you think the wedding counts as our 'meet the parents' date? We're two months in. It's about time, right?

Janie grinned. It made her nervous, the idea of meeting the entire Calhoun clan, but at least she wouldn't have to stand around and make small talk the whole time. She'd have to work. They could talk about her all they wanted while she played the reception with her quartet.

Technically, I already met your Mom. When she hired my quartet to play the wedding, Janie texted back. *I doubt she'll remember me, though.*

Of course she'll remember you, Emmett said. *You're pretty memorable*.

I hope she doesn't hate me.

She won't. But if she does, who cares? My

parents already hate me. Emmett added a winking emoji at the end of his message. Another came through before she could respond. *Are you coming over tonight?*

She smiled at the thought. They'd been spending more and more time at his place because Mallory always acted so put out when they hung out at home. But she was long overdue for a talk with her sister. For once, that had to take priority. *I have to hang with Mal for a little while. Twin bonding. But maybe after?*

K. Text me later, he responded.

Janie put down her phone just in time to hear the front door open and close. She heard Mallory's sniffles coming down the hallway and her heart lurched. She stood up, meeting her sister at the doorway to the living room, arms already outstretched. Mallory collapsed against her, her sobs coming in racking, full-bodied heaves. Janie rubbed her sister's back, shushing her gently until her tears slowed. When it seemed like she finally had a grip on things, Janie led Mallory to the couch. They sat down, legs crossed under them, and faced each other, knees touching. Just like always.

"Talk, Mal," Janie said.

Mallory sniffed. "They're getting married," she said softly.

"What?" Janie didn't even try to conceal her shock.

"I thought it was just a fling," Mallory said. "And somehow that made it feel easier. But, I guess he loves her. And they're getting married."

"How is that even possible? They've only been together, what, three months? I feel like he seriously just broke up with you."

"I know," Mallory said. "I keep counting backwards to see how long it's been. I think he must have been seeing her before he broke up with me. It's the only thing that makes sense."

"So Preston is a liar, a jerk, and also a cheat. Good. I needed another reason to hate the guy," Janie said.

"Also, he's coming back to work," Mallory said. "I thought he was gone for good, but I guess it was just a really long vacation."

Janie reached for her sister's hands. "Mallory, it's time to quit. You shouldn't have to work with him."

"I won't. I'm with Dr. Bailey now, and it's a big office. I might pass Preston in the hallway, but . . . it won't be too bad."

"You'll still have to see Tasha though, right?"

"Yeah, for scheduling and stuff. That's unavoidable. But, I don't know. There's a part of me that doesn't want them to win. He was the jerk. Why should I have to slink off with my tail between my legs, you know? I didn't do anything wrong."

"That's true."

"Besides, they pay better than anybody else. It's why I took the job in the first place."

"Also true."

Mallory shook her head. "I gotta get over it. Move past him. Show him that I'm strong enough to let him go."

Janie still hated the idea of Mallory having to deal with any unnecessary stress at work, but there was something to be said for staring down your ex with your shoulders squared and your conscience clear. She was impressed Mal was willing to push through.

"Hey, are you busy Monday night?" Mallory asked. "There's this benefit thing downtown and the office bought a table. I guess they're saying we all have to go, so I'm pretty sure Preston and Tasha will be there."

"That means you need to go looking incredibly gorgeous and poised and younger than his mother—I mean his new fiancée—and rock that party?"

"Exactly," Mallory said, her voice filled with conviction. "But I can't do it without you."

"Oh honey, you know I'm there for you. I wouldn't miss it."

"It's like a fancy dress thing. I was thinking you could wear the navy dress that you wore to Shannon's wedding? And if you don't care, I'll wear your silver dress with the open back."

"Why are we still calling the silver dress mine? You've worn it how many times now?"

Mallory smiled a wide cheesy smile. "You love me. Don't forget that."

"Of course you can wear the dress. And of course I'll be there with you," Janie said.

Mallory breathed out a sigh. "I'm really glad you were home tonight." She leaned forward and propped her head on her sister's shoulder.

"Why wouldn't I be?"

"Oh please," Mallory said. Janie could almost hear the eye roll in her voice. "You've been with Emmett every stupid day for a month. You're never home anymore."

"It's because you always act so annoyed when we're here," Janie said, a shred of defensiveness creeping into her voice.

Mallory sat up. "I'll try to be better about that," she said. "But your uber-happiness has been pretty obnoxious."

Janie swallowed her annoyance. The number of times she had listened over the years to her sister going on and on about this guy or that, endlessly patient through the highs and lows. The evenings she'd spent hiding in her room so Mallory could have the living room or the kitchen for dates. She'd put in more than her fair share of hours. But it wasn't worth arguing over. Mallory was hurting enough already. "I'm sorry," she finally said. "I'll try to be more considerate."

Mallory stood up and stretched. "I'm going to take a shower. What are you doing the rest of the night?"

Janie thought of her earlier text to Emmett. She'd love to see him, but her sister needed her, and that felt more important. "I'll be here," she said. "Want to watch a movie? I can order us some food."

Mallory nodded. "That would be amazing. Just what I need."

Early Monday afternoon, Emmett took Janie's hands, leading her slowly forward. "One more step down," he said.

"Good. You got it." He repositioned the blindfold that wrapped around her face. "You're not peeking, right? You can't see?"

"I'm not, I swear. I can't see anything."

"Good. Now, walk straight ahead."

"Please don't lead me into the water," Janie said. She knew they were close. She could hear it and smell it on the air. It wasn't beach, though. She'd guess the harbor at the base of the river.

"I promise I won't let you fall in," Emmett said.

A few more steps and he stopped her, turning her shoulders until she faced into the breeze. He wrapped his arms around her from behind, resting his chin on her shoulder. "Okay. We're here. You can look."

Janie pulled off the blindfold and looked around. They stood on a dock, looking out across the harbor, right beside the most beautiful sailboat Janie had ever seen. She gasped. "Wait, it's not yours, is it?" She'd grown pretty familiar with Emmett's disdain for the yacht club and looking around, that's exactly where they were.

"She's Deacon's," Emmett said. "But I figured I could come down off my high horse and take her out for one afternoon."

Janie spun around in his arms. "Seriously? Do you know how?"

He rolled his eyes. "I'm still a Calhoun, Janie. Sailing's like breathing."

She leaned up and kissed him, savoring the warmth of his lips against hers. Two months in, she still wasn't used to the fact that she got to kiss Emmett Calhoun. For all the times she'd dreamed of it, her dreams paled next to her new reality. "This is the best surprise ever," she said.

"I was listening when you told me how much you loved sailing with your dad," Emmett said. "And how long it's been since you've been out on the water. So. Let's go."

Janie was a novice sailor at best—her dad was always the

one doing the actual sailing while she'd tagged along for the ride—but Emmett had an easy way of teaching and explaining what she needed to do that made her feel capable, despite her lack of experience. When they finally returned to the harbor just after dark, she was exhausted, but happy.

After a picnic dinner that had magically appeared on the dock—Emmett refused to explain his secret ways—they stretched out on the deck of Deacon's boat with a couple of pillows and a blanket Janie was more than happy to use. Fall was mostly a nonevent in the South temperature wise, but once October hit, the nights finally started to cool off. Janie nestled against Emmett's shoulder and stared up at the sky, stars brilliant against the inky black. "I could get used to this," she said softly.

"Me? Or the boat?" Emmett said.

"Definitely the boat," Janie said, laughter in her voice. "I'm pretty indifferent about you."

He reached over and stole the blanket he'd given her, causing Janie to squeal, but before he could get it away completely, she grabbed hold of the corner. She yanked to get it back, but he wouldn't yield, instead pulling the blanket—and Janie—closer to him. "Indifferent, huh?" He took the blanket and wrapped it around her shoulders, then leaned her back onto the deck.

She shrugged her shoulders playfully. "Mmm? More or less."

Emmett leaned down, his breath brushing against her cheek, and placed a soft kiss below her ear. He moved slowly, leaving a trail of kisses up her jawline stopping just shy of her lips. "How about now?" he whispered.

"You're not playing fair."

He grinned. "Sure, I am."

If her hands weren't pinned inside the blanket, she'd have pulled him down and kissed the sense out of him. As it was, she was at his mercy. He continued his ministrations, this time starting on the other side of her face. Again, he stopped just shy of her lips. "What was that you said about indifference?" he said.

Janie closed her eyes, her will power completely gone. "Okay, okay, you win. I'm not indifferent. I actually really, really like you. Can you please just kiss me already?"

"That's what I thought," Emmett said with a chuckle. He dropped the edges of the blanket, freeing her arms, and lowered his lips to hers.

"So about this twin bonding thing," he said later, after they'd each eaten a slice of cheesecake out of the picnic basket. "You guys are closer than normal, aren't you?"

Janie nodded. "Does that freak you out? I mean, it's not like we finish each other's sentences or anything. But, she's definitely part of the deal. You can't be close to me without accepting that Mallory is always going to be my best friend."

Emmett nodded. "It's cool. And I sort of get it. Deacon and I are pretty close, although it's not the same thing. I like hanging out with him, but I'd hate living with him."

"I think Mal and I will always have to live close to each other. At least in the same town. She's always been there for me . . ." Janie froze. "Oh no." She stood up, scrambling toward the back of the boat in search of her purse.

Emmett hurried after her. "Janie? What's wrong? What happened?"

She shook her head, panic filling her gut like high tide during a thunderstorm. She pulled her phone from her bag, swearing when it wouldn't turn on. "The battery's dead. Where's a charger? Is there one on the boat?"

Emmett looked around. "Maybe? I don't know. Why are you freaking out?"

"Today is Monday." Janie pulled her bag over her head and across her shoulders and reached down to pick up the shoes she'd discarded earlier. "What time is it?" She climbed onto the side of the boat and reached for the dock.

Emmett glanced at his watch, then offered her a hand, steadying her as she stepped onto the dock. "It's ten thirty."

Janie groaned. "Ugggh, that's not enough time!" She hurried toward the parking lot.

Emmett hurried after her. "Would you stop for two seconds and tell me what's going on?"

"There isn't time to explain!" she said over her shoulder. "I need to find a charger and I need to get home. My sister is going to kill me."

"Janie," Emmett said, his voice firm enough, she finally stopped and turned around. "You don't have a car, or a phone. Where are you going to go without me?"

Janie turned to face him. The pained expression on his face was enough to stop her. He deserved an explanation. "I was supposed to go to a work benefit with Mallory tonight. She asked me specifically because her ex-boyfriend was going to be there with his new fiancée and she didn't think she could face him by herself. I was supposed to be there. For *her*. And I forgot."

Emmett's face fell. "That's my fault. I surprised you with

the boat." He ran a hand through his hair. "What can I do to help?"

Janie's mind started grasping at options, but it was already so late, there was only one that made sense. She heaved out a sigh. "Just take me home."

It was past eleven when Janie found Mallory sitting in the living room in the dark, moonlight glinting off the silver in her dress. Janie dropped to the floor in front of her sister. "I'm so sorry, Mal."

"You need to call Dad and tell him you're not dead," Mallory said, her voice flat.

"I did," Janie said. "I called him from the car."

"Oh, so your phone is working after all. How funny."

Janie couldn't defend herself, she knew. But she didn't want Mallory to think she'd ignored her on purpose. "I charged it in Emmett's truck. But I swear it was dead before that. Emmett surprised me with an afternoon on his brother's sailboat. We were out on the water and I guess we lost track of time—"

Mallory cut her off. "Do you even hear yourself right now?"

Janie furrowed her brow. "What? I'm trying to explain."

"Janie, you knew about this. You knew how important this was to me. Why would you even get on a boat when you knew you had somewhere to be?"

"I just . . ."

"You what? Forgot? Didn't care? I wish I could say that surprised me. But honestly, it doesn't. Not at all. Not after the way you've been acting the past two months." Mallory stood up and stormed toward her bedroom.

Janie followed quickly behind. If Mallory managed to close and lock her door, the conversation would be over and Janie was not ready for that to happen. She caught the door right before it clicked and pushed it open. "What is that even supposed to mean? How have I been acting?"

"You mean other than like a ridiculous lovesick teenager?" Mallory yanked at the zipper of her gown but gave up when it wouldn't budge past her middle back.

Janie moved in behind her and pulled the zipper the rest of the way down. "I am not a lovesick teenager."

"But that's just it," Mallory said. "You are." She pulled a t-shirt over her head, kicking the floor length gown toward her open closet. Janie stood, waiting as Mallory yanked on a pair of sweat pants and dropped onto her bed. "Just hear me out, okay? Come sit."

Janie hesitated. She didn't trust her sister's sudden change in demeanor. Angry Mallory? I-want-to-throw-something-at-your-face Mallory? Janie could handle that. But this looked more like Lecture Time Mallory. And Lecture Time Mallory sucked because she was normally right.

Janie took a long, deliberate breath. She owed her sister this. She sat down at the foot of Mal's bed.

Mallory kept her eyes down, her fingers fiddling with the edge of her comforter. Finally, she looked up. "There's something I never told you about Emmett."

Janie tensed. She and Mallory didn't keep secrets. Especially when it came to men. What could Mallory possibly know that warranted keeping it hidden? "Okay."

"The night after you gave him that note, he took it to a

party and read it to everyone."

Heat rushed to Janie's face. Even though it had been years before, the idea of so many people hearing her words was mortifying.

"He didn't know you'd written it," Mallory continued. "No one did. But he did make fun of it. Even for a couple weeks after, his friends would quote it."

Mallory's insistence that no one knew Janie had written the note only brought a small measure of relief. *She* knew. And knowing her words had been laughed at for weeks brought up all the high school hypersensitivity she'd worked so hard to leave behind. "Why didn't you tell me?"

"Come on," Mallory said. "What good would it have done for you to have known that back then? It would have killed you. And you were already so sad, I just figured I could spare you the extra pain."

Her explanation made sense, but Janie still felt like she'd been betrayed. Like a vital part of Emmett's character had been kept from her. Still, high school was a long time ago. People grew up. Changed. The Emmett she knew wasn't the kind of guy who would ever do something so cruel, *was he*?

She looked back at her sister, pretending a confidence she didn't feel. "People change, Mal. Thank you for telling me, but what do you want me to do with that? Break up with him?"

"No, that's not what I'm saying. I just want you to *think*. Keep your head on straight."

"I *am* thinking," Janie said, her voice defensive.

Mallory scoffed. "You're thinking about *Emmett*."

"Okay, seriously? What is this conversation really about?

Emmett making fun of the note? Or something else? Because it sounds to me like you're jealous."

Mallory pressed her lips together, her hands curling into fists. "Fine. Yes. There's definitely been some jealous-like feelings happening. But Janie, I've been watching you. I've never seen you so single minded. He is all you talk about. It's like everything else in your life has taken a back seat. Me. Dad. Your quartet."

"What do you mean my quartet? What do they have to do with any of this?"

"You've missed two rehearsals, Janie. Alex called me yesterday trying to figure out where you are. He says if you don't return his calls, they're asking Leslie to play the wedding with them this weekend."

"I haven't missed . . ." Janie couldn't finish her sentence. Because it wasn't true. She'd seen a voicemail come in from Alex and had meant to call him back, but she'd forgotten. "Have I really been that bad?"

"I love you. But you've been obnoxious. I mean, think about it. When do you ever miss a rehearsal? I haven't even heard you *play* your cello in ages."

Janie's face burned. She'd never meant to hurt anyone else. "I'm really sorry about tonight."

"Tonight sucked," Mallory said. "And we'll talk about that in a minute. But you gotta let me finish what I need to say right now."

Janie braced herself. "Fine. Finish. I'm listening."

"I'm afraid you don't know whether or not you actually have real feelings for Emmett."

"What? Of course I do."

"Are you sure?" Mallory said. "Because it seems to me like you're dating high school fantasy Emmett without any concern for what the man is like today. Right now."

Janie folded her arms across her chest. "That's ridiculous. This doesn't have anything to do with high school." As soon as she said the words, she started to doubt the truth of them. Because there was a certain thrill to being with Emmett that had everything to do with so many years of unrequited love.

"Does he even know about high school?" Mallory asked. "Does he know you wrote the note?"

Janie shook her head. "I thought about telling him, but . . . I don't know. It seems silly now."

"It's not silly. It's important. And you should tell him. And then you should start asking yourself some adult questions about your relationship. Does it concern you that he laughed at your letter? I know it was a long time ago, but I kinda feel like that says something about his character and I don't like that you're giving him a free pass." Mallory pulled a hair tie off her night stand and piled her hair on top of her head. "Also, I know you're impressed that he has a law degree, but it's a pretty huge red flag for me. It screams lack of commitment that he's not willing to take the bar exam. And that makes me think there's all kinds of messed up crap going on in his family."

Janie pulled a pillow from the foot of Mallory's bed onto her lap. She squeezed it tight, willing herself to swallow the defensive responses she felt like throwing back at her sister. It wasn't the time or place. Especially when her words rang with an annoying level of truth.

"If you're wading into that," Mallory continued, "you at least need to do it with your eyes open. You have to get over the twitterpation and start approaching this like the logical, intelligent human that I know you are." She huffed. "Now I'm done. Except, also you can't miss rehearsals because I cannot afford to pay the rent by myself."

On the bright side, her sister didn't sound mad anymore. But Mallory's full force call to attention almost felt worse.

Janie had some serious pondering to do.

Chapter Six

Emmett sat on his living room balcony after work and flipped through the pages of his old high school yearbook. He paused at each photo he saw of Janie. Her senior picture looked like a different person. Dark make up around her eyes, her hair dyed black. But there was a photo near the back of her playing her cello with this intense look on her face. *That* looked like the Janie he knew. *His* Janie.

"What are you looking at?" Deacon asked. He dropped into the lounge chair across from Emmett and propped his feet up on the table.

"Sure man, come on in. Don't worry about knocking."

Deacon smirked. "If you don't want people walking in, maybe don't leave your front door unlocked." He leaned over and looked at the book in Emmett's hands. "Is that a yearbook?"

"Yep. Senior year." Emmett pushed the book away,

leaning his head back onto his hands. "Long day? You look terrible."

"Killer," Deacon said. He ran his hands through his hair, mussing it even more than it already was, which was saying something. "I've got this case at work that keeps getting more complicated. And then . . . I don't know. We had a final meeting with the wedding planner today."

Emmett looked up, noting true strain in his brother's voice. "That bad, huh?"

"I swear, if Dahlia doesn't take out her mother by the end of this weekend, I might do it myself. If Lily hadn't been there today, we'd have all been throwing punches. Did you pick up the tuxes?"

Emmett nodded. "It's done. Everybody's ready to go, except for Evan, who thought they'd hemmed his pants too short, so I guess they're going to fix it before Saturday. Seriously, Deac. Evan Brinkley? When was the last time you even had a conversation with the guy?"

Deacon sighed heavily. "I know. But Dahlia has twelve bridesmaids and I guess the numbers have to be even."

"But, Evan? It's like you picked the most annoying guy in all of Charleston County."

"It was either him or Uncle Chester."

"I'd have gone with Chester, hands down. At least he'd be good for a laugh. Numbers have to be even, ties have to be a perfect cerulean blue, the cake has to be a perfect blend of fruity citrus with flowery undertones," Emmett said, sarcasm lacing his words. "Your fiancée's crazy, you know that, right?"

Deacon grinned. "She's Charleston royalty. A Ravenel

wedding is about a lot more than just what the bride wants and we both know it." He stood up. "I'm getting a drink. You want something?"

Emmett nodded. "Sure. Whatever you're having."

"Who's that?" Deacon asked, looking over his shoulder as he stood. "She looks . . . intense."

The yearbook still lay open to the photo of Janie with her cello. "Her name is Janie Middleton. Do you remember her? She was in my grade."

"She maybe looks familiar," Deacon said. "Is that the girl you've been dating?"

"Yeah. It's been a couple months now."

"Well done. You bringing her to the wedding?"

"She's *playing* the wedding," Emmett said. "She's in the quartet."

"Well that'll never do, Emmett," Deacon said, his voice a perfect mockery of their mother. "You can't date the hired help."

"She's a musician. It's not the same thing." Emmett didn't really need to defend himself to his brother. Deacon looked the part, sure, but he didn't hold his Charleston social standing to quite the same level of importance their parents did. Still, his tolerance only extended so far. He was constantly nagging Emmett about taking the bar already and coming to work with him. He appreciated Emmett's musical ability but had always been firmly on the "this should be your hobby" side of the argument.

Emmett closed his yearbook and stood to lean against the railing of his balcony. He watched as a shipping barge moved off the ocean and into the harbor. He might complain about his

Charleston social standing, but he'd never not love the city itself. Or the view from his third-floor apartment on East Bay Street.

Deacon reappeared, drink in hand, and set another on the table for Emmett. "Tell me about her," he said. "What's she like?"

"She's great," Emmett said. "Talented, beautiful, smart. And she's got this quiet confidence about her. You know how some girls seem like they're trying too hard? She's not like that."

"Sounds legit, man," Deacon said. "Are you in love with her?"

Emmett raised an eyebrow, but Deacon seemed serious about the question, so he gave him a serious answer. "It's only been a couple months."

"That's plenty of time to know. You can at least *see* it happening, right?"

An image of Janie, blanket wrapped around her shoulders, moonlight reflecting in her eyes, flashed through his mind. "Yeah. I think I can."

Deacon smiled. "Oo-hoo, my little brother's got himself a serious girlfriend."

Emmett rolled his eyes. "Shut up."

"What does she do?" Deacon tossed back the last of his drink.

"She's a cellist," Emmett said.

"Like, for her career?"

Emmett shot his brother a look. Was it so hard to believe someone could make a career out of music? "Yeah. For her career. She plays in the Charleston Symphony."

"Wow. Fancy."

"Seriously? What does that even mean?"

"Woah, down boy," Deacon said. "No need to get defensive. That's awesome that she plays in the symphony."

"Then why did you sound so judgmental?"

Deacon held up his hands. "Emmett. Chill. I was not judging her. I'm sure she's great. And I'm sure playing in the symphony isn't an easy gig. I'm impressed. That's all I was saying."

Emmett dropped back into his chair. Deacon seemed sincere, so why did he feel so defensive? "Sorry, man. I don't know where that came from."

Deacon nudged Emmett's drink a little closer. "Drink that. You seem like you need it."

They sat in silence a few minutes, long enough for Emmett to finish his drink. He put the glass on the table and leaned forward. He was tired of pretending. Tired of ignoring the truth of what he wanted. Tired of hiding from his family. Janie was right. If he wanted to make music work, he had to start doing something about it. And that meant telling his family. "Hey, Deacon?"

His brother looked up from his phone. "What's up?"

"I'm not ever going to take the bar."

Deacon put down his phone but didn't respond.

"It's not what I want and I'm not changing my mind."

His brother scrubbed a hand across his face. "Yeah, I think I saw that one coming. What are you going to do instead?"

"I'm going to try and make the music thing work. Janie's helping. She knows some people in Nashville, so . . . I have to try."

Deacon nodded his head. "Look. I'm all in, all right? I'll even back you up when you tell Mom and Dad. But so help me, if you breathe a word of this before the wedding this weekend? I'll never speak to you again."

"Deal," Emmett said. He stood and slapped his brother on the back before moving inside. "I'm going for a run."

"Hey, I'm meeting Dahlia and Lily in an hour," his brother called to his retreating form. "You care if I just chill here until then?"

"Yeah, whatever," Emmett said. He was only half dressed when his brother yelled at him, calling him back to the living room balcony.

"Hey, Emmett? You left yet?"

Emmett pulled on his gym shorts and walked, bare chested, back to where Deacon stood, looking over the balcony and down into the street. He followed his gaze to find Janie standing on East Bay, looking up at the balcony, her hands perched on her hips.

Her face lit up when she saw him. "Hey."

Emmett smiled. "Hey. What are you doing here?"

"Oh, you know. I was in the neighborhood."

Emmett looked from Janie to Deacon. "I guess you met my brother, Deacon."

"I did," Janie said. "Congrats on the wedding."

Thanks," Deacon said. "I appreciate it."

"You want to come up?" Emmett asked.

"Actually, do you want to come down? I was hoping we

could go for a walk."

He'd gladly forgo exercise for time spent with Janie. "Sure. Give me a minute to change, then I'll be right down."

He glanced at his brother on his way to his room. "Please don't say anything stupid," he whispered to Deacon.

"Come on, little brother," Deacon said with a grin. "What could I possibly say about you?"

Chapter Seven

Janie waited for Emmett, her nerves making her feel lightheaded and a little nauseous. She'd spent three days thinking about what Mallory had said. Three days keeping Emmett at a distance, claiming busyness and a need to fix things with her sister after her serious misstep Monday night. When she saw Emmett emerge from the front of his building, her heart did a little flutter thing and heat rushed to her cheeks. How was she going to get through this?

Not everything that Mallory had said was true. Janie wasn't concerned about Emmett's career. She really did believe in his music and understood the risks associated with doing something different than what your family wanted. But Mal had been right about Janie living with her head in the clouds. Missing rehearsals was so far outside of her normal. Even the symphony concert she'd played last week had been rough. She'd struggled her way through and suffered for her lack of practice. Her brain had been all Emmett, all the time. And that had to change.

Emmett was no longer shirtless, which was both a relief and a disappointment. She'd have never been able to focus on their conversation otherwise, but then, focusing on the rest of him didn't seem like such a bad way to spend the afternoon.

He stopped in front of her, and with a hint of sheepishness she found unendingly endearing, leaned forward and kissed her on the cheek. "Hey," he said, the lilt of his soft southern accent more prominent than usual.

"Hi. You sound more Southern than you usually do. Is that Deacon's influence?"

Emmett's eyebrows rose. "Do I? I don't know. Maybe it is Deacon. He's always sounded more southern than me."

"Says the guy who sings country music."

"Yeah, but Charleston Southern is a whole different animal than Nashville Southern."

"Tell me about it," Janie said. "I chose Vanderbilt because it was in Nashville and I thought it would feel like home. It was great, but it wasn't Charleston."

"No place is," Emmett said. "I couldn't get back here fast enough."

They headed down East Bay toward Waterfront Park. "This is a nice surprise," Emmett said. "I was afraid I wasn't going to see you until the wedding."

"Actually, about that," Janie said.

Emmett stopped in his tracks, concern etched into his features.

"Here, let's sit." Janie led him to a bench underneath the sprawl of a live oak. She held her hands in her lap, knowing if she were touching him, it would be harder to say everything she needed to say.

"What's going on?" Emmett asked.

"I'm not going to be at the wedding," Janie said. "My friend, Leslie, is an excellent cellist. She's covering for me with the quartet and I've already sent her the music for your song. She's happy to accompany you."

"Why? Does this have something to do with Monday night? Is Mallory still mad?"

"No, she's not mad, but I guess it does have to do with Monday." Janie had rehearsed what she wanted to say, gone over it in her mind a hundred times. She had to dive in before she lost control. "I have something I need to tell you."

"Okay," he said.

It killed her to see the confusion in his eyes. She looked down at her hands. "Back in high school, right before you graduated, you got a note in your locker." Janie's heart pounded so hard, she worried Emmett might see the pulsing right through her skin. "It was from a girl." She swallowed. "And it told you all the reasons why she was in love with you." She finally looked up to meet Emmett's gaze.

"That was you?" he said softly.

Janie nodded. "I thought by mentioning biology lab, you'd realize it was me."

"I didn't," Emmett said quickly. "I had no idea."

"Mallory told me what you did. How you read it at a party. How you . . . laughed at it."

155

"Janie, had I known . . ." He shook his head. "Regardless, I shouldn't have—"

"I know," Janie said, cutting him off. "You don't have to explain. It was a long time ago, and I'm not telling you because I feel like you owe me an apology. I just need you to see why I need to take a step back for a little while."

Emmett leaned forward, elbows on his knees. "I don't understand."

"Emmett, you were all I thought about for three years of high school. I built you up into some kind of fantasy, and then when you reappeared out of nowhere and you were actually into me, it's like my high school self was finally getting what she'd always dreamed of. It didn't even feel real."

"I'm still not following." His voice was tense, even a little shaky. "We're not in high school anymore. And this has all felt pretty real to me."

"You have to understand what high school was like for me. I wasn't the girl people noticed. I didn't turn heads. Guys didn't flirt with me or even see me, really. It's like I was watching life from the sidelines."

"Watching Mallory's life from the sidelines."

Janie winced. He hadn't said anything that wasn't the truth, but it still stung to hear the words out loud.

"Yeah, I guess so. And now, it's switched. I'm the one with the boyfriend, and she's watching me. I feel like I need to figure out whether or not what I'm feeling is based on the time you and I have spent together now, in the present, or whether I'm clinging to the past because it feels so amazing to finally have Mallory jealous of *me*."

He ran a hand across his jaw. "Wow."

The hurt was so evident in his voice, it nearly made Janie cry. But she couldn't lose her nerve. "I know that sounds awful. And I don't want to hurt you. I do care about you. I know that much. But Emmett, I'm not the girl who flakes and forgets important things. I don't forget to return phone calls. I don't ignore calls from my Dad. And yet, this past month, I've done all of that. I'm not playing my cello. I'm ignoring my sister. It's like I don't even know how to approach the relationship normally because I was in love with you before we'd even kissed for the first time."

She almost tripped on the word love. To say it out loud felt bold and crazy and painful. Especially since she was telling Emmett she needed to walk away. "I think I fast tracked my feelings for you because they were bolstered by three years of longing. I just need to take a minute and . . . refocus. Separate the past from the present. Figure out if this is even what I want right now. If this," she motioned between them, "is even real."

Emmett tensed, his lips stretched in a firm line. There were things he wanted to say, she could tell. But he only grunted before saying, "And in the meantime?"

Janie wished he would say more. Disagree with her. Convince her she already knew it was real. "I don't know. I'm not saying I don't ever want to see you again. I'm just saying I need some time."

Emmett sat silent for a long moment, his eyes staring out into the harbor. Finally, without even looking at Janie, he stood. "I gotta go."

"Emmett, wait," Janie called.

But he didn't stop.

He didn't even look back.

Chapter Eight

Saturday morning, Emmett stood in his bedroom and adjusted his bowtie. It was a great suit—light gray, cut just the way he liked it. And the cerulean blue bowtie wasn't half bad. He grabbed his guitar, his stomach tightening at the thought of playing it without Janie to accompany him. Three days later, her words still echoed in his mind. *I have to decide if this is even real.* He wasn't letting her off that easy. He patted the pocket of his suit coat; he'd show her real.

"Hey, Deacon? You ready to go?"

Dahlia had an army of family members in town for the wedding, so Deacon's place had been converted into a guesthouse, and he'd been crashing with Emmett. Better that than moving in with Mom and Dad.

"Almost," he called back. "I think I lost a cuff link."

Emmett crossed his apartment to the spare bedroom,

immediately spotting the cuff link under the bench at the foot of the bed. He reached down and picked it up, handing it to his older brother. "Looking good, man."

Deacon took a deep breath. "Thanks."

"You ready for this?"

He nodded. "Absolutely."

"Hey, if it's all right with you, I'm going to drop you off," Emmett said. "I'll be back in time for the ceremony, but there's something I have to take care of first."

Deacon's eyes narrowed. "Something Janie related?"

Emmett glanced at the floor then looked up, meeting his brothers gaze head on. "I gotta get her back, Deac."

Deacon squeezed his arm. "Fight for what you love?"

Emmett nodded. "Yeah."

Twenty minutes later, he pulled up outside Janie's condo. He reached into the pocket of his coat, making sure the note was still there, then climbed out of his truck and hurried up her front steps. He rang the doorbell, hoping against hope that Janie was home.

It was Mallory who opened the door. He'd worried, at first, that he wouldn't be able to tell them apart, but now that he really knew Janie, it was easy. Janie had more freckles and her eyebrows arched a little higher. Plus, most of the time, she wore her hair wavy instead of straight like Mallory always did. "Hey, Mallory," Emmett said. "Is Janie home?"

Mallory folded her arms across her chest. "Didn't she just ask you, like three days ago, to give her some time?"

Emmett's jaw tightened. "Please? I need to talk to her."

"It's okay, Mal," Janie said, melting out of the shadowy interior. She looked at Emmett. "Come on in."

He followed her to the living room.

"I'll just be in my room," Mallory said.

"Actually." Emmett stopped her. "Can you stay? I'd like you to hear this too."

Twin sisters as close as these two? If he was going to convince one to love him, he might as well convince the other to approve.

Mallory turned and moved next to her sister. They stood side by side and made no move to sit down, so Emmett didn't either. He took a deep breath, then pulled the note out of his pocket. He crossed the room, unfolded it and placed it on the coffee table in front of Janie.

"The day you gave me this note was the same day my father told me I would never go to Nashville. Law school, or I was cut off. No more money. No more support. I was bitter and I was angry when I went to that party. It doesn't justify my making fun of what you wrote. But it wasn't how I really felt."

"You saved it?" Janie asked, her voice soft.

"If you knew how many times I've read it, wondering who it was that understood me as well as you did . . ." He went to run a hand through his hair, then stopped himself, remembering the wedding. He could already hear Mrs. Ravenel scolding his slovenly appearance. "You think nobody saw you in high school? Nobody noticed you? You're wrong. I did. You were this beautiful untouchable mystery that I couldn't begin to understand, but I saw you." He stifled a laugh. "That time I saw you play, I just . . . Janie, you were so much more talented and mature than the rest of us. Had I known it was you that had written that note? I'd have crawled naked through a hurricane to find you."

Janie closed her eyes.

Emmett took a step forward and lifted his hand, his fingers curling softly around her cheek. "Just because you felt something in high school doesn't mean it wasn't real." He leaned down and pressed a featherlight kiss on her forehead. "Please change your mind," he whispered. "We can slow things down, make cello practice a regular part of date night, do whatever it takes. But I barely lasted three days without you, Janie. Don't make me go another."

Emmett caught sight of the clock hanging on the far wall. Stupid wedding. "I've got to go." He reached out and squeezed Janie's hand. "Just think about it, okay?"

She only nodded.

Emmett left her standing there, his heart in her hands.

Chapter Nine

"Daaaaang, that man knows how to wear a suit," Mallory said.

Janie almost laughed, but her emotions were running too high. She picked up the note, her hands trembling, and took it to the couch. She read through the first few lines and heat flooded her cheeks. High school Janie hadn't held anything back.

"I can't believe I ever gave this to him," she said.

Mallory scoffed. "Uh, obviously it did the trick."

Janie looked up. "He did look good, didn't he?"

Mallory sat down beside her sister and took both her hands. "Janie, I've had terrible luck with guys—mostly because I suck at picking good ones—so you don't have to take my advice if you don't want to. And I know I said I wasn't so sure about Emmett before. But I was wrong. That man is the real deal, and I'm pretty sure he's already in love with you."

Janie sniffed, tears brimming. "What do I do?"

"You get dressed and you go to the wedding."

Janie shook her head. "It's too late. Leslie is probably already there warming up. I can't take the gig back now."

"So go as a guest. Be the best man's date."

"I'm sure his parents would love that," Janie said, but she was already mentally digging through her closet, wondering what she could wear.

As always, Mallory was five steps ahead. "You need to wear the purple dress I wore when I met Preston's parents."

"Seriously?" Janie asked. "You love that dress."

"I did love that dress until Preston said he loved it too. Wear it. Look fantastic in it so I can have a reason to like it again."

Janie hurried out of her clothes and shimmied into the dress. The cut was perfect—cinching in her waist in just the right way and accentuating her curves. She turned to her sister. "What do you think?"

Mallory pursed her lips. "Okay, I love the dress again, but maybe I hate you for looking so good in it."

Janie grinned and hugged her sister. "Help me with my hair?"

The William-Aiken House sat right in the hustle and bustle of King Street in downtown Charleston. It had been there for 200 years, so Janie imagined it wasn't quite so hustling and bustling when the house was built, but it still managed to feel magical and secluded with its elaborate gardens and high walls. She approached the gate, discouraged to find an employee of the venue checking a guest list as people arrived. So maybe she wouldn't be crashing the wedding.

She glanced at her phone. There was still twenty minutes before everything started. Hesitating only a moment, she called Emmett.

He answered right away. "Hey."

"Hi," Janie said, happy to hear the hope ringing in his voice. "What are you up to?" It was a dumb question. He was at the wedding. How did she *think* he was going to respond?

"Um, getting ready to walk down the aisle," he said.

"Right. About that. Do you have a second to come out to the front gate?"

"What? What gate?"

"The gate where guests are being checked in? Cause, you know, I'm not officially on the invitation list, so . . . I don't think they're going to let me in."

"I'll be right there."

Janie hung up her phone and dropped it into her purse. She smoothed the front of her dress and tried to calm her nerves with some slow, intentional breathing. It was working, much to her relief, and she closed her eyes for one final breath.

"Should I come back later?" Emmett asked, his voice close to her ear.

Her eyes shot open and she stepped back, teetering on her heels.

Emmett reached out and grabbed her arm, steading her. "Sorry," he said. "I didn't mean to scare you."

She smiled, suddenly feeling shy. She'd just seen him barely an hour before, but somehow everything felt different now. "Um, I have to tell you something important. But first, I brought you something."

He raised an eyebrow. "Yeah?"

Before she could answer, a downtown walking tour stopped behind them on the sidewalk, the guide launching into a history of the William-Aiken House and the role it played in Charleston's history.

Emmett tilted his head toward the house. "Come on. We'll find a place to talk inside."

They ended up in a side garden, to the left of where guests were gathering for the ceremony. They sat on a small metal bench, a hedge giving them a tiny bit of privacy.

"You brought me something?" Emmett said, picking up their conversation where they'd left off out on the street.

"Yes." Janie picked up the Trader Joes grocery bag she'd been carrying and handed it to Emmett. Crappy as far as gift bags go, but she'd had less than an hour to prep herself for a formal party. Sometimes functionality had to win over fancy.

He opened the bag and pulled out a dark brown cowboy hat, a tiny stripe of tan, leather piping around the middle. "That's . . . nice," he said with a smile. His effort at kindness made Janie want to laugh. For all his country music singing, he'd never worn a cowboy hat. She'd teased him about it more than once. He'd always insisted he wouldn't dress the part until he had a real reason to. He put the hat on. "What do you think?"

"It looks perfect," Janie said. "I figured since a producer from Green Valley Records has your demo and has promised to give it careful consideration, you deserved a little something to celebrate."

Emmett froze. "You're kidding."

Janie grinned. "I'm not. My professor emailed me yesterday. The producer is a former colleague of his, and said she was happy to give it a listen."

Emmett shook his head. "So wait. She has the demo already? An actual producer. In Nashville."

Janie nodded. "My professor copied me on the email he sent. So yes. I can absolutely verify *your* demo is in her inbox."

"That's amazing," Emmett said. "You're amazing. Thank you for doing that for me." He moved like he was reaching for her hand but pulled back, hesitation on his face.

Janie held out her palm and gave him an encouraging smile. "Okay. That was the first thing."

Emmett took off the hat and looked at Janie, his eyes holding hers. "What's the second?"

She leaned forward and answered his question with a kiss—long and deep and satisfying. "I'm sorry if I freaked you out," she said softly, her face still close to his. "I just got scared. But the thought of being without you is way worse."

"This *is* real, Janie."

She nodded. "I know."

He kissed her again, his hands sliding up her arms to her face. "Is it too soon to tell you I love you?"

"Well I mean, I beat you to it by about seven years," Janie said with a smirk. "I actually think you're running a little behind schedule."

Emmett's phone buzzed from his pocket. "That's probably my curtain call," he said, without pulling out the phone. "Will you stay?"

"I'll happily stick around if it means getting to stare at you in that suit for an hour, but you'll have to sneak me in. I gave up my spot behind my cello."

"Are you willing to sit with my Uncle Chester? He might try and hold your hand. And will definitely smell like very expensive bourbon. And cigars."

"Hmm, that's a deal breaker," Janie said. She pulled her hand away and turned to head the opposite direction.

Emmett caught her hand and pulled her close, wrapping an arm around her waist. "You're funny." He leaned down and kissed her again.

She smiled against his lips. "You're going to miss your brother's wedding."

"Deacon will forgive me," Emmett said.

"Will his soon-to-be wife?"

Emmett shrugged casually. "Meh. I never liked her anyway."

Janie smacked his arm. "That is a terrible thing to say!"

Emmett led her to a chair about half way up his family's side of the gathering. He smiled as the photographer snapped a shot of them, knowing he'd probably never looked happier. "Will Leslie let you borrow her cello?" he asked. "Cause I really want you to play my song with me."

Janie put a hand over her chest. "I'd love to. I'm sure Leslie won't mind."

"And promise you'll dance with me tonight?" Emmett asked.

"Only with you and Uncle Chester," Janie said.

Emmett grinned and glanced at his watch. "Let me go see why this thing hasn't started yet." He kissed Janie briefly then set his new hat on top of her head. "Keep this for me?"

"For you?" Janie smiled. "Always."

Part 3: Lily and Deacon

By Becca Wilhite

Chapter One

Lily's feet automatically stepped in time to the music after all that rehearsing, or maybe it was in time to her heartbeat. She could hear the room turn to look at her as she came down the aisle, that rustle of suits and dresses, but she couldn't look at any of those people. She focused only on Deacon.

His nervousness manifested in extra-straight posture, and he seemed even taller than usual. She knew him well enough to know that this particular smile wasn't his relaxed grin but his anxious mask. The fashionable suit was a tiny bit too stylish for him to look comfortable, but the pictures were going to be gorgeous.

What was she doing, thinking about photos? No one was going to want photos of this disaster.

Walking to the front of the room took about eleven years, but when she made it, she stopped in front of him. As he looked down at her and smiled, all nerves and anticipation, she put her hand on his arm and leaned up to whisper in his ear.

"Dahlia asked me to tell you something," she said. And then her words dried up.

How exactly had she arrived here?

And what exactly did Dahlia think she was doing?

After what felt like eternities but was probably no more than a minute, she pulled her eyes from the gorgeous orchid pinned to Deacon's tuxedo and looked into his face. His expression was filled with concern. Did he know? Could he guess?

Anyone could guess, Lily thought. This leap off the traditional track was perfectly in line with all things Dahlia. Expect the unexpected and all that.

The sound in the room changed: the whisper that had become a buzz was turning to a mutter. She realized she still had her hand on Deacon's arm and dropped it down to her side.

What were her lines? Only minutes ago, Dahlia had stood with her in the bride's room, holding so still, her nose practically touching Lily's, and listened to Lily repeat the words.

"Dahlia sends her regrets, but she needs to follow her heart, and if you look around," Lily winced and her voice went softer, "you'll see that among all the flowers in this beautiful venue, you can't find a single Dahlia." The rehearsed statement came out of her mouth without any of Dahlia's spontaneity, sounding not only stiff and formal, but cruel. Shaking her head, Lily tried again, her own words this time. "I'm sorry, Deacon. Dahlia's gone."

She watched him take in her words, a little line forming

between his eyebrows. His mouth opened and then closed again. Of the million things he could be thinking, she wished she could guess the one his mind was trying to land on.

His eyes darted around the room and finally he spoke. "She left? The wedding? Her wedding? *Our* wedding?"

That burn in the back of her throat meant Lily was about to cry or throw up, and she very much wanted to do neither. She nodded.

"I'm sorry," she repeated, but she wasn't sure she'd made enough sound to be heard.

Breathe, she told herself. Just for a second.

Was that a gulp? A sob? Oh, no. Was Deacon crying? Here? In front of everyone? When she dragged her eyes up to meet his, she was relieved to see that in fact, he was trying to stifle a laugh.

"Lil," he said, and gave a tiny shake of his head. "This is really happening, isn't it?"

She wasn't ready to laugh.

"Looks like it." The heat searing her neck suggested that at least her reflexive body functions were still happening. Blushing was the most normal thing right now. "Is everyone staring at us?"

His eyes swept the room again. "Exactly everyone. Yes." Another breath of a laugh escaped him, but this one sounded tired. "Jilted? Is that the word for what just happened to me?"

"That is precisely the word." Lily wasn't sure how he could stand there and chat with her about semantics while his wedding was falling apart, but a huge part of her appreciated it. Being the messenger was the worst. The absolute worst. Well. After being the jilted. And somehow his question made the moment seem completely normal.

"I probably need to say something to everyone." He looked at her, question on his face. "Right?"

She understood all too well, from years of friendship, what his subtext was asking. "Right. Yes. You. *You* need to talk. Not me."

He nudged her. "I know. I was teasing. Okay, well, wish me luck."

She didn't have time to say another word. He moved around her and stood at the front of the aisle and smiled at the crowd. The whispering hushed when he waved. It wasn't so much a "command the room" wave as a simple "hello, there" kind of thing. A little girl a few rows from the front waved back.

"Friends," Deacon said, then cleared his throat and said it again. "Friends, I thank you for coming today. It looks like we have a slight change of plans for the main event."

How was he supposed to do this? Poor him. More than half the people in the place were there because they loved Dahlia. He couldn't say, 'hey, people, my flaky fiancée ditched me, isn't that a shame?' This was a delicate balancing act, even for someone as diplomatic as Deacon.

"Our leading lady seems to have changed her mind." He paused for the gasp and buzz that he must have known were coming. Lily watched Dahlia's mom, Aunt Camellia, go pale beneath the little pink hat perched on her perfectly sculpted hair. It happened fast—if she hadn't been watching, Lily might have missed it. Within seconds, Camellia was re-composed and had settled a slightly amused expression on her face, as if this is what she'd expected to happen all along.

To be fair, she may have expected this all along. She knew Dahlia as well as anyone. As well as Lily did.

Deacon was still talking to the crowd. Lily refocused on his words somewhere around "we're all here, and the party is prepared. You're welcome, all of you, to stick around for the evening. Let's dance. Let's eat. Let's celebrate our friendship."

Aunt Camellia took that as her cue to stand up and take Deacon's arm. She added her invitation to his with the proper sprinkling of formal amusement and Charleston charm. Uncle Benson, who'd been standing this whole time where he was told to stand, came alone down the aisle, shook Deacon's hand, and kissed his wife on the cheek. If he said what he was thinking, he said it quietly into Camellia's ear. Nobody would have heard him anyway. The gathered crowd had foregone decorum for full-tilt *discussion*, the proper title for society gossip.

Lily imagined her phone, tucked into the tiny beaded clutch in the bride's room, was positively blowing up by now. Every memory of every time she had to make excuses and take the heat from one of Dahlia's crazy exploits rushed into her mind and made her skin itch.

She felt a hand on her back and turned to see Deacon, his smile not quite reaching the level of sincerity. "You okay?" he asked.

"Sure. You?"

He made a sound that was either a laugh or that puff of air that meant someone just knocked the wind out of him. Or both.

"Dance with me," Lily said.

"Yeah. That'll fix this." The smile grew a fraction less forced.

She took his hand. "Can't make it worse, right?" As they walked through the French doors into the William-Aiken House, Deacon smiled and waved at everybody.

He went to the DJ, leaned in, and said something into his ear. Lily tried not to hear a couple of jokes from old men in suits about him not waiting long to move on to the next one, but when she let go of Deacon's hand, he grabbed her fingers tightly.

"Don't you dare make me do this alone," he whispered as he slid his arm over her shoulder. He danced in little bounces, without moving his feet. Poor guy couldn't dance at all. His only discoverable flaw.

She wrapped her arm around his waist and squeezed. Laughing up into his face, she said, "As maid of honor to the dearly departed bride, I vow to stay by your side as long as you want this party to go on."

He stopped "dancing" and dropped the fake smile. "Thank you."

She nodded.

"I mean it, Lil. Thank you. As long as you're here, I can do this." He gestured to the party, or maybe it was some kind of dance move. Whatever it was, Lily kept her arm around him. "Just stay close so nobody can ask me deep and personal questions. I might need to keep you here forever."

If only the music would blast a little louder, she thought, it could drown out the thoughts in her head. Thoughts like *I'd like to throttle Dahlia*. Like *How does a person walk away from her own wedding?* Like *I'm so glad he wants me to stay close*.

She knew it might look odd to some of the guests, maid of honor snuggled up to rejected groom. She was sure people were telling themselves and each other all kinds of stories. And she had a decent idea of the kinds of stories those might be. But Deacon was her friend, and if her friend needed her to stay close to him on his night of heartbreak, she'd stay.

She looked at him as he bounced and swayed and smiled. He didn't look heartbroken at the moment.

He looked amazing.

Lily gave herself a mental slap. Confident. That's what she'd meant. Deacon looked confident. In control. Like he could handle this. Seconds later, Kailey Pinckney glided up and stood in front of Deacon with huge, damp eyes. Lily watched with that kind of slow-motion horror as Kailey's perfectly manicured hand reached out and stroked the lapel of Deacon's suit. "I'm so sorry about today," she said, her words coming out so slowly that it seemed to take forever for her to get to the part where she was asking him out at his failed wedding reception. "If you want to talk, I'm in town all weekend. Maybe we could meet for coffee? In the morning?"

Deacon's shocked expression didn't dissuade her. "Or, if not coffee, maybe breakfast at The Palmetto?"

Lily could feel Deacon grasping for her hand. Squeezing her wrist. Silently pleading for help. She wondered what she was supposed to do. Trip her? Knock her over? Remind Deacon of some very important plans he had for the first day of his honeymoon?

Lily caught his glance. His eyes were bugging out. He was so clearly uncomfortable that Kailey removed her hand from his chest. "You've got my number. Please, I'd love to help."

How could she make those kind and generous words sound so distasteful?

Kailey walked away, swishing through the path she

created in the dancers. Men stumbled out of her way exactly as she must have planned.

Deacon subtly turned his back. "Did she just . . ." he began.

Lily put her hand over her mouth and tried to keep the laugh from reaching her eyes. "Oh, she really did." Pushing her hands through her hair, she breathed out, "Wow." She shook her head. "Just goes to prove that there are reasons for every stereotype."

"And I'd like to thank you for being absolutely no help at all," Deacon said, a little laugh in his voice.

Lily shook her head. "Are you kidding me? She's terrifying."

"Please. You've got at least eight inches on her." He spun in an awkward little move that ought to scare away any other hovering debutante vultures.

"Oh. Thank you for clarifying that my job here tonight is to literally fight off the masses of women who are lined up to take Dahlia's place." Lily immediately wanted to swallow the words back.

Deacon stopped dancing and stood quietly for a moment. Hands in his pockets, he looked up into the sky and then back at Lily.

Shaking her head, she tried to say something apologetic, but no words would form.

"I know. It's fine. How about some food?" Deacon said, his fingers grazing her back and directing her to the tables. "I hear it's both fancy and expensive, two of the words least likely to describe anything that will fill me up."

"I promise it will be delicious, and if it doesn't fill you, I'll go get you a cheeseburger."

"Deal."

Lily felt a hand on her arm. "Lily?"

"Oh, hi, Mom," she said, leaning down to kiss her mom's cheek.

"Hello, Ms. Iris, Mr. Sinclair," Deacon said, a lifetime of manners rising to the surface. "How's the party?"

Lily's dad chose to give her a hug instead of answering Deacon.

"Oh, honey," Lily's mom said, reaching her hand up to Deacon's face, "you don't have to pretend for me."

Deacon leaned down and stage-whispered in her ear, "No, actually I do. I've got to keep this act up for at least another," he checked his watch, "two hours and twenty minutes. Good thing I've got Lily here to help me."

Lily felt the kind of gratitude that comes from someone allowing themselves to be rescued.

"Come on," Deacon said, putting his arm around Iris's shoulders. "Let's go eat."

Chapter Two

Deacon glanced around as he made his way through the reception rooms. Emmett, a good sport as always, had agreed to play the song he'd written for Deacon and Dahlia. Now. Here. As people made themselves comfortable at the dinner tables and watched the carefully planned evening crumble. Deacon stood just inside the doorway, leaning against the wall. He couldn't make himself sit alone at the head table to listen to Emmett's gift.

Nodding toward his brother at the front of the room, Deacon hitched a smile onto his face and focused on breathing. Emmett sat on a stool, looking like a Calhoun man should in his perfectly tailored suit. His cellist girlfriend sat beside him, and she seemed unable to take her eyes from Emmett. Deacon had a second to wish that Dahlia looked at him like that—like she adored him—instead of her usual, which was more a look that said, "are you watching?" And Deacon always was watching. Always had been watching. Until she disappeared and there wasn't anything left to see.

Emmett strummed his guitar and as the song started, Deacon found himself unexpectedly delighted with the music. Emmett was really something. This music, this combination of his guitar, his voice, and Janie's cello, floated past the humiliation, the frustration, and the anger of the night and into a soft place inside. He forgot trying to look unfazed and confident and simply enjoyed the music. When the song ended, he clapped as loudly and sincerely as the rest of the audience. And he wished, perhaps more than anyone else, that Emmett would keep playing.

Instead, Deacon walked toward the head table to wait for the dinner service to begin.

As soon as he sat down, regret flooded through him. Regret for every part of this day. His mind filled with thoughts of what he could have done differently, what he could have done to make her stay.

But he knew better. Dahlia Ravenel wasn't a woman who'd be made to do anything. That was part of what he'd loved about her since he'd met her.

He felt his spine sag against the wood backing of the chair, as though now that he had a physical support he didn't have to hold himself upright anymore. This was a bad development. It was nowhere near the end of the night. Many hours still required him to stand up and be charming. Why did he have to come over here and sit down?

Oh. Right. Because he was starving.

Where had Lily gone off to?

He glanced through the party and saw her talking to the wedding planner who, he had to admit, was doing a great job of guiding people through what had to be the weirdest wedding in Charleston's long and vivid history. He knuckled his eyes and wished for a drink.

When a hand touched his shoulder, he cringed instinctively away, assuming it was another Charleston belle ready to help him through this trying time.

Instead, a small glass landed on the table in front of him and Emmett slapped him on the back. "So. How's your day?"

Deacon drained the glass before he decided not to bother answering his brother. "Any chance you're hiding another one of these in that suit?" he asked, rattling the ice in the otherwise empty glass.

Emmett patted his pockets. "Sorry."

Shaking his head, Deacon said, "I'm getting tired of that word. I've heard it from just about everyone. Everyone but Dahlia."

Distinctly and visibly uncomfortable, Emmett said, "Do you, you know, want to talk about it?"

"No."

"Good." Emmett pulled a chair out from the table and sat in it, his elbow touching Deacon's. "You're allowed to be mad, you know."

Deacon scrunched up a handful of tablecloth and then smoothed it out again. "Almost true. I'm allowed to be mad tomorrow. Tonight, I am required to be charming and jovial and—what else are Calhoun men?"

"What do I know about it? I'm the black sheep, right?"

Deacon almost laughed. "The black sheep with the gold star after that performance." He sat back and stretched his arm across his brother's chair.

"You liked it?" Emmett's voice betrayed the same little-brother need for approval Deacon had heard for decades.

"Are you kidding me? It was perfect. Best thing to come out of this wedding."

He didn't say anything, but Emmett's smile suggested Deacon had said the right thing.

Lily slipped into the chair next to Emmett and slid a drink past him to Deacon. "Thought you might need this," she said. He drained it, choosing not to mention Emmett's contribution.

"So Emmett," Lily said, "In the last three minutes, I've had every single woman here and a few who aren't single ask me about your musical aspirations."

Emmett blushed and said something about being recently off the market. Deacon was glad he didn't need to respond. He knew what Lily was doing and he was grateful. For the next few minutes while Emmett and Lily talked, Deacon could look into the middle distance between them and pretend to listen while reminding himself to stay upright.

That first moment, the second Lily walked down the aisle alone and leaned in to whisper to him, Deacon felt a tiny shiver of relief wash over him. He hadn't thought too hard about it, but now he realized it was something he should at least try to explore. Had he actually been relieved that Dahlia ditched him? Had he been holding his breath waiting for this? Was he glad she'd gone away? Or only glad that she didn't say it to his face? That she didn't make a firework display out of it and tell him she was leaving in the middle of the wedding ceremony? In front of all of Charleston? Because Deacon well knew that something like that was not out of character for Dahlia.

Nothing was impossible for her. Nothing should be unexpected.

That was why he'd been in love with her since he was fourteen.

She was as unpredictable as a summer rain storm, and sometimes as destructive. A force of nature. He'd lived his whole life following the path his parents had set for him. Dahlia was the arrow pointing off into the woods: "Adventure this way."

She was fearless. She was exciting. She was astounding.

She was gone.

His stomach dropped. This was the part where he slid his head onto the table linens and never sat up again until all the guests had gone home.

He nearly let himself sink down, but he heard his father's voice out there in the party somewhere and sat up straighter. Another drink appeared in front of him and Deacon glanced up from it long enough to see a waiter walking away.

Walking away like Dahlia had.

He felt his spine softening.

Pathetic. He was being pitiful, and he knew he was. He stood up. He heard Emmett say, "Is he okay?"

Lily answered him. "Reality appears to be setting in. Come on." They both stood beside him, one on each side.

When Lily slipped her arm around his waist again, he put his arms on her shoulders and held her. He'd been hugging Lily for years. All the years. "Thanks for sticking with me," he said.

She pulled away enough to make room for Emmett. "I didn't have any other plans for tonight."

At the same time that he laughed at her joke, he felt the

loss of her closeness. Smarten up, he told himself. It's not that Lily's comfort is so amazing. You're just relieved you don't have to circulate through this crowd alone.

Alone had never been Deacon's strong suit. He'd never enjoyed being by himself; he was a people person. The thought flitted across his mind that maybe that label was a coverup for something else. Maybe he was entirely too comfortable with his decision to never be alone with his thoughts. Perhaps a guy ought to spend some time with himself now and then.

But not now.

Now, right now, he ought to walk through this party of people who were having a good time despite the wake of destruction that Dahlia left and apparently only he could see. He ought to thank them for coming. He ought to go be pleasant to Dahlia's mom and dad.

He thought he'd like to throw up first.

But there they were, only a few feet away. Lily wasn't leading him there, exactly, but she was making it possible for him to do what he knew he had to do.

Eventually.

He looked around for another waiter carrying a drink tray. It's possible his look was desperate, because Emmett shook his head. He made a signal that Deacon knew was supposed to remind him that he'd had enough and people were watching.

Leaning close, Emmett said, "You have to talk to everyone. And you have to do it carefully. Every word you say is going to be passed back and forth by these people for as long as it takes this scandal to be replaced by the next one."

Deacon nodded. "Thanks, counsel. You should have been

a lawyer."

Emmett punched his arm. "Shut up."

Playing stupid, Deacon said, "Has anyone ever told you that before?"

"Not for the last fifteen minutes."

Lily slipped out from under Deacon's arm and hugged her aunt. Dahlia's mom. Camellia.

Deacon panicked. What was he supposed to say? How was he even supposed to address them? Camellia had been pressuring him to call her Mom ever since the engagement. It had never happened yet, and he was pretty sure it would be weird to start now. He stifled a nervous laugh.

Thank goodness Emmett had talked him out of that last drink.

Benson Ravenel put out his hand. "Son," he said, and then didn't finish, because that word hung so heavily in the humid evening air. He just stood there, shaking Deacon's hand and shaking his head. He looked like he could use another drink. Emmett muttered something about finding someone as he squirmed out of the awkward little group.

"Oh, honey," Camellia said, taking an unsteady step between the two men and straightening Deacon's tie. "This is just a hot mess. But the food and the flowers are lovely."

And she, Deacon thought, looked like she'd found a few drinks already too.

Not that he could blame her.

Lily said, "Aunt Camellia, it was a good idea to keep the party going."

Deacon watched Camellia's face registering the new

understanding that this was her own idea.

"And," Lily said, "I'm glad you've decided to serve the wedding cake. Once it's cut and put on plates, people won't be able to tell the difference between it and any other cake. And it's so delicious." The more she talked, the more Camellia nodded. Deacon had seen her do this with Dahlia on more than one occasion—convince her that something she'd not planned to do was, in fact, her brain child.

"Let's go make sure Harper's on board," Lily said, and she pulled her aunt across the lawn to talk to the wedding planner, leaving Deacon standing next to Dahlia's father. No one could expect the two of them to have anything to say to each other, so Deacon enjoyed the moment of quiet.

"You're not going to sue, are you?"

Deacon wasn't sure he'd heard Benson Ravenel correctly. "Sir?"

"For defamation? Or breach of contract?"

Deacon had no intention of correcting Mr. Ravenel's legal misunderstandings. "Of course not."

Benson nodded, breathing an audible sigh of relief. "Of course not. Of course not," he said. "Well. Don't be a stranger." And he walked away, smoothing the silver sideburns that lay already perfectly smooth against his face.

Lily came back and stood again by his side. "Good?"

"This has been a weird day," Deacon said, shaking his head. "Any chance I could sneak out the back?"

Lily seemed to be weighing the odds. "No chance at all."

"Actually, there's no chance I could have done this without you." Deacon bent his head from side to side and let his neck crack. "Thank you again."

Lily turned so she was standing directly in front of him. She was so much taller than Dahlia, it was easier to look her in the face.

"I'm not going to lie," she said. "I wish things had gone better. But this isn't like one of those nasty breakups where you have to divide up the dishes and the furniture and the friends." She hugged out a breath of annoyance. "Tonight Dahlia left us both, and I'm yours."

She seemed to realize very quickly that what she'd said might not be exactly what she'd intended. "I mean," she said, "that I'm here for you. I'm your friend, and I'll always be that."

"I get it, Lil." Deacon wrapped his arms around Lily one more time, and as he held her, he had a moment to realize that he'd hugged her more in the past hour than he had in a long time.

And that he liked it.

He definitely needed another drink.

Chapter Three

Lily swore under her breath and vowed to never, ever again agree to be a maid of honor. Not even a bridesmaid. This was dumb. And totally not worth the dress she'd never wear again. She liked the necklace, though.

She walked through the debris of the William-Aiken House, relieved at least that fixing overturned glasses and sticky chairs both inside and outside were not part of her job description.

She'd heard a few whispers that Dahlia had used her honeymoon plane ticket. Bali? Alone? It was exactly something Dahlia would do. Lily knew it was partly her fault. That year right after nursing school when she took six months to do humanitarian nursing in Indonesia, she'd called Dahlia and demanded that she make her way there—immediately, if not sooner. She'd packed a bag or three or four and flown around the world to see this paradise, and she'd decided on the spot that it was the place she'd honeymoon with Deacon someday.

Well. No honeymoon. No Deacon. But Lily hoped she'd have a great vacation.

She slid into a chair. She was too tired to be angry at Dahlia.

No, that wasn't true. She was just tired enough to be angry at Dahlia. It wasn't her usual reaction to Dahlia's usual nonsense. She'd spent her whole life walking just behind, clearing away the detritus of all the "watch this, you're going to love it" moments.

Starting with the little rebellions of their childhood, like stealing chocolate bars from the convenience store, and moving up to that hit and run on a parked car. Uncle Ben had fixed that with the authorities by explaining there were faulty lightbulbs on the street corner. Dahlia was able to deny her participation in the high school gambling ring (even though every student knew she was running the whole thing), but she didn't get kicked out of their prestigious private school until she stole and then sold Mr. Keane's physics test questions. Lily had denied knowledge of any of it, but she refused to go any farther. She wouldn't agree to testify that it had been someone else. Dahlia pretended she didn't care and kept her rebellions in the new high school to a quiet roar.

Over the past few months, all the warning signs had flashed in Lily's face, and she had shaken it off over and over. That was her whole action plan, until it seemed way too serious. It started with Dahlia's drinking more and at strange times of the day, then grew to lying about where she'd been and who she'd been with. Then she'd started walking out of stores with things she hadn't bought—her own specialty of accidental shoplifting. When Lily told Deacon about her worries, he'd listened with half attention, knowing that any of those things could signal a spiral— or not.

So even though this is all my fault, Lily thought, *it's not really my fault. Just because I should have seen it coming doesn't mean I could* actually *see it coming.*

And now she was gone. Overseas and across the world, if an all-expense paid ticket was any indication and if the rumors were to be believed. She should feel sad. She got left too. But all Lily could feel was exhausted. And, if she were being honest, a little grateful.

She looked around to see if anyone had heard her think that. But nobody else was left. She peeled herself off the chair and walked to the parking lot, thinking the whole way that she hadn't meant it. She didn't want Dahlia to disappear from her life. She loved Dahlia. She had always loved Dahlia. Sometimes to a dangerously worshipful degree. But as she unlocked her car and a soft breeze ruffled her hair, she could admit, if only in her mind, that it would be a relief to go a few weeks, even a few months without worrying about cleaning up after Dahlia.

The next morning, she drove over to Camellia and Ben's house. She decided to knock on the front door and let the housekeeper announce her instead of walking through the kitchen entry like she'd done nearly every day of her life. She was here as the maid of honor, not simply as Lily.

"Hi, darling," Camellia said, leaning over to kiss her cheek.

"Morning, Camellia." She didn't ask any polite,

meaningless questions that Camellia would have to lie to answer. "Ready to get started?"

Her sigh floated out. "Ready as I'm likely to be."

They sat at the formal dining room table surrounded by wedding gifts ranging from the ordinary (at least three really nice toasters) to the practical (towels and sheet sets) to the profane (who needed so many heavy silver platters?). At Lily's feet stood a tower of cardboard boxes, mounds of bubble wrap, and a carton full of sticky labels and permanent markers.

Lily would choose a gift, read the card, and start wrapping it for return. Aunt Camellia found the giver's name and address on her invitation spreadsheet and hand-wrote an address label. They got into a groove, and several hours passed in which they said very little about anything other than what was related to the packaging and labeling of gifts.

When Camellia's marker ran dry of ink, she capped it and placed it beside her and then said a curse word Lily had never heard from her before. Lily blinked in surprise.

"Sorry about that, honey. I've been holding that in for," she checked her watch, "about nineteen hours now."

Lily didn't know whether to laugh or not. In no way was this funny, after all. Except that it had turned her aunt into a dockworker. Playing it safe, she kept wrapping. Camellia kept talking.

"Can you believe this? How could she? What was she thinking? Obviously, she wasn't thinking at all. She took no thought for what this would do to her father. Or me. Or Deacon, that poor boy. This will change him forever, mark my words. How will he ever recover from the shock of this?"

Lily thought about letting her continue muttering

complaints, but that last one was a question, after all.

"I can't imagine Deacon was completely shocked. None of us should have been entirely surprised." She couldn't quite make herself look at Aunt Camellia. "I think he'll recover."

"Lily, I'm surprised at you."

She felt her face flush. "I don't mean that he's not sad. I know he is. But I don't think it's irreparable damage."

Camellia did a sniffy little breath. "You misunderstand me."

Lily looked up. Camellia was smiling.

"I'm surprised because I've never heard you speak with anything approaching backbone about our Dahlia. She's pulled you along after her harebrained schemes your whole life." Only someone with Aunt Camellia's charm and charisma could use a phrase like "harebrained schemes" without sounding like a living, breathing cartoon character. She reached over and patted Lily's cheek with soft hands. "Good for you." She looked around the piles of packaged boxes. "I think we should call it a day. What do you say? Lunch? Let's call your mom and go find something made of white bread carbs."

"You sure you want to face the town?" Lily asked.

Camellia paused and shook her head. "We'll have something delivered. A girl has got to eat."

A few minutes later, Lily heard the front door open and heard her mother's voice. "Hey," she called.

Camellia answered, "We're in here, Iris." The sisters kissed the air beside each other's faces. "I'll call for sandwiches," Camellia said.

When she was out of the room, Lily's mom slid into a chair

and heaved a theatrical sigh. "Oh, sweetheart. What a night. You handled all that maid of honor business like a pro."

Lily laughed. "Thanks, but I really don't want to go professional with the maid of honor business. In fact, I'd be thrilled to never, ever do that again."

Iris leaned over and patted Lily's knee. "We'll see. Maybe now you can focus on yourself."

"Mom. You are not going to use Dahlia's runaway bride incident to springboard into a conversation about my fantasy wedding."

Iris looked a little self-conscious. "Sorry. I know. It's just that for the first time in years," she looked over her shoulder to assure herself they were alone, "you can stop following after Dahlia and Deacon and deal with your own life."

Lily did not roll her eyes. She behaved herself with grace and decorum, just as Iris had taught her. She smiled at her mom and said, "I will start dealing with my own life right after lunch. I promise."

Even though the afternoon spent with both Camellia and her mom went smoothly, and was even fun, Lily found herself checking her phone every few minutes. Why hadn't Deacon called? Or at least answered the text she'd sent when she woke up? She was glad she'd waited to text him until morning, because she could come off way more breezy and casual after a few good hours of sleep. Her message, **Let me know when natural light hits you**, seemed miles better than what she would have sent if she'd written something in the night.

So where was he?

Obviously, he wasn't expecting to go into work. He'd planned two weeks off for the honeymoon. And if he'd gone into the office, he'd have seen her text and could respond that he was fine.

Which, of course he was.

Probably.

But he didn't respond. And he hadn't called.

She couldn't even go break down the door, because she didn't know where he'd gone home to. Was he at the single house just off Vanderhorst Street that Dahlia's parents had given them as a wedding gift? She couldn't quite see it, Deacon hiding out in the single house by himself. Lily couldn't imagine that he'd go there to escape the specter of Dahlia. Her fingerprints were literally and figuratively all over the house.

His old apartment, then? Last she heard, extended family in for the wedding was staying at his place. Emmett's place? A hotel? His parents' house? None of those seemed like good options.

So what did that leave? Waiting.

She hated waiting.

She wondered if any of the groomsmen had stuck around. Maybe one of those friends had changed plans and stayed in Charleston to keep Deacon company. How hard would it be for him to tell her so?

Unless he wasn't okay.

But he was okay.

Of course he was.

Lily didn't have a shift at the hospital until the next

morning. What, she asked herself, would she be doing this afternoon if the wedding had happened and Deacon and Dahlia were in Bali? Certainly not obsessively checking for a text that wouldn't likely come.

Grocery shopping. That's what she'd be doing if everything had happened like it was going to. She almost thought "like it was supposed to," but stopped herself. *Was* it supposed to happen? Or did it all implode because cosmic forces were opposed to the marriage in the first place?

Wait. Did she *think* cosmic forces were opposed? Of course not. That was ridiculous.

Maybe.

She pulled out her phone and made a shopping list.

Or, if not cosmic forces, was Lily herself opposed to the marriage?

Huh. She grabbed a cloth bag from under the sink and walked to the market. Pulling stir-fry ingredients into her basket, she tried to forget that Deacon was ignoring her.

Deacon-and-Dahlia was a fact of Lily's existence. They'd been together so long that sometimes Lily thought of them as one, as a unit. Their marriage would have only cemented that. And it hadn't happened. And they were entirely Not Together now. And Lily was way more concerned with where he'd spent his day, and with whom, and whether he was fine, than she was with any question of Dahlia.

What did any of this even mean? She asked herself that question several times over the next ten minutes as she walked down grocery aisles from which she needed nothing.

Then, walking past the canned peaches, Lily had an

epiphany. An honest-to-God epiphany. It stopped her still, between the pears and the mandarin oranges.

She hadn't had a Dahlia-free thought in years.

Every day, life's goodness or badness was measured by how Dahlia's actions affected Lily. Her nursing job at the Medical University of South Carolina was the only thing that felt unaffected by the dramas Dahlia inspired. In every other moment of Lily's life, Dahlia's happiness led to Lily's satisfaction; Dahlia's dejection led to Lily's unhappiness. Today's deepest concern, outside of Deacon's whereabouts, was that she wasn't at all sure how she should react to a world where Dahlia was absent.

And that was wrong. Unfair.

"No." She said the words aloud. "I am not the sidekick in Dahlia Ravenel's life."

She laughed and looked around to see who heard her. No one.

She picked up a box of herbal tea on the way to the checkout lane—the kind of tea that Dahlia would have called an old lady drink. Lily held the box to her heart until the cashier was ready to ring her up.

"You know what?" Lily asked the guy. "It's a really great day."

Chapter Four

Deacon's relief when his phone battery died equaled his concern when his bottle ran dry.

He answered a few calls in those first twenty-four hours but didn't remember anything he'd said. He'd felt responsible enough to tell Emmett where he was going, and he remembered that Max called to make sure he was all right. He vaguely remembered wondering exactly how right he had to be to qualify as "all right." After a couple of calls in which he was pretty sure there was some shouting, he ignored the phone. Even on silent, he could tell every time a text came in, and there was nothing—nothing at all—that anyone had to say to him that he wanted to hear. So he did what he could do so he wouldn't hear.

He wasn't, in general, a big drinker. His job was too demanding, and he could see by looking in every direction the results of southern lawyers drinking. In his experience at his father's firm, a guy worked hard until he got really good at law, at which point he allowed himself to spend afternoons in the bar when not in court, until the boozy haze killed any desire or ability to perform in court. Then he got his name on a building and retired. To the bar.

"I'm not in court this week," he thought. "Looks like I'm behaving as expected."

He closed his eyes and let himself sink into sleep. When he woke, he'd roll over and sleep again. If the sunlight seemed too bright, he'd pull his T-shirt over his head or use a pillow to block some of it out. When he could be bothered to think about it at all, he considered the possibility of sleeping for the rest of his life.

After many sleep/wake/sleep repeats, he pulled himself out of bed. He wandered around the sparsely furnished hunting cabin wondering if there was anything to eat. The kitchen corner had a few cans of soup that expired years ago, but he hadn't found a can opener. There were boxes of cereal, but mice had claimed them. Half a bottle of whiskey hadn't lasted long, and the bourbon in the cupboard made him feel like a legitimate southern gentleman until he stopped feeling anything at all.

That was two days ago, and now he was starving.

Wallowing was hard work.

"What am I trying to prove?" he asked the empty cabin. That he was heartbroken? Check. He was so weighed down he couldn't even stand up straight. That he'd become tragic? He'd caught a reflection of himself in the window. His two-day beard made his face look sunken, and the circles around his eyes could have been painted in ink.

"No wonder she left." When this pathetic sentence left his mouth, he flopped down on the couch and determined that he'd never get up again.

Except he was really, really hungry.

Hauling himself back up off the couch, he slumped into the bathroom. Under his funk of depression and self-pity he had the thought that he was grateful his family not only kept this place, but they kept the electricity and water hooked up. He splashed cold water on his face and fished a toothbrush out of a drawer. "Don't think too hard about it," he told himself as he wondered who'd used the toothbrush last, and when.

He grabbed his dead phone and his keys and headed out to the car, which he did not remember parking that close to the cabin. Close enough to leave a wrinkle in the BMW's front bumper.

"One more thing I've messed up." His muttering startled a bird, who left him a streaky white present on the back window. "I deserve that," he said.

The engine started with a comforting hum. Patting the steering wheel, he said to the car, "I love you. I really do. Don't leave me." He checked his mirror before backing out and caught sight of himself again. This time, he had to laugh. It was a pitiful laugh, but it beat the alternative. "All right, D. Pull it together." He plugged his dead phone in to charge and drove to find food.

When his phone had enough charge to turn back on, the first thing he saw was a text from Lily: ***You need to eat.***

She had that right. After a few more minutes of driving, he pulled into the parking lot at Barry's, a dingy diner that had made the world's best pancakes for about a thousand years. It was possible the same woman had been serving the pancakes for that whole time. A bell announced his entrance, and he was hit with the comforting scents of toast, bacon, and coffee.

"Seat yourself, honey," an ancient voice called out, and Deacon slid into a booth. The tiny woman with white cotton-candy hair bounced over within a minute and pulled out one of those ancient paper order pads.

"Need a menu?" she asked.

"No thanks." He held his hands out, one a couple of inches above the other. "I need a stack of pancakes. Can you make that happen?"

She leaned in and lifted his upper hand a few inches higher. "Big stack?"

He nodded and raised it a bit more. His hands indicated nearly a foot of hot, buttered carbs.

"You're easy to please. Coming right up, honey." She patted his shoulder, and he used all his strength to resist pulling her into a hug. Clearly Deacon didn't do *alone* well.

While he waited for his pancakes, he scrolled through his missed calls and texts.

So many missed calls and texts.

Although he could pretend he wasn't looking for anything in particular, it didn't take long to realize that none of them were from Dahlia. Many of them were from his mother, all on the theme of, *Are you finished pouting?*

And quite a few from Lily. He looked through them quickly, reading the newest first: **You need to eat.**

Did you take food with you?
Just give me a hint.
Did you leave the city or possibly the country?
Apartment?
Not the house, right?

Where are you?

Emmett says he knows but he's not telling.

Where are you, I mean it.

Your mom said you're not with her.

I'm trying not to get worried.

Did you wake up?

Let me know when you wake up.

Please note that I waited 24hrs to send another message.

Please?

Tell me you're okay.

Are you okay?

Not our best day, am I right?

Where are you staying?

Did you make it home?

Sorry.

I know you're tired of 'sorry' but . . .

Tell me when you're home safe.

Three days' worth of concern from Lily, who was only a friend. And from Dahlia? Not a thing.

He sent three texts: to Emmett, his mom, and Lily. All three said the same thing. **I'm fine. Having breakfast. Coming home soon.**

His mom responded immediately. **Home here? I'll have a room ready.**

Emmett's reply came a minute later. In typical Emmett fashion, his was a mixture of comedy and concern. **Don't go home. Mom will eat you whole.**

The waitress brought Deacon his breakfast, set it down in

front of him, and started walking away.

"Wait," he said.

"Need something else, honey?"

He glanced around the otherwise deserted diner. "Can you sit for a minute?"

She looked at him from the corner of her eye. "If I sat down with every handsome man who invited me, I'd never get a single bit of work done."

He nodded and laughed, wondering what had made him ask her that in the first place. "Sure. Thanks. This smells perfect."

He'd shoveled a great deal of food into his mouth but barely made a dent in the pile of pancakes when she returned. She slid a bowl of sliced strawberries and a can of aerosol whipped cream onto the table. "A little something extra for you. Looks like you could use it."

"That bad, huh?" His hand reflexively smoothed out his hair and ran along his jaw.

She shrugged. "Doesn't have to be all that bad to leave a mark."

He helped himself to berries and cream, relishing the slurpy sound the can made as he sprayed. It was one of the happy sounds of childhood. Good to be reminded that there were at least a few good things (okay, at least one) unconnected to Dahlia Ravenel. He looked around again, saw nobody, and tipped the bottle so the nozzle was pointing into his mouth. He shot a tentative spray which came out mostly air.

"Tip your chin up, honey. Gotta be straight up and down."

Where was she?

How could she see him if he couldn't see her?

Oh, well. Too late to play it cool. Chin up, he squirted cream into his mouth and smiled.

Chapter Five

Balancing a cafeteria salad and her water bottle in one hand, Lily turned on her phone with the other. Helping to change bandages on a burn patient had taken up fifteen minutes of her lunch break.

Texts from her mom, Aunt Camellia, and a guy she had dinner with a month ago. And at the bottom, finally, a reply from Deacon. It wasn't much, but he was okay. Responsive. Upright, apparently.

She shot him a message telling him she was on a shift until seven. She started typing more: how she was glad he was okay. Delete, delete, delete. How she hoped he wasn't annoyed by her barrage of messages over the past few days. Delete, delete, delete. How she'd been so angry and now she wasn't. Delete, delete, delete.

An alarm buzzed on her hand, startling her, and she checked the time. She only had five minutes left to eat her wilty, mostly-white-lettuce salad. Shoveling a few bites into her mouth, she hoped it would fuel her for another six hours. It would have to do.

Walking to her car after work, she noticed how pleasant the evening felt. She pulled the ponytail out of her hair and ran her fingers over her scalp, scratching out the stress of the day and letting the breeze blow through.

A voice called out from the hospital parking lot. "Is there a doctor in the house? Or at least a nurse?"

Deacon stepped out from behind an old red minivan.

"You need medical attention?" she asked, smiling at the grin on his face.

"I need all kinds of attention," he said. Almost immediately she saw his face flush and he looked at his shoes, clearly embarrassed by any number of wrong ways she could have taken that.

"Come here, you. Bring it in." She opened her arms and he hugged her long and tight. Oh. His arms fit around her so perfectly. And she had no desire to let go any time soon. She noticed the scent of his skin, his clothes . . . and then she remembered who she was. "Sorry I smell like work," she said.

He breathed in while she was still in his arms. "You smell like . . . is that baby shampoo?"

She pulled back and ducked away. "There was possibly a little bit more human biology happening today than I'd expected."

"Mmm." He pretended to be intrigued. "Got a little on you, did you?"

"Gross. But yes. Baby shampoo was all they had in the

locker room showers."

He came close and put his arm around her. "I like it. It suits you."

Why was she so aware of both Deacon's arm and her shoulder? He'd walked with his arm around her shoulders for years. This should feel normal, she told herself.

Lily kept walking toward her car. "What brings you here?" She found that she was holding her breath, both hoping and fearing that she knew what he'd say.

"I was lonely." That was the fear, right there. That he'd come because there was nothing else to do. That he was here only because she was his secondary default. "It's weird for me, being alone." He tried to laugh it off, but she knew he wasn't kidding. "I don't like it."

Lily understood what he was trying hard not to say. She was still riding the wave of her realization about being the main character in her own life story, but Deacon hadn't had any such revelation. He wasn't ready for it yet.

"Remember that time Christmas of junior year, I think it was, when you and I spent every day together?" He didn't say her name. He didn't say "because Dahlia and her family had gone to Vail to ski," but the specter of her hung there in the parking lot anyway.

"I do remember," Lily said. "We watched a lot of really terrible movies that week."

"No, you must be thinking of something else. No, we watched all those Steve McQueen car chase films that winter."

"Oh, was I unclear? Those are the movies I was talking about. They were terrible."

Shaking his head, Deacon sighed. "Poor Lily. You don't know an amazing piece of art when you see one."

"I maintain that the movies were awful. Company was great, though," she said, bumping him with her elbow.

Deacon nodded. "I will allow you your incorrect opinion of Steve McQueen." He went around to the passenger side of her car. "Can I ride home with you?"

She worried her surprise would come across as disinterest, so she answered carefully. "Of course. Are you leaving your car here?" Why was it so hard to be normal?

Oh. Right. Because *normal* contained another person. One who drove every decision, steered every conversation, and dominated every aspect of every day. That.

"I dropped her at the shop for a little shine-up and walked over."

This, Lily knew, was code. A "shine-up" was what Dahlia got every time she crashed her car into something: fire hydrants, parked cars, trees, light poles.

"What'd you hit?" she asked as she clicked her seatbelt.

"I didn't hit anything. I nudged."

"Right. Got it." If he didn't want to tell, she wasn't going to pester him about it.

They'd been together for fewer than five minutes, and already she was tense from being so careful about what she did and did not say. Not to mention from the memory of how she'd reacted to that hug. The hug that she'd shared with her cousin's ex-fiancé. Her old friend. This grieving man.

"Can you lead this conversation, please?" she said. "I don't want to say any of the wrong things, and I'm drawing a blank on what the right things might be."

From the corner of her eye, she saw him shift in the passenger seat.

"What were you planning to do about dinner?" he asked.

Good. Food was easy.

"I'm making grilled cheese sandwiches, and no comments about four-year-old taste. It's a very good sandwich."

He nodded. "I almost believe you, but I'm willing to let you prove it to me."

"Did you just invite yourself over for dinner?"

He scratched his jawline. "Do normal people not do that?"

She laughed. "Is that what you're aiming for? Normal?"

He did not laugh. His hands covered his face and he spoke from behind them. "Lil, I don't even remember my life without her in it. I don't know how to be a person who isn't her person."

I do! She wanted to shout it out her open window. *I know how to be me without her.* But his wound was different than hers, and he needed to figure it out on his own. And if Lily were being honest with herself, she still had some figuring out to do when it came to how she behaved around Deacon. This was obvious. She wasn't finished with the process yet, she knew.

"I need to do a few things," Deacon said.

Lily nodded, assuming he meant errands he wanted to take care of tonight. Possibly in her car.

"I need a new apartment."

"Oh." This, she knew, was not an intelligent response. But it was what she had available to her in the moment.

"I've lived with my parents for seven hours now, and I'm about at my limit."

She laughed. "How many of those hours were you actually in the house?"

"Four. Don't laugh." But he was laughing too.

She forced her face into a stoic expression. "I hear the Holiday Inn by the airport has rooms, if you're feeling desperate."

"Nah. Mom's excited to cook for me, and Emmett's here, so I can probably survive a little longer." He reached up and tweaked the angle of her rearview mirror. "But not forever. So. You know the Charleston apartment scene. Where do I want to look?"

"I'm not sure. There are lots of options, but . . . why don't you buy a house?" She didn't say what she was thinking, which was something along the line of *you have all the money in the world and didn't the Ravenels just buy you a house and nobody's going to live in it while Dahlia's on the other side of the planet,* mainly because he still had not said her name.

"I'm looking for a short-term thing, I think."

What did that mean? This tiptoeing around was making her crazy. There had never been a time since they were kids that Lily had felt like she couldn't just say what she meant or ask what he was thinking.

"Okay," she said, glad that exasperation was absent from her tone. "Close to work? Close to the water?" Was she supposed to be a real estate agent?

He shrugged. "I like your place."

What?

"I already have a roommate, and no."

"Not your apartment. But maybe your building. Or your

neighborhood."

She nodded. "Let's Google it and see if there's anything around here."

Did that sound like she was giving him permission? Like she thought he needed her permission? This was making her skin itch.

She pulled into her parking garage while he was still looking at his phone, and when she got out, he followed her up to her place.

"Sandwich?"

"Sure."

Those two words? That was the most comfortable exchange they'd had since the . . . party. It was hard to think of it as a reception without all the correlated baggage.

He sat on a stool in the kitchen looking at apartments on her laptop while she chopped onions, spinach, and mushrooms, and sliced gruyere. In a few minutes she had two steaming grilled cheese sandwiches and put them on plates.

"Drink?" she asked, sliding him a sandwich.

He shook his head, then said, "Water?"

She wanted to ask all the questions but knew she couldn't without tipping the balance. This new territory riddled with emotional pitfalls contained too many mysterious dark places, and above it all hung the fear that she'd say or do the one thing that would turn Deacon away from her. And without him, she feared, there was so little left.

Wow. The drama.

She shook it off and sat down to eat. Deacon made all the appropriate noises of appreciation for the sandwich.

"When you call this 'grilled cheese' you might be underselling it."

She shrugged. "It's got cheese. It's grilled."

"I'm not saying it's not true," he said. "I just think you could make it more appealing."

Her heart thumped with anxiety. It sounded like he was channeling her mother, who occasionally said things like, "You've got so much potential. I wish you'd try a little harder to show it to men." Unfortunately, her mom had a different visual attached to "showing her potential," and it almost always required expensive clothes and absolutely never included scrubs. But she didn't need to think about that right now.

"How about you give this sandwich a name," Lily said, "and I promise I'll always call it whatever you say it's supposed to be."

"And whenever I come over and ask for the Baltic, you'll make this one?"

"Really? The Baltic? As in eastern Europe?" She picked off a corner of her sandwich and nibbled it, looking at the ceiling and trying to find anything Baltic about it.

He shook his head. "Or not. Maybe it will be called the Geisha."

"Why?" Lily couldn't even begin to imagine how spinach and onions conjured up Geisha feelings.

"The Yucatan?"

"You're really reaching now."

He smiled and took another bite. "Madagascar."

"You keep saying words that reflect cultures and places that are not in any way contained in this sandwich. Also, you might need to call a travel agent and take a trip." She put the last piece of her sandwich in her mouth.

"It's on the list," he said through a large bite. He gestured to his phone. "Get an apartment. Take a vacation. Fall out of love."

Lily was unsurprised but a little embarrassed when tears sprang to her eyes. "Oh, Deacon," she said, but didn't know how to finish.

"Have you noticed," he asked, "that I have not once said her name this evening?"

The tears came a little faster. "Of course I've noticed. This is the most awkward we've ever been."

He held his hand out, fingers pinched almost together to show a tiny space. "The time you threw up in front of me might have been as awkward."

She nodded and wiped her eyes with her napkin. "Close second."

"I'm running on the theory that if I don't mention her, don't actually ever say her name, my heart will zip itself back together and everything will be natural again."

She folded the napkin in half, then in half again. "That's so repressive and adorable."

"So in your medical opinion, I'm on the right track?"

He couldn't keep his face straight for long.

She gathered the two plates and carried them to the sink.

Deacon leaned back from the counter, stretching his arms over his head. "I've been thinking." He was quiet for a minute.

She asked the question she'd been avoiding. "When you were gone the last few days?"

"Nah, mostly since I got home this morning. While I was gone, I mostly drank to excess and slept as much as possible."

"In my medical opinion, you had it half right." She wiped her hands dry and stood watching him from the other side of the counter.

He nodded. "I actually guessed that's what you'd say." Now he leaned forward again, closer to her. "But what I've been thinking is that I need to do a little revisiting."

She waited.

"I think I want to go back to some of the places where my memories are strongest so I can lay those things to rest."

The fact that he still had not spoken Dahlia's name did not escape Lily's notice.

She nodded, hoping he'd go on to explain, clarify, or at least something.

"So you'll come?"

What?

"What?"

"You'll come with me?" he asked. "You'll help me?"

Lily turned back to the sink and closed her eyes for a second, settling into the strange balancing act. Could she do this for him? With him? And why was it even a difficult question? Of course she could. She would. He was her friend. He needed her. She would be there for him. She wrapped her arms around herself, trying not to feel the memory of his arms. When she turned back to him, he was watching her with an eager expression.

When she spoke, her voice came out more quietly than she'd anticipated. "I'll come if you think it will help."

He got up off his stool and walked around the counter. "Are you kidding me?" he asked. "Having you with me makes everything better." When he put his arms around her yet again, she found herself trying not to stiffen.

This was an entirely new problem, and one she had not anticipated. Deacon had always, all the time she'd known him, been affectionate. As a little kid, he'd wrestle with her, dunk her in the pool, bump her arm to show he'd noticed her. He was the most huggy teenage boy in all their group of friends, and his affection was never, ever weird. The way he'd always cuddled with Dahlia was different, but now that there was no Dahlia, Lily felt the strangeness of all of this.

Come on, she told herself. He needed comfort. His world had just changed forever. He was re-figuring his whole life. She understood that.

But why did she find herself both craving and evading his touch? What was it about the way she felt in the circle of his arms that gave her a sense of both comfort and fear? What was she afraid of?

She knew, much too well, the answer to that.

Chapter Six

A never-ending stream of juicy bugs smacked against the Jeep's windshield as Deacon drove the winding road through the woods. His stomach felt full of hornets—butterflies were too tame. Beside him in the passenger seat, Lily sat forward, like she was trying to get there before him.

"I can't believe we're going back. It's been twelve years since I've been to Lafayette." She gasped and squealed. "Look! The sign. We're really here."

Deacon drove under the wooden arch signaling entrance to Camp Lafayette, where he'd spent a month every summer from ages eight to fifteen.

Lily clapped her hands. "There's the admin building. Remember that lady who ran the camp when we were like nine? She was the worst."

Deacon shook his head. "You think everyone was the worst."

"Maybe. But she was a terror. I was convinced that when she told us she sent someone home, she really chained them up in the admin building's basement and forced them to write letters to parents telling them how much fun Lafayette's service week was."

Deacon almost laughed. "Service week. Yeah, I don't think we were ever mature enough to appreciate the nuances of that particular project."

It had taken Deacon a month to schedule and arrange this visit back to Lafayette. Or at least it had taken a month for the actual visit to happen. He wanted to do it. It was his idea. But there was something about taking this trip back in time that made him nervous.

Lily looked anything but nervous. She was practically leaping out of the moving car. She pointed to a parking space by the front door, not a difficult find, since it was midweek in autumn and no one else was around.

He pulled in and yanked up the parking break, checking to make sure the windows were all the way up and all knobs and switches were off.

Lily was jiggling the key he'd gotten from the property manager in the door handle.

"I'm in," she said, only then looking back over her shoulder to find him still inside the car. When she noticed that his seatbelt was still fastened, she gave him a thumbs-up and went inside. Deacon felt a bit of that prickle of anxiety loosen. It was nice to have Lily around. She never hurried him.

The subtext of the rest of that thought hung in the car like Dahlia's ghost. Well, the ghost of their relationship anyway. After the wedding debacle, Deacon started to realize how fast Dahlia's pace had always been. He spent all his life running to keep up with her, and as soon as she was gone, he settled into what felt to him like a more natural rhythm. And today, more than a month after what should have been their wedding day, he was here to say goodbye to one part of their history.

The door to the admin building creaked in precisely the same way he remembered it. The rush of stale air that blew past him smelled like every summer in his childhood—a mixture of chlorine and fire smoke with hints of pine sap and skunk.

"Isn't it perfect?" Lily stood in the center of the building's main room, a large open area with a purpose that was never quite clear to Deacon. Lily spread her arms wide and turned in a slow circle. "I think I lied to adults in this building more than anywhere else all the days of my entire life combined."

She pointed to one side of the room. "In that chair I denied knowing anything about the fireworks for three years in a row. In that one, I denied the streaking. Over there, I sat and looked into the eyes of a very sincere counselor and assured him I knew nothing about the breakout scheme for the next night. Everyone always believed me."

Deacon laughed. "That's why you were the front man. First line of defense with grownups. Dahlia could never have done that. Everyone could always tell when she was lying. Besides, she couldn't sit still. Her fidgeting would have given her away every time."

Lily walked the perimeter of the room, checking the view from every window. "The trees are bigger. There's a new parking lot over there. There's the trailhead to the lake. Remember that kid who tried to sleep in the tree? When he fell, he broke both collarbones. Ouch."

Deacon appreciated the steady stream of chatter and general memories. He still had to gather his resolve for what came next.

When he was ready, he and Lily took the trail past the girls' cabins, past the amphitheater, and over the bridge to the grassy hill near the lake. She looked in every window, pointed out all the bunks she'd had, and reminded him of things he'd forgotten. He paid as much attention as he could. At the hill, he walked up to the fire ring and sat on a stone.

"Right here," he said. "This is where I kissed Dahlia for the first time."

Lily nodded and sat on a stone opposite. They were only a few feet apart, but Deacon appreciated the distance, because it would help him with something he needed to do.

Pulling his wallet out of his pocket, he said, "Don't laugh."

She shrugged up her shoulders as if she hadn't yet determined whether to go along with his demands. "Don't be funny."

"I solemnly swear I will not be funny."

Lily's tiny smile created a dimple in her cheek that drew his eyes.

He looked down at the grass by his feet and said, "Okay, but seriously, my therapist is making me do this, and now I feel like I'm twelve years old again so please be nice to me."

"I'll be nice." She folded her hands on her knees.

He unfolded the letter he'd handwritten and shoved in his wallet. This was draft four, because the first three were, chronologically, horrifying, shameful, and angsty. This one wasn't perfect, but it wasn't required to be perfect. According to his therapist, it was only required to be completed.

So.

He cleared his throat. "Dear Dahlia," he read. "There are a few things I need to say to you. I'm working on getting over you, but you are tied up in every memory of my life. Untying those strings is scary, because everything in my history, and therefore in my present, might actually fall apart.

"Today I'm at Camp Lafayette, and I need to walk through a memory so I can let you out of it. Remember the night you organized the breakout? When you brought your cabin of girls to meet my cabin of boys at the lake? And we had our first kiss? I have a confession.

"That was not my first kiss."

He looked at Lily, who was inspecting her fingernails.

"When we made the plan, while we were canoeing that afternoon, I wasn't lying when I said I'd never kissed anyone."

If he hadn't promised his therapist that he'd read this aloud, he'd tear the letter up right now. But keeping promises had become imperative to Deacon lately, so he kept reading.

"I kissed Lily behind the meal hall at dinner that night."

The sounds of birds and breeze through trees grew louder as Deacon's voice went silent. Lily tore tiny pieces from a fallen leaf and didn't look up. Even when the silence grew uncomfortable, she continued to stare at the leaf pieces in her hands.

He picked up reading again. "I wanted to impress you so badly that I asked Lily to help me. And I've never thanked her for how helpful she was, because I never mentioned it again ever. To anyone. That night I decided that my kiss with Lily didn't count.

That it was only warm-up. And I've always told everyone that you were my first kiss. But you weren't."

He cleared his throat. "And now, here in this place, I need to say the truth. The story I told, to you and everyone else, was not the real story. You were not my first kiss. And although it doesn't change how I always felt about you, it does change the story of us. You were not my first kiss, and you will not be my last."

Deacon folded the letter on its creases and slipped it back into his wallet.

He leaned forward and put his arms across his knees, staring into the memory of a fire. He didn't know how long they sat there like that, saying nothing, looking at the ground, lost in their own memories of those summers in this place, but when his legs started to tingle, he stood to wake them up.

On the other side of the fire pit, he saw Lily wipe her eyes.

Oh, no. Which part of what he'd said had made her cry? How did he manage to mess this up? His therapist was going to hear about this. Stupid idea.

He stood up and stopped in front of Lily, shoved his hands in his pockets, and waited. She was so good about waiting for him, he figured he could return the favor.

When she finally looked at him, her red eyes were leaky and swollen.

"Lil, I'm sorry. I'm not sure exactly what I did, but if you tell me I won't do it again."

She shook her head.

Great. Maybe she was more like Dahlia than she used to be. One of Dahlia's favorite tricks was to withhold her reasons for being angry so he would apologize for everything, anything, and nothing. He didn't think Lily would do this. That she was even capable of it.

But then she reached out and put her hand on his arm. A beam of afternoon light filtered through the trees and touched the crown of her head, making her auburn hair glow. She smiled at him, and that smile reminded him of so many good things about this place.

"Thank you," she said, her voice damp and cracking.

"What?" He knew he sounded like a dumb guy, but he must have misheard her.

"Thank you for telling that part of the story." She rubbed her sleeve against her eyes. "Every time I've ever heard you talk about that night, you say that Dahlia was your first kiss. You might be surprised how many times I've heard you tell that story over the years." She sniffed. "Here's a hint—a lot of times. I've felt erased from your history for half of my life." Her voice did a little hiccup. "Sometimes I wondered if I'd imagined it, if it never really happened. But it did. It happened. We were each other's first kiss. You've just given me back one of my missing memories."

Deacon stood in the clearing and watched Lily pull herself back together. He hadn't even known his lie had hurt her, but she called him out and forgave him in the same breath.

"How do you feel?" she asked him, with her Lily-skill of turning the conversation back to him.

He thought for a second and then told her the truth. "I untied a piece and I didn't fall apart."

Chapter Seven

Lily washed her hands for what must have been the thousandth time. "Do you think it's true that Christmas season is sicker than any other season?" she asked the hospital locker room in general.

No one answered. Everyone was too tired.

Some kind of nasty flu dropped in on Charleston for the whole month of December, so not only was the ER full of spiking fevers, broken and sprained limbs from dizzy falls, and patients who couldn't get office appointments during overfull days, but inpatient beds filled up at a far more rapid rate than usual. Add to that the number of health care providers who fell victim to the wretched bug, and it was a Merry Christmas at MUSC. Lily felt like she'd been holding her breath all month.

The ladies of Charleston had come out in full force to bring Christmas to the hospital. Trees lined the perimeter of the lobbies and a stocking filled with candy canes, gold-foil paper crackers, and silly trinkets hung from every room's door handle.

Lily's mom had made sure to put a few extra gifts in the stockings that would come to Lily's hall. She included paperback books, earbuds, and vials of essential oils to "make the rooms smell homey." Lily wasn't sure whose home smelled like oranges and eucalyptus, but she certainly appreciated the gesture. It was fun to see her parents come into the hallways, her dad in a horrible white Santa beard on an elastic band and both wearing elf caps with jingle bells dangling off the points.

"If anyone needs nonspecific winter holiday gifts, we have these," her dad said, holding up a box full of blue paper gift bags covered with cut out snowflakes. "All the same stuff is inside," he told her, leaning in close like it was a secret.

"That's very thoughtful of you, Dad. Thanks. I'm sure everyone will appreciate the kindness." If a person made a list of her dad's qualities, kindness would always top it. His gentle nature in no way got in the way of his business success, but everyone who knew him recognized the tenderness he always displayed.

Lily always appreciated her parents' examples of community service and humanitarian aid. Like any southern gentleman of means, her dad hoped that she'd settle down and marry a wealthy man, raise a house full of babies, and eat lunch with her mom twice a week. But he couldn't be more supportive of her decision to go to nursing school and work in the hospital. He always told people Lily was walking in the path of kindness. She couldn't think of a better compliment.

For two days, Lily had picked up shifts for nurses who had gotten sick or had family holiday obligations. She knew this was standard at Christmas time. The nurses who had no children were working, mostly without complaint, so those with kids at home could be there for the holidays.

With two days left until Christmas, the manufactured cheer filled up the halls. Lily found it best to stick to the rooms and the hallways and avoid the locker rooms as much as possible. The exhaustion generally collected there, where no patients could see it. And it was as contagious as the flu.

For the last hour of her shift, Lily violated her own Cardinal Rule: she checked the clock every few minutes. She felt like whimpering every time, because she knew the time would never pass that way, and she was right. All she wanted was a seamless shift change, a quick drive home, and a bath that lasted about six hours. Or at least something to eat that hadn't come from a cellophane wrapper.

At seven, she breathed a huge sigh of relief and pulled off the latest pair of gloves. Checking the schedule at the nurses' station, she saw that Elise was scheduled to relieve her. She made a few notes about the patients so Elise would know the things that didn't show up on the stats charts (like the little girl in 4127 who handled the pressure cuff much better on her right arm than on her left, and the man in 4133 whose legal name was Francis but preferred to be called Jojo). When the only thing left for Lily to do was see Elise's face and say goodnight, Nancy Anne, the shift coordinator, came around a corner shaking her head.

"Sorry, Lily. Bad news. Elise is sick. Stomach bug. She called in half an hour ago, but I couldn't find you. I had to cover Celeste's patients because she broke out in hives after doing a shift at her church's soup kitchen. Please tell me you can stay."

Several hundred ways to say no crossed her mind in the few seconds before she answered. "Are you kidding me? Twenty-four hours straight during a flu epidemic the day before

Christmas Eve? I can't think of anything I'd rather do." She held out her fist and Nancy Anne punched her knuckles.

"Don't call it an epidemic where anyone can hear you," Nancy Anne said. "Thank you for being willing. I will not forget this, at least not before I forget to eat, shower, and shave my legs. Oh, wait . . ."

Lily breathed out a single syllable laugh. "Yeah, I know. Okay. Coffee. Then I'll go back and tell my friends on the east hall that we're going to party all night long."

But instead of eating or drinking anything, Lily went into the locker room and did a few minutes of yoga stretches, washed her face, and texted Deacon.

Remember how we're having pre-Christmas dinner and a Jason Bourne marathon tonight? We're not. Gotta stay and heal the sick. Sorry. Happy Christmas anyway.

Then, because she could, she changed into a new set of scrubs and brushed and braided her hair. Finally, in an effort at merriment, lipstick. It helped a little.

Maybe it was the holiday music playing in the hallways. Maybe it was more visitors than usual. Maybe it was just good karma, but the first six hours went faster than she had any reason to expect. At her 2:00 a.m. break, she ran down and back up the stairs twice before heading for the cafeteria.

One guy was sitting alone at a table with his back to the door when she walked in. At least there wasn't a line for food.

"Hi. What kind of sandwiches do you have tonight?" she asked the sleepy-looking man behind the counter. Even the instrumental Christmas music playing through the cafeteria speakers seemed tired.

Saying nothing, he pointed to a computer print-out with nearly every option crossed out.

Better and better. "So, I could have tuna or pastrami?"

He pulled the printed menu over the counter and crossed out pastrami.

"Tuna or tuna."

A voice over her shoulder said, "I'd recommend the tuna."

She spun around at the sound of his voice. "Deacon," she said. "What are you doing here?"

He gave her a grin that looked too awake for two in the morning. He was wearing a plaid flannel over an untucked T-shirt, which was opposite his working day-wear, but typical for his time off lately. She thought that lawyerly Deacon had a sharp and fancy attractiveness, and previously-casual Deacon, in his ironed button-ups and khakis, looked the part of Charleston Man-about-town, but recent casual Deacon, Deacon after Dahlia, looked more like himself. "Watching you order a tuna sandwich, I think. Or, if you're not in the mood, maybe a plate of fried chicken from Uncle Jimmy's gas station on Fifth and Main."

Gasping, she looked at his hands, which were holding two paper bags spotted with grease.

"You didn't."

He shrugged and held the bags up higher. "I think I did."

She almost didn't dare ask it. "Are there fries in there?"

"Both traditional and sweet potato. With a cup of gravy for the lady."

She grabbed his arm and led him to a table. "If I start crying, you'll know it's from basic gratitude and serious sleep deprivation, right?"

He pulled out her chair and then sat in the seat beside her. "I'd still much prefer it if you didn't."

They unpacked the cheap, greasy, wonderful fried chicken from the bags and placed it on Uncle Jimmy's branded foil pie tins.

"Corn muffins? Seriously? What is this, Christmas?"

He smiled and unfolded a tiny, papery, brown Uncle Jimmy's napkin which they both knew was woefully inadequate for the task at hand.

The first bite made Lily moan with delight. "It's so hot. It's so delicious. How did you do this?"

Deacon gave a little modest shrug. "I know a guy."

"Is his name by any chance Uncle Jimmy?" she said through a mouthful of chicken.

"Excellent guess."

"But really. You are here. With the world's most perfect two-in-the-morning food." She wiped her mouth with a napkin, which she was pretty sure was as ineffective as she feared it to be.

He didn't deny it. "And you are here. Saving lives and comforting the weary. We're both pretty spectacular."

She couldn't deny it, mostly because her mouth was full. When she'd shoveled in as much as she could handle, she checked the time. "Why do the minutes pass so quickly when I'm eating chicken and gravy fries?"

"The most commonly asked question in the universe. Sadly, also an unanswerable one." He handed her a couple more nearly useless napkins. "Here. You've got a little gravy . . ." he gestured toward her mouth and she mopped herself up.

As she picked up the garbage she'd managed to create, she

said, "You are welcome to stay here sitting on this plastic chair for as long as you'd like, but I have pressing social obligations to attend to, so I've got to run."

Folding her foil plate over on itself, she snatched one more fry off his plate before tossing her garbage into the trash. "Thanks," she said over her shoulder as she started to jog out of the cafeteria.

But that didn't seem like nearly enough.

She walked back to the little round table.

Kneeling next to his chair, she waited until he swallowed his bite so she knew she had his full attention. "Deacon Calhoun, you are a stand-up guy. Thank you for dinner. Thank you for excellent company. Thank you for being my friend." Why did she feel like she was going to cry?

Oh, right. Sleep deprivation.

"Really. Thanks again for this few minutes of pure happiness tonight." She squeezed his wrist, hoping to avoid getting her hands even messier. "You did good."

The look on his face showed her that coming back for a real thank you was the right thing to do.

He asked, "Will I see you tomorrow? Can we reschedule Jason Bourne?"

"Sure you don't need a day off from me?" She smiled, hoping he'd understand that she wasn't suggesting she wanted to have a break from him.

"I'm doing better. Having some time alone is good. A little. But we shouldn't make Jason Bourne wait." Was he leaning toward her?

"I don't think he'll mind waiting twenty-four hours, but I

have to eat Christmas Eve dinner with my parents. So yes to the movie, but I won't need food."

"Sounds good. I'll bring a bucket of ice cream and one of those bins of popcorn the firm's been getting all month."

She loved that he understood that hungry wasn't a prerequisite for movie snacks. "Perfect."

"See you tomorrow," he said. "Do good in there."

"Drive safely," she said back.

Why was it taking her so long to leave? She had to get back onto her hall.

Well, she said to herself, *he's not keeping me.*

But she didn't want to go. Not that she didn't want to get back to work. She didn't want to leave his side.

Nothing strange about that, she told herself.

Right?

Chapter Eight

As Deacon pulled up to the Carolina Ice Palace, he felt a sensation he hadn't noticed in many months: anticipation.

"It appears," he said to Lily as he unbuckled his seat belt, "that I am excited."

Lily looked carsick. "Coincidentally, it appears," she said, "that I am terrified."

Deacon turned to her. "If you want, we can cancel."

Please, he thought, *don't say you want to cancel.*

"No way," she said. "This is a big day. We have to make it perfect." Her smile was shaky, but her little dimple showed through. He was finding more and more reasons to make that dimple appear.

He gave her a grateful smile and jumped out of the car. He had to force himself not to run up the front walkway.

"The last time I had my birthday party here, I was eleven," Deacon said.

"I've booked you a clown who does balloon animals."

He was pretty sure she was kidding, since the only people invited to this birthday party were Deacon and Lily. Add to that the fact that she was terrified of clowns, and he thought probably not.

Walking in the door together they must have looked like complete opposites. He was eager and rushing to the counter. She tried to hold the door for everyone going both in and out, but there weren't very many people exiting at the moment.

"Two adult packages with skates, please," he said, trying to keep the adult in his voice.

Lily came up behind him and leaned over his shoulder. "It's his birthday," she told the teenage boy with the scrawny chin beard. He nodded at Deacon, who assumed this was a standard Ice Palace birthday greeting.

He could see her warming up to this embarrassing little game of hers. "In fact," Lily went on, "he's been celebrating his birthday here for decades."

This was technically true—he had, in fact, had parties here in two different decades. And if it helped her with her ice-skating jitters, well, he didn't mind being the punch line.

"Not only that," she continued, "but he happens to represent the legal team that underwrites all the liability waivers that you make people sign."

This was not technically true, but Deacon didn't stop her.

"Which means," she said, "that Mr. Calhoun here is your lawyer."

Chin Beard failed to look impressed. Lily was unfazed. "And do you know the policy for entertaining your lawyer on his birthday at the Ice Palace?"

The poor kid. He looked at her for the first time as though maybe he was supposed to be paying attention to her. "Uh, no?" His response seemed like an invitation and she jumped on it.

"Well, aside from the obvious," she started counting on her fingers, "choosing the playlist, getting a photo with the staff, and a round of "Happy Birthday" from everyone in the rink, he also gets to ride the Zamboni when it's time to clean the ice."

She put her hands on the counter and tapped her fingernails against the glass, waiting for a confirmation of her demands. Deacon kept a straight face but couldn't pretend he wasn't amused. He watched her stare down the kid, who had no idea how to deal with a woman like Lily. Oh, who was Deacon kidding? There was no other woman like Lily in all of Charleston. Or anywhere else.

"Uh, well, the Zamboni guy doesn't come until after we close," the kid said. "But we can do the other things, no problem."

Lily's sigh was an almost perfect imitation of Dahlia's exasperated noise. Deacon had to turn away so he didn't laugh out loud. "Fine, we'll take the playlist, photo, and birthday-song options today, and a reservation for the Zamboni ride will appear on your next legal retainer statement."

"That'll be seventeen fifty," the kid said, clearly hoping Lily would stop talking to him.

Deacon pulled out his wallet, but Lily pushed his arm away. "No way, man. My treat."

As they were lacing up their skates, Deacon said, "So, are you aware that you perjured yourself to a minor about legal representation of a public entertainment facility?"

She opened her eyes wide to look more innocent. "Oh, did I?" Then she winked at him. "I think it's going to get you a couple of laps on the Zamboni, though. So, worth it." She held up her hand for a high five, and he found it a little bit of a struggle to breathe evenly. Maybe it was her playfulness. Maybe it was how willing she was to come do something she was totally not into because he wanted to. Maybe it was the way her loose braid hung over her shoulder or how her beanie slipped just above the curve of her eyebrow.

Or he was excited to be skating again. Probably it was simple as that.

"I think I need a different size," she said. "Go take a few warm-up laps so you'll be ready to keep up with me when I get out there."

As Deacon slid onto the ice, a knot loosened. This kind of freedom, reminiscent of restraint-free childhood and happy days, gave him a release he hadn't known he needed. Added to that was the ease with which he and Lily could hang out and be together. He realized how incredible it felt to not second-guess what Lily said. If Dahlia had told him to go ahead, he would have to wonder what that meant, what she was really thinking, what she intended to punish him for, or at least hold against him later.

When Lily said she'd be there in a minute, she meant that she'd be there in a minute.

It had been a few minutes, though, and she wasn't on the ice yet. He skated to a stop at the place he'd entered the rink and leaned over the partition. "Hey, Lil."

"I'm not afraid to skate; what are you talking about?" she said.

"Want to get up out of fetal position and give it a try?" He held out his hand.

She pulled herself off the floor and took his hand, squeezing his fingers. Her smile, though shaky, seemed sincere. "I would like to remind you of several things I am good at before you watch me lose all my credibility and all my coolness." She cleared her throat and counted on her fingers. "I can backflip. I am an excellent speller. I have great taste in music. I make a fantastic grilled cheese sandwich."

"I'll keep all of that in mind," he said, not letting go of her hand. He was pleased that her grip on his fingers only got tighter.

"So what's the secret?" she asked. "How do people propel themselves with grace on a friction-free surface?"

He shrugged. "You just do it," he said.

"Wow. You should have been a hockey coach." She took an audible breath and put one foot on the ice.

"You've got this. Propulsion and balance. That's all there is to it."

Turning around, he took her other hand and started skating backward, pulling her slowly onto the sheet of ice. "Don't worry, just keep your eyes on me."

Holding her hands and her eyes, Deacon felt his stress and anxiety slip down a few more notches. "You're doing great," he told her.

"You realize I'm doing literally nothing? You're pulling me and holding me up. I'm neither propelling nor balancing."

"If I let go, you'll be doing both. Ready?"

She let out a laugh that sounded terrified. "No. Not remotely." Gripping his hands tighter, she kept her eyes on his face.

"As long as you need," he said. Rounding the corner, he glanced over his shoulder to assure himself the path was clear. He loved how she depended on him. It was a new sensation, to have a woman physically leaning on him and emotionally counting on him. Dahlia had been the alpha personality in every way, and categorically refused to do anything at which she didn't already excel. In all instances, she was proving that she didn't need him. *Lily*, he thought, *is a brilliant and capable woman, but she's letting me support her and hold her up*. He was surprised how much that pleased him, filled him.

"Is that a smile?" he asked her.

"If I grind my back teeth together really hard, it sometimes resembles a smile," she said. "Easy mistake."

"Can you maybe relax your shoulders a little?" he asked, jiggling her arms to help loosen her up. "Just bring them down from around your ears."

He watched her inch her way toward comfortable posture. She eventually took a big enough breath to invite a real smile onto her face.

"There, that's better. Isn't this—?" He didn't finish asking, because before he knew what was happening, he had fallen over something and pulled her onto the ice with him. Ouch. It took only a few seconds to realize that falling on the ice as a little kid was a much different concern than doing the same at twenty-seven. He still had one of Lily's hands in his. She wasn't laughing, exactly, but she definitely wasn't screaming, swearing, or even complaining. Wiggling limbs and a high-pitched shout suggested that the thing he'd fallen over was a kid. He rolled himself away from the wreckage and pulled the kid out. He looked about nine years old, and he was laughing. What a relief.

"Sorry, man," the kid said. He pointed to a group of laughing kids. "We were seeing how close we could skate to you before you noticed."

People skated around the pile of them like they were a stone in a stream.

"Did you win?" Lily asked the kid, rubbing her knee.

"Well, you noticed me," the kid said, pulling himself onto his feet. "So probably not. But I did get closer than any of them," he said, indicating his buddies.

Deacon still hadn't said anything. What was he supposed to say? He felt foolish and worried that, despite her unruffled appearance, Lily might be hurt. He pulled himself up onto his feet and leaned down to help her stand.

"Deacon," she said, checking her limbs, "I am required to thank you for your help, but I could have done that myself."

He shook his head. "I don't know. It's really hard to get up when you're in skates."

"Not the getting up. The falling down. I have falling handled."

He pulled her into a hug and was pleased to feel her arms tighten around him. "Sorry about that," he said, his mouth close to her ear. "I'd promise it won't happen again, but I guess I can't control that kind of thing." He stood and breathed in the air around her, the feeling of closeness, and the happiness he felt being with Lily.

As his words replayed in his head, he thought of other things he wasn't controlling all that well. Like his heart rate. Or his desire to tilt her head up so he could kiss her.

Not that this was the first time he'd had that feeling. This wasn't even the first time this week that he'd thought about it, but something was always in the way. Every word, every conversation, every activity held the specter of Dahlia, and Deacon couldn't be sure how to navigate this kind of territory with Lily.

Could he just push thoughts of Dahlia out of his mind? Could he ignore the years of memories that intruded with every conversation? With every event?

Lily looked into his face, a small smile lifting the corner of her mouth.

He was beginning to love that smile.

And he wanted to see it more and more often.

But at the same time, he was finding himself comfortable and confident when he was on his own. He was putting himself together.

He let her go and took her hand again. "Ready to take another lap?" he asked.

"I'm ready whenever you are," she answered, and he couldn't be certain if she was talking about skating or something else.

But he hoped.

Chapter Nine

When Lily's hair was pinned up to perfection, she angled herself so she could see the back. It looked great.

It had been so long since she'd had an excuse to get really dressed up, she could hardly remember what came next.

Her last day of spending this much time on her appearance was the wedding last fall. Now, nearly six months later, she realized that she could think about it without feeling sweaty or anxious. Her part in Dahlia's runaway scheme felt like a fading nightmare—she knew she'd actually been the one to tell Deacon what was happening, but she no longer carried the shame and horror of breaking his heart on Dahlia's behalf.

Good thing, too, or this evening would be very awkward.

Deacon had come over to her apartment earlier in the week. "I have a huge favor to ask you," he'd said.

"Anything," she answered. Obviously.

"You might want to know what I need before you sign up."

He had smiled that smile Lily knew would convince her of just about anything.

He went on. "There's this thing. Event. Shindig."

Lily held up her hand. "Hold on," she said. "Give me a second to process the fact that you just used that word."

He started to speak again, but she kept her hand up, making him wait.

Finally, she said, "All right. Shindig. Continue."

He shook his head. "It's the annual firm banquet. They do a Christmas family thing and a summertime family thing, but this is the big formal event."

"Okay." Lily wasn't one hundred percent certain he was asking her to be his date, but she one hundred percent hoped he was. She pictured herself zipping herself into a dress far more elegant than anything she got to wear regularly. Not that "more elegant" was much of a leap when "regular" meant scrubs or yoga sweats. But she pictured something sleek. Something with a little sparkle to it.

"For the last few months," Deacon said, "I was pretty sure I was just going to skip it, but the partners are making it clear that skipping it is unacceptable. So. Um."

She loved the way he scratched the back of his neck when he was nervous.

"Would you consider coming with me? Like, as my, uh, companion?"

She felt an uncomfortable heat wash up her chest and neck. Companion? Like a guide dog? Like a hired assistant? Was it so horrible to consider her a date?

She didn't answer him, and he didn't keep asking. The

room was very quiet, only the hum of her fridge and a clock ticking.

Finally, he cleared his throat and ran his fingers over his jaw. "Okay, well, don't worry. Please don't feel bad. I understand."

A nervous laugh broke out of her. "You understand? Good thing. Because I don't. What just happened? You uninvited me to your firm dinner?"

"I didn't mean that."

Gathering courage in an inhale, she looked at him. "It almost sounded," she said, picking up a pen from the counter and twisting it in her fingers, "and I almost dared to hope that you were asking me on a date." She felt unable to meet his eye, but she looked at the wall just above his shoulder.

There went his hand to the back of his neck again. "I was."

She laughed, relief mixing with a rising anticipation. Leaning closer to him, she whispered, "You're not very good at it."

His sigh sounded like the first real breath he'd drawn that night. "I'm a little out of practice."

"We can fix that," she said, leaning back against the counter. "Try again."

"Are you serious?" he asked.

She gave him a stone-faced look. "Don't I look serious?"

"Can you come to my stuffy, formal work event with me?" he said, gritting his teeth in an almost-smile.

She tipped her hand from side to side. "Not quite there. One more try."

He sighed, pretending to be exasperated. Or maybe he

really was. She didn't care. This was fun.

He stepped in front of her and took her hand in both of his. The shiver that ran up her arm might have been visible. He squared his shoulders and looked into her eyes. "Lily, nothing would please me more than to have you by my side at the firm dinner. I would be honored if you'd consent to be my date."

And now, five days, one pedicure, three dress changes, and several averted "anxiety moments" later, it was time. Deacon was on his way to pick her up for a real, actual date. She checked her teeth in the mirror. Clean.

Nancy Anne, her supervisor at the hospital, had asked for a picture, so she snapped a couple of shots of herself in the dress, a shimmering deep purple that gave the impression of glitter without any actual bling.

When she heard the knock at the door, her stomach gave a thump of equal parts anticipation and fear. Well, maybe a little more anticipation than fear.

She opened the door and Deacon stood there, that perfect Calhoun hair, that immaculately fitted tuxedo, that nervous smile. He did a double take when he looked at her and leaned slightly forward.

"Wow," he said. "You look magnificent." He managed to say it without any surprise, and he didn't break eye contact, even when he handed her the gorgeous bouquet of flowers he'd been holding.

"These are lovely," she said, aware that her voice held a little more air than usual. "Come in real quick and I'll put them in water." She turned and walked into the kitchen, glad to have her back to him for a few seconds. Why couldn't she catch her breath? She wasn't surprised to see him looking so perfect.

Looking perfect was kind of Deacon's thing. But something in the way he looked at her gave her the feeling that he really saw her tonight. Not just the hair and the dress, but all of her, inside and out.

The drive to Belmond, the refined hotel where the Calhouns' firm held its dinner, was awkward enough to remind Lily that she was, in fact, on a first date. She tried to make casual small talk, but every time she looked at Deacon and saw him glance at her, she felt the weight of her own hope pressing against her and stealing her words. At a red light, he turned and looked at her, his eyes on her face. He moved his mouth like he wanted to say something, but the light turned green and he reached for the shifter. He missed. As his hand grazed her knee, she felt that shudder of electricity again.

Keep it together, she told herself. It was an accidental knee graze.

But she couldn't deny how nice it felt.

Pulling up to the valet stand, Deacon met her eyes again. "Ready for this?"

"Are you kidding?" she said. "I've never been more ready to accompany you to an event you don't want to go to. This is going to be amazing."

The valet opened her door and offered his hand. Nothing electrical there, she noticed.

Deacon came around the car, and she put her hand in the bend of his arm. Because of the heels, she told herself. So I don't stumble, she told herself. That's all, she told herself. But when he reached across and squeezed her fingers with his other hand, she knew she'd been lying to herself. For all the times, millions of times over the years, that they'd touched each other, bumped into each other, wrestled, hugged, something was different now.

Everything was different now.

The room was filling with people from Deacon's firm, and Lily kept her hand on Deacon's arm as they walked through the room. She smiled when she recognized Harper Day from the . . . well, the event planner. Harper's eyes fell to where Lily's hand rested on Deacon's sleeve. The other woman's eyes widened the tiniest bit before she shot her an approving smile and made a subtle way-to-go gesture before she turned her attention to a waiter.

Lily blushed, but fortunately Deacon didn't notice. He introduced her to a few people, and it didn't get weird until they reached the table they were assigned—across from his parents, Melanie and Everett. Deacon shook his dad's hand and kissed his mom on the cheek. Lily had eaten countless meals at the Calhoun home. She'd slept in the backyard hundreds of weekends of her childhood. But somehow, she didn't know how to say hello tonight.

Melanie stepped over to her, pulling her away from Deacon. Lily's hand suddenly felt cold.

Leaning up to kiss Lily on the cheek, Melanie said, "Hi, honey. I'm glad you're here tonight." She cupped the side of Lily's face in her hand. "This is all a little strange, isn't it?"

Which part was strange? What did she mean? Was she disappointed that Lily was here with Deacon? All the possible meanings of the words she didn't say weighed heavy in Lily's ears.

She could stand there worrying about Melanie's subtext, or she could behave in the way she was raised to. "You look beautiful, Miss Melanie. I love your dress," Lily said, and that was the right thing, apparently, because Deacon's mom shook her head in a 'this old thing' gesture and started telling a long and detailed story about the dress she was supposed to be wearing tonight and the various tiny disasters that led to this second choice.

Nodding and smiling and making small noises of sympathy came more naturally as the story went on. Lily's heart rate had nearly returned to normal when she felt Deacon step beside her and take her hand.

He didn't say anything to her. His dad was talking to him about something Lily didn't pay attention to. She was still nodding at Mrs. Calhoun's story. Everything was the same. And everything—everything—was different.

Here she stood in the ballroom of this fancy hotel, wearing a fabulous dress, making small talk, and holding Deacon Calhoun's hand.

Someone called for everyone to take their seats, and Deacon let go of Lily's hand to pull out her chair. When he'd seated himself beside her, he shifted to better see the speaker at the front of the room. It might have been an accident that the move brought his chair closer to hers. But it probably wasn't an accident that he draped his arm over the back of her seat. And she couldn't imagine it was an accident when he brushed his hand across her neck and fingered the loose curl trailing down her back.

If anyone had asked Lily to report what was said that evening, she couldn't have done it. The speeches washed over her as she sat inside the curve of Deacon's arm. She didn't want to move, because she didn't want him to move. She wasn't sure she even wanted to breathe.

At the end of a speech, Deacon moved his arm to applaud. She added her polite clapping to the rest, sure that the moment had passed. But as the next speaker stood, Deacon's arm came back around her shoulders.

She was certain she could get used to this.

After the speeches ended, dinner was served. Deacon shifted his chair again, this time so he could face the table. Lily felt the loss of his touch immediately, until he moved so close that his leg leaned against hers. He put his napkin in his lap and smoothed it, letting his hand linger on her knee for a few heart-racing seconds.

He had to know what he was doing to her. Nobody did things like this on accident. But she couldn't simply sit here and wait for him to touch her, could she? As salads were placed in front of them, she picked up a fork and speared a small bite. Her other hand found Deacon's leg under the table. She felt his muscle tense under her hand, and then his knee pressed against hers.

"Delicious salad," Deacon said, and his mother answered with a comment about the caterer that reminded her of a story. She talked to the table as a whole, gesturing and laughing. Lily smiled and didn't hear a word. Her heartbeat thrummed in her ears and she had no intention of trying to change that.

When Deacon put his fork down, his hand slipped over the back of her chair again. He leaned over and whispered in her ear, "This isn't nearly as bad as I worried it would be." His other hand slid on top of her fingers under the table. "In fact, I'm enjoying myself."

"I'm kind of enjoying yourself, too," Lily whispered back, twining her fingers with his.

Chapter Ten

Deacon understood that dating rules required (or at least suggested) waiting twenty-four hours before calling. He couldn't wait ten minutes after he woke the next morning.

He knew Lily had a shift at the hospital, so he sent a text.

Good morning. Thank you again for making last night so much more wonderful than I had any reason to expect it to be.

He tried not to stare at his phone obsessively for the next several hours.

He failed.

When she answered, her text said, **Any chance you'll be hungry after seven?**

Always a very good chance, he responded. **Can I meet you?**

I'll come to your place. And I'll bring dinner.

Better and better. Have a great day.

Now that I have this to look forward to, how could I not?

He loved the way her words made him feel.

Looking around his living room, he realized that it could use some work. He'd never finished unpacking his bookshelves, and there was a pile of mail growing on a side table. He spent a couple of hours organizing the room and then realized that what was missing was a lamp. And maybe a painting for the wall.

He got in the car and headed to the furniture store he passed every day on the way to the office. After buying two lamps and a framed mirror, he stopped at the home improvement place for a couple of plants. Unloading these things into the sterile apartment Lily helped him find months ago made him realize that he had been waiting for something to change. This room had been a place to watch TV, to sit and wait for something to happen, to kill time before he went to work, or to Lily's place. But now he wanted to make it warm and welcoming. He wanted Lily to come inside and feel like she wanted to stay. If not forever, at least for a couple of hours. He looked at the decorations and realized they made it feel like a home.

He checked his watch and hurried to the shower. She'd be there any minute.

When he was cleaned up, he heard music playing.

"Are you here?" he asked, even though he knew the answer.

"Hi," she called. "It looks great in here. Come on. Pizza's hot."

He walked in and saw her sitting on his couch in her sweats, mouth full of pizza, and thought she'd never been more beautiful.

She gestured to the box and he helped himself to a slice, sitting on the edge of the coffee table facing her.

"Mm," she said, swallowing. "This was at the door." She tossed him a small, flat package.

He glanced at the return address and didn't recognize the name. He put the package on the table.

"What are you doing? Open it," she said, reaching for another slice of pizza.

"I don't even know what it is," he said, sliding it farther away.

"That is why," she said slowly, as if she were explaining something very simple to someone who still couldn't understand, "you need to open it."

"You're not much into delayed gratification, are you?" he asked, laughing.

"Surprised?" she said. There was something new in her smile. Something expectant. Flirty. Well, *that* was a bit of a surprise.

He picked up a second slice of pizza and folded it in half. "Okay," he said, taking a huge bite. "I'll open it," he said through a mouthful of cheese and sauce.

She clapped and wiped her hands on a napkin. Grabbing the package, she held it out to him. Her eyes sparkled.

"Do you know what this is?" he asked, wondering at her excitement.

"Course not," she said. "I just love mail."

"You love mail? Like, ads and bills?" He watched her wiggle the package in her hands, making it dance as he ate another bite.

She sighed. "Nobody loves bills, weirdo. But getting a package in the mail? Even when I order it myself? It's one of life's simple pleasures."

He made himself a mental note to send Lily something in the mail.

He brushed crumbs off his hands and tore into the padded envelope. The return address was New York. Inside was a rectangle of brown paper sealed with wax and tied with twine.

"That is so cute," Lily said, fingering the corner.

Deacon slid his finger under the seal to break it open and let the paper fall. Inside was a book.

A photo book.

Of the wedding.

He tossed it onto the pile of mail on the side table.

Lily's eyes were wide. Mood killed.

Only one thing to do now. Deacon pulled out another piece of pizza.

Lily watched him eat, her eyes darting every few seconds to the side table.

Finally, she asked, "Are you going to look at it?"

He didn't say anything, just shoved another bite into his mouth and shook his head.

She fidgeted on the couch. "I can go, if you want to look at it alone." She was doing her best to make this sudden awkwardness disappear, and he wasn't helping at all.

"I don't want you to go." His voice came out strange, strangled and weak.

She patted the couch beside her. "Come here."

He moved over to the couch.

"Do you want to see?" She pointed to the side table, just in case he'd managed to forget where the book had landed.

"Kind of?" he said, not at all sure this was a good idea.

"Me too." She stood up and picked up the book and sat beside him. Almost close enough.

The cover was a photo of the groomsmen, Deacon in the middle. The guys stood in a casual line, arms slung over each other's shoulders, laughing. He watched Lily run her finger over his smiling face in the picture.

She turned the cover to see the pages. Photo after photo of Deacon and the wedding guests. Deacon and Emmett. Deacon and his parents. Deacon and Lily, dancing at the "reception," eating dinner, greeting guests. Pictures the photographer had taken, and others that were obviously from guests' phones—casual captures of the evening.

Lily made a small sound of happiness. "This is amazing," she said. Then she turned the page. She gasped. The photograph had caught the moment Lily had walked down the aisle to tell Deacon the news. Lily, standing on her toes to whisper in his ear that Dahlia was gone. Lily, hand on his arm, head tilted toward him. He looked at his own image in the picture, gazing down into Lily's face, his eyes full of trust and anticipation. The moment *before*.

Deacon stared at the picture. Every feeling from that day flew through him, past him. He felt the shock, the humiliation, the relief, and the exhaustion, and then they were all gone. His sigh cleared out all the past emotions.

Lily started to turn the page.

"Wait," he said, putting his hand over hers to stop her. "Look."

She looked. They looked together.

"I know I was there and everything," he said, his voice strained, "but I didn't know what I was looking at." He slipped his finger along the image of Lily's face.

Lily cleared her throat and sniffled. Was she crying?

He took his eyes from the picture and turned to face her. "Are you okay?"

She swiped at her eyes. "Sure. But look at this beautiful thing." She gestured at the book. "Look at all these people who love you."

He felt a ripple of happiness flutter inside him. But her tears worried him. "You're not sad?"

"I'm not," she said, running her finger over the photograph of the two of them, his hand on her waist, her hand on his arm, heads tilted toward each other.

"This is kind of an amazing picture," he said.

"You look incredible," she said. "I love that suit."

"You look pretty good yourself," he said, his voice a whisper.

She wiped at her eyes again. "It kind of looks like we . . ."

He waited, but she didn't finish.

He knew what she meant. "There's a little chemistry going on there," he said. He didn't take his eyes off the book.

Her laugh took him off guard. "Yeah, I guess you could say that." She pointed to her face in the picture. "This girl looks ready to kiss you."

"And I look ready to pick you up and carry you away."

Lily looked up from the book. "I think I'd let you," she said. He couldn't tell if she was talking about the picture or not.

He reached over and closed the book.

"Would you?"

He saw her swallow. "Would I what?"

Turning so he faced her completely, Deacon said, "Would you let me?"

Lily's face lit up in the smile he'd seen so many times through the years, the smile that made him feel like he was himself, he was enough, he was home.

He put his hands on either side of Lily's beautiful face. His eyes flickered from her eyes to her mouth and back to her eyes again.

"The last time I kissed you," he said, his voice softer and deeper than usual, "I had no idea what I was doing."

Her laugh was low and fragile, trusting. "No kidding. But now you've learned all the tricks?"

He shook his head. "That's not what I meant."

Gazing into her eyes, he slid his thumb along the curve of her cheekbone.

"I was a dumb kid that day. And I didn't realize what I had right in front of me."

He felt her breath catch, a tiny shiver.

"Now I'm not a kid anymore. And I see that it's been you, all the time." He closed the distance between them, his lips meeting hers in a soft, gentle touch. He pulled back, still holding her face in his hands.

He breathed an audible sigh. "Oh, Lily. You are in every good memory of my life. You have laughed with me, run around with me, teased me, protected me, and caught me when I fell." He brushed a piece of hair away from her forehead.

"My life doesn't make any sense without you," he continued, leaning in and kissing her again, deeper. He felt her lean closer, her fingers at the back of his neck. He bent his head and rested his forehead against hers. "I wouldn't know how to function in a world without you."

"You don't need to," she said, and his heart swelled with the weight of her implication. "I'm right here."

She reached up and twined her fingers with his. He brought her hand to his lips, kissing her fingertips.

"I can't promise I won't ever be dumb like I used to be," he said, kissing the tip of her nose. "Habits are hard to break. But, Lily," he said, holding her gaze, "I will never, ever fail to see you again."

As he wrapped her in his arms and kissed her again, he knew it was true.

Part 4: Sutton and Max

By Brittany Larsen

Chapter One

Sutton aimed her camera at Lily's face. Lily whispered in Deacon's ear, her long tapered fingers with their rosy pink nails resting on his arm. She knew she shouldn't click, but she couldn't miss out on such a compelling shot. Maid-of-Honor Delivering Bad News. Why else had Lily half-run, half-marched down the aisle in her very high heels?

The look on Deacon's face as he'd watched Lily's advance said everything. The closer Lily got, the less Deacon's eyes danced with nervous excitement and the more his brow creased with worry. By the time Lily had finished whispering to him, his eyes were wide with disbelief.

But there was a glance between Deacon and Lily that Sutton hoped she had captured. A moment of electricity in the breath between Lily laying her hand on his arm and then leaning close to whisper in his ear. Sutton hadn't caught anything close to that kind of tenderness in the hundreds of pre-wedding shots she'd taken of Deacon and Dahlia.

The hundreds of shots that all looked contrived and forced, except when Dahlia was looking in the distance. Those were the most honest pictures. They were the ones that made Sutton wonder whether Dahlia would actually make it down the aisle.

Sutton had buried her doubts about Dahlia saying *I do* underneath her relief that Dahlia was paying her more for one job than she'd made in months. Of course, giving in to Dahlia's pleas to come back to Charleston for the bridal and wedding photos had cost Sutton a chance to network with other photographers at the opening of her brother's show in Soho.

But good friendship required sacrifice, and Dahlia would have done the same for her.

On the other hand, with Dahlia's failure to appear, Sutton's wedding job had turned into a typical Dahlia event. Dahlia always pitched her ideas as benefitting everyone else more than herself, yet somehow always came out on top.

"No one is as good as you," she'd said to Sutton six months before, even though she knew Sutton's number one goal in moving to New York, aside from escaping Brett—her crazy ex-husband—was to get as far away as possible from the wedding photography industry. Sutton wanted to be a real artist, even if reaching her goals meant riding her brother's coattails for a while.

"I'll pay you double what you used to charge, plus travel expenses," Dahlia had promised, knowing things hadn't been easy for Sutton since moving.

"Hadley has to be my flower girl. She's my god daughter," she'd pleaded. Sutton's daughter loved her "Aunt Dolly." Being in her wedding would be the highlight of her five-year-old life. And that little girl deserved some highlights.

Dahlia must have felt Sutton's resolve slipping, because then she'd pulled out the big guns. "I helped you out when you needed it most."

And Sutton couldn't say no, because Dahlia wasn't exaggerating.

So here she was. Taking photos of the groom and maid-of-honor. No bride in sight.

Deacon motioned for the music to stop as Lily stood by his side. Sutton heard Deacon say something about Dahlia not coming, but everything after that went blurry. She didn't hear him say why or what next. If Dahlia had bolted, like Sutton suspected she had, Hadley might be alone.

Hadley hated being alone. Ever since the night her father had lost his temper with her, she clung to Sutton. If the bride had been anyone besides her Aunt Dolly, Hadley wouldn't have left her mother's side long enough to walk down any aisle, no matter how pretty the dress. Sutton didn't like her being alone either, especially when she wasn't one hundred percent sure her ex wouldn't show up.

She swallowed hard, pushing back the fear making its way to her chest, threatening to fill her heart with the same darkness pulsing through her brain. Dahlia had promised not to let Hadley out of her sight until she sent her down the aisle. Hopefully she'd kept that promise.

Sutton ran by the candle and magnolia decorated tables ready for dinner guests who likely wouldn't be eating. She turned down the hall and ran to the bridal suite where she'd taken the pictures of Dahlia in her dress and Camellia helping her with her veil. The same room where she'd held open Hadley's crinoline and helped her shimmy into her "princess" dress. The final touch—and Hadley's favorite—was the crown of flowers Sutton had pinned on top of her curls.

Sutton threw open the door, expecting to see her little girl, though the silence hinted at the worst. The door swung wide, hitting the wall with a loud thunk and revealing a room empty except for the chaos left by twelve bridesmaids, two flower girls and one bride. A wild array of flowers, hair products, and a lacy wedding gown draped over a chair that served as a testament to the way Dahlia lived her life. Go big and leave the clean-up for someone else.

Hadley had to be close, but the mansion was huge. Sutton cursed the venue and Dahlia all in one breath as she thought about how scared her little girl must be.

She backed into the hallway, then ran around the corner into a large foyer with a grand staircase. She slowed when she saw a man in a tux—one of the groomsmen—on the bottom step. She recognized him. He'd given Hadley a high five and told her great job at the rehearsal after she'd tripped.

A puff of white dress on the other side of him caught her attention, followed by a shock of dark curls as the owner of the flouncy dress leaned forward to retrieve her flower crown. The groomsman said Hadley's name. The sound rippled through the foyer in a gentle wave.

Sutton stopped to collect herself. At only five years old, Hadley had the uncanny ability to pick up on Sutton's energy and take on her emotions, good or bad. Hadley had felt enough fear in her lifetime, so Sutton was careful about letting her baby girl see that in her mama. Hadley let out a giggle, the first one in a long time, and Sutton knew she couldn't ruin the moment. She stepped behind a massive potted palm and listened.

"You would have done a great job sprinkling those rose petals," the groomsman was saying to her. "Did you try out for the job? You were a natural at the rehearsal."

"I'm Dahlia's god daughter, so I didn't have to try out." Hadley rested her chin in her hands and stared at her basket, her giggle gone. "She had to choose me."

"Her god daughter? And her flower girl?" Mr. Tux whistled. "You're a VIP. Probably the most VIP person here now that the bride's gone."

"What's a VIP?" Hadley asked with the lisp that tugged at Sutton's heart every time her little girl slipped into it.

"A Very Important Person." The groomsman emphasized each word and nudged Hadley with his knee. "Except you're the VMIP – very most important person."

Hadley sighed. "I guess, but I still don't get to do the rose petals."

Sutton stepped from behind the palm, calm enough to embrace her daughter and not let her out of her sight again until they were out of Charleston and back safely to her brother's place in New York. But the man's next words made her stop.

"What do you mean you don't get to do them?" He noticed Sutton and gave a tiny wave followed by a thumb's up. "You can do them right here," he continued. "I'll do the music." He hummed the first bars of "Canon in D" and picked up Hadley's flower basket, handing it to her as she stood.

Sutton put her camera to her eye and focused. Hadley still hadn't noticed her, which meant Sutton could get a natural shot of her. She snapped the photo when Hadley, grinning, put the flower crown back on her head and took the basket. The man's lips were curved into his own grin as he continued to hum. Sutton took as many pictures as she could before Hadley saw her and stopped her procession.

"There's the prettiest flower girl I've ever seen!" Sutton said as Hadley ran to her with rose petals spilling out of the tipped basket.

"I've been looking for you." Hadley wrapped her arms around her mom

"Who's your friend?" Sutton asked, picking her up.

"Max," Hadley answered as he wandered over.

"Hi." He flicked his hand in a wave, and Sutton let Hadley slide off her waist.

"Thanks for looking out for my girl," she said without offering her name. She was grateful he'd found Hadley, and he seemed like a nice guy, but she needed to keep a low profile. Brett knew a lot of people, and she couldn't be sure he wasn't still in Charleston.

"Dahlia promised to keep an eye on her," she continued, suddenly remembering there was still someone missing. "But I guess she had other places to be. Or something."

"Yeah, what happened?" His brow creased with a concern that seemed genuine. She hoped it was. She liked his eyes—deep brown, almost as dark as his hair.

"I don't know—"

"—I do!" Hadley yelled and let go of Sutton's hand to step between her and Max. She pointed her dimpled chin up to him and spilled. "She told me she remembered being a flower girl too, then she said she wasn't ready to get married. I think she still wants to be a flower girl!"

"That sounds about right," Sutton muttered, and Max let out a short laugh.

"You know her pretty well?"

"Well enough I should have predicted she'd do something like this before I let her convince me to be her photographer."

Music filled the air as Sutton finished her words. Not the rich sounds of the cellist, whose performance had been cut short, but the pulsing bass of the DJ.

"What's that, Mama?" Hadley asked, grabbing Sutton's hand and yanking her in the direction of the music.

"I don't—"

"—Maybe Aunt Dolly is back and they're still having the party!" Hadley kept yanking, and Sutton reluctantly followed, glancing back at Max with a question.

He shrugged and followed them to the ballroom. Heavy bass pulsed through the closed doors followed by rhythmic clapping and stomping. Sutton knew before Max opened the doors, the room would be filled with people line dancing. She also knew exactly what Hadley's reaction would be.

"Let's dance, Mama!" Hadley squealed, predictably, and pulled her mom toward the dance floor, but Sutton resisted.

Dahlia had already paid in full. The DJ was playing music, the waiters were serving food, Sutton needed to work. She wasn't going to take any more charity from Dahlia, even if Dahlia wasn't there to be part of the pictures.

That is, if Deacon wanted pictures.

"I can't right now, baby." She pulled Hadley in the

opposite direction. "I've got to talk to Deacon."

"Please, Mama. I want to dance!" Hadley cried before yanking her hand from Sutton's. "This is my favorite song, and it's almost over!" She ran to the dance floor while Sutton stared helplessly after her.

"I can keep an eye on her," Max offered.

Sutton bit her lip. She didn't know this guy, but she also didn't get a creepy vibe from him. Then again, given her history with Brett, she wasn't entirely sure she could trust her ability to read people's vibes.

"If you're comfortable with that." Max held up his hands to prove his trustworthiness, as if he wanted to show he didn't have anything up his sleeve. "I promise not to let her go anywhere but the dance floor."

Sutton glanced from the dance floor to Deacon. Hadley would be within her line of sight no matter where in the room she went. She took a deep breath and pointed to Deacon and Lily.

"I'll be right over there, and I'll be back as soon as I find out what's going on."

The clapping song faded into "Celebration" and Max said, "looks like . . ." before singing along with the music "there's a party going on right here . . ." in a high falsetto.

She laughed, and the last of her worries about leaving Hadley with Max floated away with the disco beat. Dahlia, for all her anti-establishment aspirations, had chosen the most mainstream wedding playlist ever.

For the first time in years, Sutton actually felt like dancing. She had to force herself not to move to the music as she made her way across the room. The closer she got to Deacon, the closer Lily moved to him, like a mama cat with brand new kittens.

"Hey, Deacon," Sutton said, meant to sound soothing, but the music forced her to yell. "You okay?"

He nodded along with Lily who answered for him. "He's going to be fine. This is all for the best."

Despite her years of friendship with Dahlia, Sutton really didn't know Deacon. The look on his face told her today wasn't the day to rectify that situation, even if she'd wanted to. Instead, she turned toward Lily. They weren't necessarily friends, but at least they'd spent some time together the few times Sutton had hung out at Dahlia's house.

"So, the dinner and reception are still happening?" Sutton asked, though the answer seemed pretty obvious.

"Aunt Camellia said they'd already paid for everything, so there was no use having all the food and the DJ go to waste." Lily answered while Deacon shoved his hands in his pockets and stared at the ceiling.

"Does she still want me to do the pictures?" Sutton leaned close to Lily in a vain attempt to keep Deacon from hearing.

Lily took half a step toward Sutton, blocking Deacon from their conversation. "Do it. I'll send them all to Dahlia, so she can see the world went right ahead and kept on turning without her."

Sutton raised her eyebrow. "Good plan. Any idea where she is?"

Lily shook her head. "Don't really care at the moment."

"Okay. I'll go do my job then."

Sutton left Deacon and Lily, heading back to the dance floor with her camera raised. She scanned the floor for Max and

Hadley, then seeing Hadley was safe, Sutton began snapping shots of people milling around the room. She turned to the dance floor and took more shots of guests doing the Electric Slide. Dahlia hated The Electric Slide. That had to be Deacon's doing.

The perfect shot presented itself a few minutes later when she spotted Hadley ducking under Max's arm before he twirled her around, her flower crown clinging for dear life to the ends of her curls. The pure joy on Hadley's face reminded Sutton of the first time her parents took her to Disney World and she'd met all the princesses, a million years ago when she still believed princes existed.

She'd long since given up on that dream, but watching Max sparked an ember of hope. Prince Charming didn't exist, but maybe some good guys still did.

Sutton focused in on Max, getting her first shot of him without Hadley. Two years had passed since she and Hadley had fled to New York; it had been longer than that since she'd seen Hadley so happy. Sutton had vowed when she left Charleston that the only two things she would ever care about again were Hadley and her career. Men and relationships were out.

But if more guys like Max were out there, then someday she might be ready for love again. Someday . . .

Chapter Two

From the first moment he'd seen the photographer, Max had wanted to know her. He'd been watching her take picture after picture the entire day, trying to work up the courage to introduce himself. Then, once he had the chance, he'd bungled it. Now he was on his way to being remembered as the babysitting groomsman instead of the hot groomsman.

Or nice . . . he'd take nice.

He saw her now at the edge of the dance floor, her camera obscuring most of her face except for her mouth. She chewed her bottom lip when she concentrated. He'd seen her teeth go to her lip every time she took a picture. Why that had endeared her to him he didn't know, but he couldn't keep from watching to see if she'd do it again whenever she reached for her camera.

"Spin me again, Max!" Hadley yelled above the music. He'd spun her about a million times and should have been tired of it, but every time she giggled he saw her mother's smile. He wondered if Hadley's laugh matched her mother's too.

Her mother. Max still didn't know her name. The smooth way she maneuvered around giving it to him hadn't escaped his attention. She was smart, but also afraid. He saw that maternal fear as she clung to Hadley even when she didn't have her hand, watching him with her from across the room. Fear made her protective, but not scared. Everything about her—from her dark cropped hair to the black cocktail dress she wore in a sea of floral—screamed *I am not a victim.*

Max didn't know what drove her fear, but he guessed it was a man. As a prosecuting attorney, he'd worked with countless women who had been in and out of abusive relationships. They all put up invisible barriers whenever a man came within ten feet of them. Their shoulders tensed, or their posture stiffened, or they clenched their fists. Every woman did something different, but there was always some slight physical shift given as an instinctual warning to stay away. Like a skittish horse with its ears flicking back and forth looking for a source of danger.

He respected those barriers. He respected her for not offering him her name the moment they met, but her secrecy didn't make him want to know it any less. Her secrecy didn't make him want to know *her* any less. If anything, his desire to know her and her story had only increased. He wanted to help her feel safe again, even if that meant keeping his distance.

The dance music faded into a slow song, and suddenly the woman who'd fascinated him from afar stood by his side.

"Thanks for keeping an eye on her," she said and took Hadley's hand.

"No problem." Max stepped back to make space for

Hadley's mom. "We had a great time."

"I want to keep dancing!" Hadley took Max's hand and pulled away from her mom. "You dance with Max," she said and pushed her toward him.

"I don't think—"

"I'd love to dance with you." He held up his hand and waited for her to take it before lightly resting his other hand on her back. Hadley wrapped an arm around each of their waists, forcing them to step closer to each other.

Their eyes met, and she let out a breath of a laugh.

"She knows how to get what she wants, doesn't she?" Max asked.

"You have no idea." She closed her eyes and shook her head. When her eyes fluttered back open he saw they were blue. From far away they looked so dark he couldn't tell. But this close, they were cobalt, same as the Smoky Mountains.

She looked down and a silence fell between them that he wanted to fill with all the questions he had about her. He resisted the urge. He liked the feeling of having her close.

"My name is Sutton, by the way. I don't think I told you that."

"Sutton." He liked the sound of it. Liked the way she said it; softly, despite the hard syllables. Like she felt comfortable enough to let down her tough exterior. "Nice to meet you."

She took a breath and he felt her shoulders relax. "Thanks again for your help with Hadley."

"She's a great kid." He glanced at the dancing girl and wanted to ask about her. Where was her father? Did Hadley know him? Sutton didn't have a ring on her finger and judging from the way Hadley kept pushing him and Sutton closer, her mother and her father weren't still together.

"What did you find out about Deacon and Dahlia?" he asked instead.

"Nobody knows where she is, but everything is paid for, so Camellia said the show must go on. At least, I think that's what she said. It sounds like something she'd say." Sutton smiled, and Max moved to create some space between them because that smile made him want to pull her closer. To be honest, that smile had him thinking he'd like to kiss her.

He cleared his throat and asked, "How do you know Dahlia?"

"High school. We got to be friends after she transferred from Ashley Hall to Porter-Gaud. I was a scholarship kid and she was a new kid, so we were both kind of outsiders."

"You know Deacon too then?"

"Not really. Dahlia and I didn't run in the same social circles outside of school. She lived in Charleston proper and I . . . didn't." Sutton bit her lip, but then her face brightened. "We were each other's support system at school though. I don't think either one of us would have made it through without the other."

"Were you surprised she ran?"

Sutton considered his question, then slowly shook her head. "She didn't tell me anything, but it's Dahlia, so nothing really surprises me. I love her, but she has a blind spot the size of Texas when it comes to recognizing she's not the center of the universe."

"That's God's honest truth." Max slipped into the North Carolina accent he'd worked hard to lose since moving to New

York. "She knows how to fill a room even when she's not in it." He tipped his chin, and Sutton looked around the ballroom stuffed shoulder to shoulder with people there to celebrate Deacon and Dahlia.

"How do you know her?" Sutton asked.

"I don't really. I was roommates with Deacon in college, so I only know her from the Skype sessions I couldn't help but overhear on a nightly basis for four years."

"Every night?"

Max nodded.

"And you're still friends with him?"

"I'm nothing if not loyal," he answered. "Or a glutton for punishment."

She made a noise that could have been a laugh if she'd let it, then pulled away from him as the song ended. But she didn't leave, and Max didn't want her to. A fast song started and Hadley danced between them, giving Max just the excuse he needed to stay. He followed Hadley's crazy moves and Sutton joined in, finally letting him hear her laugh. The sound brought to mind the wind chimes and ocean breezes of the Outer Banks, musical and refreshing all at once.

They danced through another three songs before Hadley pulled them both off the floor to find the "guys carrying around food."

"When do we get cake?" she asked.

Max looked over Hadley's head to Sutton who rolled her eyes at what Max could only assume was the ridiculousness of serving the wedding cake at a bride-less reception.

"I don't know if there's going to be cake at this party,

baby," Sutton answered. At the same time, Max grabbed two flutes of champagne from a waiter passing by and handed one to her.

"To Dahlia," he said. "She knows how to throw a great party."

"To Dahlia," Sutton replied and clinked her glass to his. He watched, admiring the line of her neck as she tipped her head back and drank.

"Mama, I'm hungry." Hadley wrapped her arms around Sutton's waist and rested her forehead on her belly.

"I've got to feed this girl. We're at T minus three minutes until meltdown." She untangled the flower crown from Hadley's curls, then rubbed Hadley's back. Sutton hadn't asked for help with words, but Max could see the question in her eyes.

"I'm on it," he said. "Wait here, and I'll find something."

"No shellfish. She's allergic."

"Got it." He wheeled around ready to set out on his mission.

"Oh, and no fish at all. She doesn't like it," she called, stopping him in his tracks.

He turned to face her again. "Shouldn't be a problem." Who would serve only seafood at a wedding reception?

Dahlia. That's who.

Every appetizer he found was some Asian fusion version of shrimp cocktail, crab puff or scallop. The clock was ticking and any minute he expected to hear a wail of hunger coming from the spot where he'd left Sutton and Hadley. When he had less than thirty seconds left, he finally stopped a waiter.

"Have you got anything a five-year-old will eat?" he asked.

"Only if they like fish." The waiter glanced back and forth, making sure no one could hear him. "But the chef's in the kitchen. He might be able to help you out."

The waiter hustled away, offering appetizers to more than one wary guest, and Max returned to Sutton empty-handed and late. Hadley was in the beginning stages of her meltdown.

"It's all fish, shellfish or more fish."

"Ugh, I forgot," Sutton moaned. "Dahlia's vegetarian now. Deacon had to beg her to be pescatarian for the night."

Hadley let out a whimper. "I'm hungry!"

Max scooped her up and put his fingers lightly on Sutton's back. "Let's find the kitchen. I've got top secret info the chef might be able to help us."

He guided her out of the room, hoping he'd guessed right about which hallway led to the kitchen. As he turned to try the opposite direction, a waiter emerged out of a door followed by the sounds of clattering dishes.

"Bingo." Max quickened his pace, then slowed down to let Sutton catch up.

"Don't wait for me! Just go!" She waved him ahead at the same time Hadley let out another cry.

"I'm hungry."

Max pushed open the door to the kitchen but stopped short when he saw a man and woman kissing on the other side of the room. Their kissing was definitely on the PG-13 side, and Hadley was definitely *not* thirteen.

"What are they doing?" Hadley loud whispered, and Max quickly covered her eyes

The door hit him in the back and he stepped forward.

"Did you find some—" Sutton stopped behind him. "Oh. . ."

Max cleared his throat to get the couple's attention, but they were too wrapped up—literally—in what they were doing to notice.

"What's happening?" Hadley squirmed to see around the hand he still had covering her eyes. Her voice echoed off the stainless counters and appliances, and the man and woman broke apart faster than a Kardashian marriage.

The tall Asian man pushed his sleeves up while the blonde woman wiped her mouth. "Can I help you with something?" he asked more politely than any man should whose make-out session had been interrupted.

"I'm hungry," Hadley answered. "Do you have something besides fish? Because I don't like fish unless it's the stick kind."

The guy smiled and shook his head. "Sorry. Seafood is all I've got. There's an excellent barbecue place down the street though. Do you like mac and cheese?"

Hadley sighed. "I love mac and cheese. But only the Kraft kind that's in the blue box." She wriggled out of Max's arms, then stuck her hand in his. "Can we take Max to get some mac and cheese, Mama?" she asked Sutton.

"It probably won't be Kraft, but . . ." Sutton hesitated, then nodded. "Max can come with us if he wants."

"Oh good." She held up her arms to Max. "Can you carry me again? I'm too tired to walk."

Max didn't wait. He took off his jacket then stooped down and picked her up. She wrapped her little arms, still pudgy with baby fat, around his neck. They were damp and sticky with sweat, but he didn't mind. He loved it when his sisters' kids did the same thing. There was an innocence to it that helped him forget the bad stuff he saw every day.

Someday he hoped to have his own kids to remind him how good the world was, but the moment Hadley rested her head on his shoulder she restored his faith in humanity.

If he was lucky he'd be able to hold on to that faith for a few days once he was back at work.

Chapter Three

Sutton followed Max through the French doors to the grounds where Deacon and Dahlia should have exchanged vows. The chairs had been taken down and the flowers were gone leaving no evidence of Deacon's dashed hopes or Dahlia's recklessness. Like always, someone had cleaned up Dahlia's mess.

The sun hung on the horizon turning the sky a soft pink as it clung to the last bits of daylight. Sutton breathed in the air heavy with honeysuckle, watching Max shift Hadley to a more comfortable position. She held back a sigh, remembering that this is how she'd pictured parenthood when she'd walked down her own aisle. Maybe Dahlia was smart to run—Sutton's own walk had led to disaster. But it had also led to motherhood. She'd never regret that.

Sutton walked with Max without saying a word, but she heard Hadley's heavy breaths and knew the little girl would be asleep before they got to the barbecue place. She wanted to worry about Hadley's sudden attachment to this man she'd just met. It seemed like the right thing to do as a mother—to worry. To be less trusting.

But her instincts told her she could trust him. That was a new feeling. Besides, they'd be leaving in the morning, before Hadley could get too attached.

"It's a block or two away. Will you be okay?" Max asked over his shoulder after they'd walked from the back of the house to the sidewalk on King Street.

"I'll be fine." She stopped and slipped off her shoes then hurried the few steps to catch up.

"I think this one is almost asleep," he said, and Hadley's arm slipped off his shoulder as if to confirm his suspicion.

"Dancing will do that to a girl."

"You know from experience?" His sleeve brushed her bare arm and the soft fabric reminded her of the blanket she used to curl up under during thunderstorms.

She thought about his question then laughed as she caught the threads of a memory. "For my eighteenth birthday Dahlia talked me into signing ourselves out of school and driving to Atlanta to go clubbing at a place she swore she could talk her way into."

"And did she?"

"Almost, but I looked way too young." Sutton still couldn't believe some of the things Dahlia had convinced her to do. "The bouncers didn't even check our IDs, just sent us on our way." She'd worn the only thing she had that came close to being club wear but looked every bit the prom dress it actually was.

"From what I know of Dahlia, I'm guessing you didn't turn

around and go home." He drifted closer to Sutton, so they were almost touching. Normally she would have put some space between herself and any other man that close. Creating distance was instinctive for her now. But for some reason, not with Max.

"Sounds like you know Dahlia better than you think you do." Her arm brushed his again, and this time shivers ran up it. She rubbed them away and went on with her story. "We saw a restaurant a few doors down with kids all dressed up coming out of it." She rubbed her arm again because the goose bumps were still there.

"Are you cold?" He stopped and held out his arm with his jacket slung over it. "You can take my jacket."

"Thanks." She slipped her arms through the sleeves. The silk lining felt too nice for the tux to be a rental. Its warmth and slight hint of cedar made her shiver in a different way.

"So, you and Dahlia see the kids coming out of the restaurant, and then what?" he asked, and they continued walking.

"Dahlia saunters up to them and starts talking. I'm still hanging back because one rejection was enough for me, but within minutes she's friends with all of them and she's got us an invite to their school's prom."

"You went to a random prom?"

"And the after party, where I fell asleep because I'd danced so hard. She woke me up at three a.m. to drive the four hours home."

Max laughed, startling Hadley. He laid his hand on her head and she nestled back into his shoulder.

Sutton's breath caught watching how tender he was with

her baby in a way Brett had never been. When she could breathe again, she continued her story, using happier recollections to push back darker memories of her ex-husband. Memories that threatened to steal a feeling of comfort she hadn't felt in years with a man.

"If I hadn't officially been an adult that day, my parents would have murdered me for coming home so late . . . or early. The sun was rising by the time Dahlia dropped me off. I ran inside long enough to change clothes before we left to grab breakfast."

Max slowed his walk as they left the grounds of William-Aiken House into the lights, noise and crowds coming from stores and restaurants surrounding the venue. "Deacon always described Dahlia as the flame that drew in every moth in a hundred-mile radius. I could never tell if he loved or hated that about her."

"You're definitely going to get burned the longer you're around her," Sutton answered, her voice lowering as they approached the busy street corner, as though everything would get quieter if she did. The longer Hadley slept, the more time she'd have Max to herself. "Usually it's worth it though."

"You've been burned by her?" He hit the button to cross the street.

Sutton waited until they were on the other side, gathering her thoughts—and emotions—before answering. "She introduced me to Hadley's father."

"That wasn't a good thing?"

Sutton could feel him looking at her, but she kept her eyes on the sidewalk. "Good and bad. I got Hadley out of it. I wouldn't change that."

"But you blame Dahlia for the bad stuff?" Max's arm brushed hers again, and Sutton's stomach simmered with a familiar anxiousness she hadn't felt in months. She hadn't missed it either. Talking to Max had forced her to think about Brett and thinking about Brett made her worry about being back in the city he'd sworn to never leave.

Sutton shook her head and quickened her pace. "She introduced us, but my choices were my own."

She moved to the side to let people pass between her and Max, then widened the gap even more. She never wanted to talk about her ex, but right now she didn't want to talk about Dahlia either. She didn't deserve to be lumped with Brett.

Dahlia, despite all her faults, was probably the best friend she had. Dahlia had given—not loaned—Sutton the money to take Hadley and finally leave Brett. Dahlia had hired an attorney for Sutton once Sutton discovered Brett had stolen all her wedding photography money. She never could have afforded an attorney skilled enough to show Brett as the abuser he was. By the time her lawyer had finished with Brett, no judge would have granted him any parental rights.

Knowing Brett wasn't in Charleston anymore should have made her feel safe, but once she'd left the security of William-Aiken House, a thousand *what if*'s started running through her head. *What if he'd heard about Dahlia's wedding? What if he showed up assuming—correctly—she and Hadley would be there?* He knew everything Dahlia had paid for, including Sutton and Hadley's move. She hoped he still didn't know that move was to New York. Just like she hoped he didn't know where she was right now.

Thinking about Brett got her so distracted she didn't

notice Max had stopped.

"This is it," he called to her, and she turned to see him standing in front of a nondescript storefront with only the smell of woodsmoke and vinegar to indicate they'd found the right place.

Sutton looked at Hadley sleeping peacefully on Max's shoulder and unclenched the fingers she hadn't realized were curled into her palms. Hadley's chest rose and fell in a contented breath, and Sutton didn't want to wake her. Or didn't want to end her time alone with Max. Maybe both.

"Do you want to sit down for a minute and let her sleep a little longer?" Sutton pointed to a bench a few stores away where there were fewer people.

"I'd love to." He let her pass to sit down first then sat beside her and laid Hadley's head on her lap and draped her legs over his.

"Not for too long though," Sutton blurted when his knee touched hers. "I'm supposed to be taking pictures."

"Got it. I'll get the food to go."

His sleeve grazed her shoulders as he rested his arm on the back of the bench. The brush of his arm had been so light, she doubted he realized he'd touched her, but she'd felt it. Felt it all the way to her fingertips, and her longing to lean into him surprised her. Lean into his arms and rest her cheek where Hadley's had been.

"So . . ." Max drew out the word, and Sutton could almost guess what would follow. "Her dad's not around anymore?"

Sutton had the urge to tell him everything, how she'd known she shouldn't marry Brett, but she did anyway. How he'd promised to quit drinking once they got married, but his bingeing had only gotten worse. So had the way he talked. The memory of his words was still more painful than his fists had been. Hadley was the only good thing that she'd taken from her marriage.

She wanted to tell him all that and to believe he'd understand, but she didn't trust her judgment anymore. Instead she stumbled over the words, "It's complicated."

"Yeah?" He answered so softly she almost wished she'd let herself trust him with her story. "Well, Hadley's a great kid. He'd be crazy to not want to be part of her life."

Her cell buzzed in her camera bag, and she leaned over to unzip the bag and search for the phone. Looking for it gave her an excuse to move away from him and the feelings he brought out in her.

"It's Dahlia," she said when she saw the name on the screen.

"Dahlia?"

She nodded and for another half a second debated whether to answer. But of course, she answered. She always answered Dahlia's calls, even when she knew she shouldn't.

"Sutton!" The way Dahlia drew out Sutton's name would have given her away even if her name and number hadn't. "How pissed is everyone?"

Her question was one of curiosity, not concern, and Sutton answered with the same absence of care.

"Not too pissed. They're dancing and drinking all the champagne and eating all the food you ordered."

A pause followed, long enough to make Sutton consider

whether she'd been too harsh.

"Good." Dahlia's voice, when she finally answered, was as lilting and seductive as always. And as loud. Whispering wasn't in her wheelhouse. "I fought Mama hard on that food. I hope she told them to eat all of it. That's the one part I'm sorry to miss. She's the one who wanted the fancy party anyway."

"Uh huh. I'm sure she's real pleased about getting her party. That oughta make up for you taking off and not telling anyone where you are." Sutton glanced at Max who stared hard at her phone like he wanted Dahlia to know that he, at least, was pissed at her.

"Don't lecture me, Sutton. I couldn't do it, and Deacon will be better off because I'm the one who had the guts not to." Her voice rose loud enough to stir Hadley.

"Guts?" Max said toward the phone. "Or maybe he's not a big enough tool to leave her at the altar."

"Who's that?" Dahlia asked.

"No one." Sutton turned her back to Max to get some privacy, however little it might be. Dahlia had been about as hurtful as one person could be, but Sutton didn't disagree with her that Deacon would be better off. The two were oil and water, and she'd never been able to figure out why they kept trying to mix.

"Is Deacon okay?" Dahlia's voice lost some of its music, and Sutton made her wait for her answer.

"He will be, but it's going to take a while."

"I know."

Sutton thought she heard a sniffle, but she couldn't be sure, and before she could say anything else Dahlia was back to herself.

"Listen, I need a huge favor from you."

Sutton took a deep breath. She wanted to say no, but Dahlia had done her a million favors without Sutton having to ask.

"What is it?"

"I left my handbag there, and I need my passport from it."

"Where are you going?" Sutton shouldn't have been surprised, but Dahlia had a great capacity for surprises.

"On my honeymoon. I'm already at the airport. I need you to bring me my handbag so I can get on the plane." She spoke casually, as though the most obvious thing in the world would be for her to go on her honeymoon without her groom.

"You're still going to Bali?"

"Deacon didn't want to go in the first place. He's getting the party he and my mom wanted, so I'll take the trip I wanted."

Her explanation made sense . . . in a Dahlia sort of way.

"Yeah, I'll do it. I guess you don't need me to take pictures anymore." Sutton's legs were tingling, so she sat Hadley upright, who promptly tipped over and leaned her head back on Max's shoulder.

"Of what? Who's going to want pictures of a wedding reception without the bride?"

Of course, Dahlia would think the party couldn't be a memorable event without her, but Sutton couldn't disagree.

She got directions for where to meet her then hung up. Dahlia's flight wouldn't be boarding for hours, but Sutton knew she'd keep calling if she didn't have the passport in the next half hour.

Despite knowing Sutton was on her way, Dahlia called back thirty seconds later. "Will you just make sure people use the app to upload pics? Make an announcement or something."

"Sure," she answered, not questioning why. Dahlia had the worst case of FOMO Sutton had ever seen, even when she'd chosen to miss out.

Sutton tucked her phone away without meeting Max's eye.

"You have to go?" Max asked.

Sutton nodded and stood.

"Can I get mac and cheese now, Mama?" Hadley rubbed her eyes and sat up.

"We're going on a drive. I'll find you a McDonald's." Sutton took Hadley's hand and helped her off the bench.

"You want me to carry her?" Max stood, ready to pick up the little girl, but Sutton shook her head and crouched in front of Hadley.

"Jump on baby, and I'll give you a piggy-back."

Hadley tried to climb on Sutton's back, but slipped off her satin dress, so Max helped her back on. Once she had a good hold on Sutton's shoulders, Max held out his hand to pull Sutton up. Her brain told her to refuse. *Say No* was a mantra she'd cultivated over six years being married to Brett and two years of living on her own. Accepting help never turned out well.

She took Max's hand anyway, then worried about how much she didn't want to let go.

Chapter Four

Max walked Sutton and Hadley back to William-Aiken House wanting the whole time to ask Sutton for her number, but he'd seen her hesitation when he offered his hand to help her. If she didn't want to take his hand long enough to steady her while she stood up, why would she want to give him her number? And why should he ask when he had a ticket back to New York in the morning, and she'd be staying in Charleston?

Their walk back was quiet except for Hadley's occasional demands for Sutton to go faster, followed by her squeals when Sutton trotted, bouncing her up and down. The music drew them closer to the party as the distance between them grew. Sutton walked ahead near the grass lining the sidewalk while Max followed behind, his steps hugging the curb.

She headed toward the front door instead of taking the trail to the back, and Max wasn't sure whether to follow her. He stood at the bottom of the porch steps while she climbed them and bent to let Hadley slide off her back.

Sutton turned when she reached the door. "I'm going to get Dahlia's stuff and slip out. If I see Deacon I'll have to tell him where Dahlia is, and his heart will be broken all over again. Or worse, he might try to stop her. I think it's best if he just lets her go."

The last line came out almost as a question, like she needed him to agree. So he did. Because she was right. The only people who hadn't seen Deacon and Dahlia weren't meant for each other were Deacon and Dahlia.

"And Dahlia wanted me to make sure people were uploading pictures to her site through that wedding app." Sutton closed her eyes and rubbed her forehead. "It makes no sense anymore, but she's already paid me. I have to follow through."

Max had seen her take at least a hundred pictures of all the pre-wedding stuff and the wedding party. She'd taken a ton while they were on the dance floor. She'd more than done her job photographing an event no one would want to remember anyway.

"I'll make sure that happens." He stuck his hands in his pockets and gazed up at her, wanting to stretch out the moment before he had to say good-bye.

"Thanks." Her smile almost gave him the courage to ask for her number. Instead he watched her open the door, take Hadley's hand, and step inside. "I had fun tonight," she said over her shoulder before walking away.

Hadley turned and waved good-bye as the door shut behind them, and he wasn't sure who he felt more sad to see go, the little girl or her mother.

He sighed and walked the trail to the back of the mansion

and the ballroom. The music had stopped, and as he rounded the corner he almost ran smack into Deacon.

"Jake Lawrence Maxfield, as I live and breathe, where've you been?" The only time Deacon called Max by his full name was when he was drunk. And he was definitely drunk. Like walking distillery drunk.

"Had a little bit to drink, bro?" Max swung his arm around Deacon and caught him as he stumbled.

"A little." Deacon slung his arm over Max's shoulder. "It's all good though. I'm glad she's gone." He patted Max's chest. "I'm glad she's gone, but I'm glad you're here." Another pat and another near fall.

Max helped him to a nearby seat on the patio and set him down. Deacon tipped his head back and stared at the sky and the few stars sprinkled across it. Soon there would be more. There couldn't be a more perfect night for a wedding, which made Max feel worse for Deacon.

The patio had separate sets of glass doors which led into the dining room and the ballroom on the other side where guests spilled off the dance floor as Camellia announced dessert was being served. People would be wondering where Deacon had gone, but Max figured no one would blame him for skipping out on the wedding cake. Some of them noticed him sprawled on the seat, but no one said anything to him.

"Did you get some dinner? Or do we need to get some food in you?" Max asked and put his arm behind Deacon's head to help him sit up.

Instead of answering the question, Deacon slumped forward with his elbows on his knees and his head down. "I just wish I knew where she was." He turned his head to look at Max.

"I don't want to see her, but I want to know she's okay."

"She is, buddy." Max squeezed Deacon's shoulder.

"How do you know?" Deacon asked, suddenly clear, and Max knew he'd made a mistake.

"She called Sutton."

"Where's Dahlia?" Deacon tried to stand too fast and fell back into the seat.

Max hesitated telling Deacon what he wanted to know, but he couldn't keep the information from him. "She's at the airport. She's using the ticket to Bali. Sutton is taking her passport to her."

"She's going? I should go." He stood again, but this time renewed hope steadied him. "We should just go on the honeymoon and forget about the wedding. We don't have to get married. I shouldn't have pushed her."

Max stood and grabbed Deacon's arm to stop him from walking away from the people who had stood by his side in favor of the woman who didn't deserve to have him by hers.

"That's not a good idea, Deacon. It's not the wedding she didn't want." Max hadn't meant to be so harsh. Dahlia was the one he wanted to hurt, not Deacon. But he saw in Deacon's eyes that his words had dealt the final blow to his dreams of spending his life with Dahlia.

"She's gone for good, isn't she?" Deacon's voice cracked.

"I don't know, but you need to let her go for good."

Deacon blinked, then straightened his shoulders and nodded. "Let's get some cake. Looks like they started without me." He jutted his head toward the room full of tables and the people sitting at them.

"Tomorrow's a new day. A new start. You can do this." Max pulled his phone out of his jacket pocket and opened the camera. "Come on." He pulled Deacon close and held the camera at an angle above them. "We're documenting this moment. I want you to remember it as the night your life began, not ended."

They smiled, Max wider than Deacon, and Max snapped the picture. Deacon's smile dropped as soon as Max lowered his arm, but he pulled Max into a hug.

"Thanks, man. You're a good friend."

Max threw his arm around Deacon's shoulder and helped him inside to the spot Lily had saved for him. He left Deacon in Lily's care and headed to the one seat left at the opposite end of the table, taking a last look at Deacon. Lily already had him smiling. Deacon was in good hands. If anyone knew how to pull him out of despair, it would be Lily. Deacon talked about her almost as much as he talked about Dahlia.

Max wished Sutton were still there to make *him* smile, but his selfie with Deacon had given him an idea. He hadn't wanted to scare Sutton away by asking for her number, but he also hated the idea of not seeing her again. But he could put the ball in her court. He'd promised her pictures in the wedding app, and he'd deliver.

If Dahlia wanted Sutton to do something with all the guests' pictures, he'd give her plenty to work with. He guessed Sutton would be looking at those pictures long before Dahlia— honeymooning by herself in Bali—ever would. If Sutton liked his pictures—liked *him*—she could make the first move.

He started with the plate of food Camellia had saved for him. He had another guest snap a photo of him taking a bite of the spring peas and another of him making a face at the fish because he hated fish. One more reason to be mad at Dahlia. Then he moved onto getting selfies with guests and encouraging them to take their own. Once he got people going, he made sure to photo bomb as many pictures as possible.

By the end of the night Max felt confident he'd kept his promise to Sutton. Not only kept it but told her things about himself that he wished he could tell her in person. Things like he could eat a lot of chocolate, he could pull off a duck face like a boss, and he loved sitting under a star-filled sky. He even got a shot with fireflies. That one took a lot of tries.

The last shot he took was the most important. The one he hoped she'd see soon. He had grabbed a couple drink napkins and found a Sharpie—the one meant for signing Deacon and Dahlia's wedding portrait. He unfolded the napkins and scrawled his phone number across them, along with *Sutton, Call Me,* then arranged them on the table in front of the candles and flowers. Sutton was a photographer after all, so the shot had to look good.

He uploaded his pictures along with a string of prayers that she'd see them soon. Then he sent up another prayer that he hadn't misread their mutual attraction. A bunch of good selfies and prayer; that's what he needed for a chance at ever seeing Sutton again.

Chapter Five

Sutton sat on the train staring at the subway map and its intersecting lines spread across Manhattan, without really seeing them. The subway system had taken her a few weeks to figure out—which route ran fastest, which trains were on time, which stations were always crowded, and which ones smelled the worst—but two years into being a New Yorker, she was a subway pro.

She'd fallen in love with New York her first day living with her brother and hadn't thought twice about leaving her past behind in Charleston. That had changed in the two weeks since she'd come back from Dahlia's un-wedding. She couldn't stop thinking about Charleston and, more specifically, Max. She didn't know very much about him, but she felt like she *knew* him.

The first thing she'd done when she came home from Charleston was download Dahlia's wedding pictures from her camera. She didn't bother looking at any of the photos guests had uploaded. She had other projects to work on, and she doubted Dahlia or anyone else would be anxiously waiting to see the un-wedding photos. Anyway, she wasn't interested in other people's pictures.

Sutton wanted the pictures she'd taken of Max.

One in particular. The only one without Hadley in it that she'd taken of him on the dance floor. She used Photoshop to change the shot from color to black and white, and the change sharpened the line of his jaw and the dimple in his cheek when he smiled. She left the photo on her computer—she felt less stalkerish looking at it on a screen a hundred times a day rather than staring at an actual copy.

The shot she did print was the one she'd taken of him sitting on the steps of the grand staircase handing Hadley her basket of flower petals. That one she'd kept in color to highlight Hadley's dark curls against her white dress and the bright pink roses in her flower crown. Max's dimple wasn't as noticeable in that shot, but he looked as good in color as he did in black and white.

Hadley tapped her leg as they approached their station. "When will we see Max again?" She'd asked at least a thousand times since they'd come home. Maybe that's why Sutton couldn't forget about him, but the fact that Hadley felt a connection to him meant something. Her little girl was a much better judge of character than she was.

"I don't know if we will, baby." She didn't even know Max's last name or where he lived. She assumed Charleston, but maybe Columbia since he and Deacon had been roommates at USC.

The train screeched to a stop, and Sutton gripped

Hadley's hand as they stepped onto the platform. Crowds made Sutton nervous when she had Hadley with her. Her little girl could be lost so easily.

Brett had never been really invested in raising Hadley, so being her daughter's only protector wasn't new to Sutton. But seeing how good Max was with Hadley had her thinking about what parenting would be like with a partner.

When she'd said good-bye to him, she'd been determined to walk away without making any new attachments. She'd been relieved he hadn't asked for her number.

Now, she regretted not asking for his.

"I liked him, Mama. I think we should visit him." Hadley's voice pulled Sutton out of her thoughts but did little to distract her from them. Swinging Sutton's hand, she prattled on about Max, repeating everything she'd said about him a million times since they'd been back.

They walked out of the dirty subway station into the bright sunlight that insisted on warming her skin as though November weren't right around the corner. The leaves in Central Park had turned, so she and Hadley had planned a picnic in the park. Along with a thousand other New Yorkers. Sutton had been raised in the open spaces just outside of Charleston. She should have hated New York, but she loved the community of strangers. If this many people could coexist and appreciate the beauty of a park together, maybe she could find one person to share her life with? Even if the first time she'd tried had been a disaster?

Sutton and Hadley found a shady spot on a hill with a view of The Metropolitan Museum of Art, one of Sutton's favorite places. While Hadley gathered fallen leaves that still held their color, Sutton spread an old quilt across the grass and unpacked their lunch basket. Once she'd found enough leaves to satisfy her, Hadley plopped next to Sutton and laid them all out for her.

"This one is my favorite." She held up a leaf that looked identical to the others. "I'm saving it for Max."

Sutton handed her a sandwich and helped her with the wrapper before uncorking the question that had been bubbling in her brain almost from the moment she'd said good-bye to Max.

"Should we try to call him?" she asked.

Hadley wasn't the most reasonable person for Sutton to ask that question, but Sutton hadn't made a lot of girlfriends in New York, and her brother was definitely out of the question. Seth would say no. He'd appointed himself her protector and got defensive when any man came close to glancing at her.

"Yes. Then we should visit him," Hadley answered, bouncing on her knees.

"The problem is, I don't know his phone number or where he lives." Sutton tucked Hadley's hair behind her ear. She knew she shouldn't treat her five-year-old like a confidant, but the fact was, her baby had pretty good advice.

"You can just type his name into Google and get his number that way." She wiggled her fingers over an imaginary keyboard. "Let me have your phone." She reached across Sutton's lap to pick up the phone beside her. Her little fingers were barely long enough to wrap around the phone, but she had no trouble unlocking the home screen and opening the Google app.

"How do you know my password?" Sutton asked, tempted to take the phone back but too curious to see what Hadley had planned.

"I used my fingerprint."

"You little sneak." Sutton poked her side and Hadley giggled and squirmed away, but then frowned.

"There are too many Maxes." She turned the phone to Sutton to show her the long list Google had created for the word Max. Sutton reached to take the phone from her, but Hadley pulled it back.

"I know! I'll put in New York with his name so Google can find the right Max."

Sutton peeked over Hadley's shoulder to see if she knew how to spell New York, feeling more than a little proud when Hadley got it right.

"What makes you think he lives in New York?" she asked with a spark of hope that maybe Hadley knew something she didn't.

"Everyone lives in New York, Mama," Hadley said with an exasperated breath.

Google brought up too many possibilities again, and Hadley's face fell.

"Don't worry. I have an idea that might actually work." She took her phone back from Hadley and opened her email. "I'm going to ask Aunt Dolly if she knows how to find Max."

The problem with that was the solution depended entirely on Dahlia actually checking her email. Sutton hadn't heard from her since she'd dropped off Dahlia's passport at the airport and waved good-bye as she went through the security line to catch her flight to Bali. She'd tried texting Dahlia but hadn't gotten a response. She doubted Dahlia had an international plan or would think to add one if she didn't.

She emailed her anyway, asking if she knew Max or how to get ahold of him, then crossed her fingers and said a Hail Mary that Dahlia would check her messages soon. Once the message was on its way, however, Sutton thought of another idea.

Deacon would know where Max was. She could track him down through work.

Sutton tucked her phone in her pocket and turned her attention back to her little girl. "Don't worry, Had, I've got a plan. We'll find Max."

They spent the rest of the afternoon in the park eating, feeding ducks, and people watching. Sutton felt at peace for the first time in weeks knowing as soon as she got home she could find a number for Deacon in a matter of minutes, and minutes after that, she'd have a number for Max.

She waited until Hadley and Seth were absorbed in the World Series before googling Deacon. She found him and his law firm without a problem, but she doubted he'd be in his office on a Sunday night. It wasn't impossible, but she decided to do a little Facebook and Insta stalking first.

She had shut down all her social media while going through her divorce to keep Brett from harassing her. Finding Max meant opening new accounts, but she used her given first name and her maiden name: Jessica Harris. She ran the risk of Brett finding her, but she took it anyway.

In a matter of minutes, she'd found Deacon on Facebook and done a search of his friends for a Max. The closest she'd found was a Jake Maxfield who didn't have a profile picture or any recent posts and had his privacy settings set so high she couldn't see any personal info. He could be her Max, but she doubted it. The man she'd met wasn't shy about opening up to strangers.

Deacon's Instagram privacy settings, on the other hand, were non-existent. She could see everything about him, including a picture of the Charleston skyline from a few hours before with the caption, *Working on a Sunday, but at least I've got a view.*

She took a deep breath. Finding Max was suddenly a real possibility. She stood and paced a circle behind her desk, shaking her hands and pepping herself up with the same words she'd used before a big swim meet.

Finally, she picked up her phone and dialed Deacon's work number. Every ring that went unanswered made her heart beat faster, but just before she went to voicemail, Deacon picked up.

"Hello?" The sharpness in his voice startled her.

"Deacon? It's Sutton, Dahlia's friend." She knew he knew her, but her nerves were a jumble of live wires all buzzing with electricity.

"I know who you are." His voice sounded strange, slurred. "You're the reason Dahlia left me. You screwed me over worse than she did."

Sutton wasn't sure how to respond, and the more he talked the more she understood the reason he sounded like he had a mouthful of marshmallows. He'd been drinking. A lot. She heard *drunk* in every *s* he turned into a *sh* sound. He reminded her of Brett. She didn't want to think about Brett when she'd finally worked up the courage to take a chance on a new relationship.

"I'm so sorry, Deacon. I know she really hurt—"

"—You knew," he snapped. "You knew, and you didn't tell me. You helped her make me look like an idiot."

"I had no idea, I promise." Sutton scrambled to soothe him while at the same time wondering if she *had* been complicit. Dahlia hadn't said anything to her, but Sutton had wondered if she'd bolt. Maybe she should have warned Deacon.

"You knew, and you helped her. You took her passport to her, so don't pretend like you're sorry."

She couldn't deny that part. She had helped Dahlia get to Bali without even thinking about how that might hurt Deacon. Before she could think of any way to defend herself, Deacon spoke again.

"If you're calling to apologize, don't bother. I don't want to see or talk to you or Dahlia again." He ended by putting a string of words and names together that she'd never been called before and then hanging up.

Sutton stared at her phone. Of all the scenarios she had come up with for when she asked for Max's number, that hadn't been one of them. He'd been her best chance, and he'd shredded that hope into microscopic pieces.

A few photos and a night of memories might be all she'd ever have of Max.

No . . . that didn't feel right.

She wasn't ready to give up looking for him yet.

That thought made the wall she'd built around her heart feel less impenetrable. She could sense the cracks and the imminent exposure they would bring, the certain vulnerability.

So why did the crumbling feel like freedom?

Chapter Six

Max gazed out his apartment window at Central Park. He only had a peek-a-boo view that required a lot of neck craning, but he could see the leaves had changed into their full autumn glory. Their reddish-orange color shone brighter against the green shrubs and grass. He loved this time of year before the weather turned from pleasant to biting cold. Families and couples came out in droves to picnic in the Park; seeing them dot the grass made Max think about Hadley and Sutton.

Not that he needed much encouragement to think about Sutton. He hadn't stopped doing that since the moment they'd said good-bye. He'd given her two weeks to find the pictures he'd left for her, but he couldn't wait any longer. He didn't want to obsess over her. Either she'd seen the pictures and was ignoring him, or she hadn't seen them. Whichever one, he had to know.

He'd tried finding her on Facebook and Instagram. Nothing. Not knowing her last name didn't help, but with a name like Sutton he'd thought he'd easily find her among Dahlia's friends. Wrong. Out of 2,500 "friends," Dahlia had three named Sutton and none of them was the one he wanted to find.

Deacon was his last hope. He hadn't talked to him since the wedding—or not-wedding. (There needed to be a word for life's biggest events that didn't happen). He'd tried texting, but Deacon hadn't responded. That wasn't unusual but it still worried Max and gave him another reason to call besides asking about Sutton.

He'd seen on Instagram that Deacon was spending his Sunday working, so he wasn't surprised when Deacon took more than three rings to pick up. But instead of a hello, Max heard a crashing sound, followed by a curse and finally an apology from Deacon.

"You doing alright, buddy?" Max asked.

"I'm a little drunk," he answered.

"A little?"

A beat passed before Deacon answered. "A lot. And I'm at work."

"It's Sunday."

"It's the only place that doesn't remind me of Dahlia." Deacon sighed. "I can't get her out of my head. She's been there so long, I don't know if I ever will."

"You will . . . eventually."

Max let Deacon pour out his soul, which took a while. A long while, but it sobered him up. There was a lot in there that Max suspected Deacon had been keeping in for years.

"It's good you're getting this all out, man. Get it out and let it go," Max said, once he was sure Deacon was done. "And I hate to even ask this right now, but I'm wondering if you know anything about her friend, Sutton. We kind of connected—"

"Stay away from her," he growled. "I never want to see her again. She's poison."

"Poison? That's harsh."

"Trust me. She was always getting Dahlia into trouble. I didn't want her to be our photographer. Dahlia wouldn't have anybody else. Now I know why. Sutton was all part of the plan to make me look stupid in front of everyone." A glass clinked in the background while Deacon spoke and when he stopped, Max heard a deep swallow. "She's married anyway."

"Married?" She hadn't acted married when he met her, and she wasn't wearing a ring. He'd checked.

"Maybe she's divorced now. I don't remember." Deacon hiccupped. "Excuse me."

"Do you have a ride home?" Max asked.

"I don't need one."

He definitely needed one. Max didn't have to be in the same room, or even the same city, to know that. After he ended his call with Deacon, he texted Emmett to give him a heads up that his brother wasn't fit to drive.

As he typed his message to Emmett, Max thought about everything Deacon had said about Sutton. None of his descriptions sounded like the Sutton he had met, but Deacon had known her a lot longer. Deacon was also angry, drunk and broken-hearted, making him the worst possible matchmaker. Max would have to find Sutton without his help.

In the meantime, the Apple Universe conspired to make sure he never forgot about the wedding everyone wanted to forget. A notification from the wedding app popped up reminding him to upload all his wedding shots to Dahlia's site before the two-week window closed. He shook his head at the absurdity of the whole situation and was about to delete the app when a thought occurred to him.

He could go back to Deacon and Dahlia's wedding website where he remembered seeing a list of the vendors who were part of the event. Flipping open his laptop, Max typed DahliaandDeacon.com and whispered a *yes* when a link for vendors appeared on the home page. He scrolled through the long list—who knew a wedding took so many people?—until he saw her name, Sutton Bradley, with her website address next to it.

Bradley. Her last name was Bradley.

Max clicked on the link for her website and Sutton Studios Wedding Photography popped up. He scrolled through the pictures on the home page, admiring her work but also looking for an address or phone number. He found them under the contacts tab, and he unconsciously bounced his leg as he stared at them.

Her business was located in Charleston, which meant— like he'd thought—she was too. It didn't matter. Having his dream of finding her so close to becoming a reality helped him realize how much he wanted it. If Sutton's address had been on the moon he'd still be trying to contact her.

He wished she had an email address listed rather than a contact form. Email would be less threatening to her than a phone call, he felt sure. But a phone call would put him out of his misery sooner. He'd know right away if she'd felt the same spark or not. Then, he'd be able to go forward or move on.

He dialed her number before he could talk himself out of it. The phone rang once before switching to a robot voice announcing the line had been disconnected.

That was not what he had expected. He ended the call, double-checking he hadn't put in the wrong number, then dialed again anyway. He got the same result and was just as disappointed as he'd been the first time.

He wondered how she stayed in business without a working number, and disappointment threatened to bury his hopes. Fighting the feeling off, he went to Google and typed *Sutton Bradley* into the search bar, then crossed his fingers. Apparently, old school superstition didn't work because the only links that popped up were for Sutton's website and a bunch of five-star reviews of her business.

The contact form on her website was his last chance. Putting in his info was easy, but when he reached the comment box, Max sat back and thought about what to write. He wanted to tell her everything he'd been feeling since the night they met, but as he started to type, the words didn't feel right.

He erased everything and started again.

And again.

Two more drafts followed before he was satisfied with his message.

Dear Sutton,

I can't stop thinking about you.

Max

He hit send before he could be tempted to repeat his write

and erase process. Then the waiting game started all over again.

Except he only had to wait for as long as it took his form to travel across the ethernet and back again with an automated response that said the site was no longer active.

"Dammit." How could the whole world be connected, and he couldn't find the only person on earth he cared about finding? His studio apartment felt too small, and the world felt too big.

He closed his laptop and pushed it aside. Leaning his head against the back of his chair, Max let his gaze wander to the bike parked in his entryway. A ride around Central Park would clear his head and help him sort out what to do next. He wasn't ready to give up on finding Sutton.

Without checking the weather or bothering to change into something better suited to biking than jeans, he slung his bike on his shoulder and headed down the stairs. The lightbulb moment he was hoping for came before he made it out of his building.

Max had one more chance to connect with Sutton in her language: pictures. The wedding app hadn't closed, and Sutton would eventually see all the photos uploaded to Dahlia's website, if she hadn't already. Maybe he could help her get to know him a little better.

If she'd seen the pictures he'd uploaded to the wedding site she knew that he liked chocolate, stars, and fireflies, but not fish. She even knew his phone number.

But she didn't know him. Not really. He'd seen her in her environment doing what she loved; maybe she needed to see him in his city doing what he loved. Maybe seeing that would make her feel safe enough to call him. Maybe knowing he lived in another city would be enough distance for her to not feel threatened by him. They could get to know each other slowly, long distance . . .

Maybe.

Unless, of course, she was married.

That thought didn't feel right to him. He might be crazy for not believing Deacon, but Sutton didn't seem like the kind of girl who'd dance with him all night if she were married. She seemed like the kind of girl who had a reason for not giving out her name or number. And maybe that reason was that she'd been in a bad marriage, not because she was still married. And Hadley definitely didn't seem like the kind of little girl who had a loving father, not with the way she'd attached herself to him so quickly.

He took a picture outside his apartment building, then pushed his bike a block to the park. His favorite spot in Central Park was on the bridge overlooking the lake, so he headed there first. He handed his iPhone to a tourist to take a shot of him with his bike. When he saw the result, he knew he'd chosen a legit photographer. It was definitely good enough to share with Sutton.

His next shot was with the statue of Hans Christian Anderson. He had another tourist take the picture of him sitting next to Hans on the copper bench and pretended to feed the ugly duckling. Then he moved on to the puppet theater where he took a selfie with the puppets. Hadley would love seeing a show there if Sutton ever brought her to New York.

At the thought of Hadley, he noticed a little girl about her size with dark curly hair. She was too far away to really tell, but she looked so much like Hadley, he almost said her name. But why would Hadley be in New York without her mom? And he didn't see anyone who looked like Sutton. He'd checked as soon as he'd seen the girl.

Brushing off the thought as wishful thinking, Max moved on to his next shot. He posed and snapped a picture in front of Alexander Hamilton. He was a fan. Sutton needed to know that.

He took a dozen more shots around the park, ignoring thoughts that he might be approaching overkill. Once he got close to the Met, he decided to get a last shot right outside the museum in front of the best hot dog stand in New York. He pedaled to the park exit, then walked his bike across the street and waited in line. Mustard, onions and pickles, just the way he liked his dogs. He took a selfie of his first bite, then had someone take a another shot of him holding the half-eaten dog with one hand and making a thumbs up with the other hand.

Max sat on the museum steps long enough to finish his lunch while the pictures uploaded to the wedding site. If he'd remembered to bring his bike lock, he would have spent some time taking shots next to his favorite paintings in the Met. But that would have to wait for another day.

Clouds that had spent the day threatening to block the sun finally succeeded, and heavy drops of rain left their individual marks on the sidewalk. He pulled up the hood of his sweatshirt and rolled his bike to the curb, watching his phone to make sure the pictures finished uploading. The progress bar hit one hundred percent as he stepped off the curb.

He never saw the taxi skidding through the light, unable to stop on the wet pavement before it hit him.

Chapter Seven

The mild autumn turned into one of the coldest winters on record and blizzard after blizzard kept Sutton and Hadley shut indoors. During one of those blizzards, the city had come to a stop, and Sutton and Hadley were watching TV in front of the fire when Sutton opened her email to find a surprise.

Three months after the fact, Dahlia had finally answered Sutton's email asking about Max.

Sutton hadn't forgotten him. The picture she'd printed of him and Hadley was the only one of Dahlia's wedding pictures she'd done anything with. Camellia had called her a few weeks after the wedding and said she had no interest in seeing any of the pictures she'd paid for. She also had no interest in ever seeing or hearing from Sutton again since Sutton had "taken it upon herself to encourage Dahlia in her half-cocked plan to go to Bali by herself." That stung, but Sutton had always gotten the feeling Camellia didn't *quite* approve of her friendship with Dahlia.

In all honesty, Sutton didn't have time to edit the pictures even if Camellia had wanted her to. She'd been invited to show her work at a gallery opening that had led to other showings and some commissioned work. Between that and taking care of Hadley, Sutton's days and nights were booked.

She also didn't have time to pursue any relationships, particularly not with a stranger who'd made himself impossible to find.

But when she saw Dahlia's email, her pulse quickened with the thought she might finally have Max's number. She may not have had time to look for him, but she hadn't forgotten him. The picture of him and Hadley wouldn't let her. Neither would Hadley, although her questions about him had slowed to a few dozen per week.

Sutton opened the email and quickly scanned it. When she didn't see a phone number, she slowed down and read Dahlia's words more carefully, trying to ignore the tightness in her chest.

Hey Girl!

My yogi says true happiness comes from looking outside of yourself, so I'm giving it a try. You've been a good friend, and I'm sorry for all the trouble I've caused you over the years.

Sutton double-checked the sender before reading on. Dahlia had never apologized to her before.

As I've become more enlightened over the past four months, I've realized something. You've been the one person who's always stood by me, and I'm hoping I can still count on you, because I need a HUGE favor, and you're the only person who can do it.

Of course, she wanted something from Sutton. She really

wouldn't be Dahlia if she didn't.

I made a mistake when I left Deacon. I don't regret leaving, just the way I did it. I should have told him long before our wedding day we weren't right for each other. I chickened out and ran. He didn't deserve that. He deserves to know how loved he is, not just by me, by everyone who stayed the night I left.

Sutton had to give Dahlia credit. She really had gained some enlightenment.

Deacon needs proof of this. Photographic evidence. And you're the only person who can do it the way it should be done.

Sutton continued reading. Dahlia wanted her to put together a photo book of all the reception pictures. She'd skimmed through them and knew Sutton would do something amazing enough to convince Deacon to forgive her for running away. But Dahlia knew he'd never open anything from her, so it would have to be from Sutton.

Based on her last conversation with Deacon, Sutton wasn't sure he'd open anything from her either, but she was willing to try. She owed him an apology too. She should have told him where Dahlia went instead of sneaking out of the reception the way she had to help Dahlia.

I don't know when I'll be back, but when I do, I want to be able to face Deacon with no regrets for either of us. I've made a lot of mistakes and have a lot of relationships to repair, but this thing with Deacon is the first thing I need to fix.

Love,

Your Dolly

P.S. I don't have Max's number, but I think he lives in

Chicago. Or maybe Baltimore. And Max is a nickname. His real name is Jacob.

Jacob? Max was a Jacob?

Sutton read Dahlia's P.S. a second time, then a third. Sure, she still didn't know Max's number, but she had learned his real name. Wasn't that a step forward?

For some reason it didn't feel like it. Maybe because there were so many more Jacobs than Maxes. His real name only made him harder to find.

Nearly four months had already passed since they'd met. She shouldn't still be thinking about him as often as she did. Or regretting that she hadn't asked for his number—or given him hers—every time she did think of him.

But she also hadn't forgotten his promise to get the wedding guests to upload pictures to Dahlia's site. If he'd followed through, maybe he'd also taken some selfies and she'd have some more photos of him other than the few she'd taken. She wouldn't mind a few more reminders of what he looked like.

Sutton logged into the account and opened the file. A feeling of dread spread over her as she scrolled through the thumbnails. There were over a thousand pictures. It would take months to look through and Photoshop them.

Closing her eyes, she took a deep breath to keep from cursing Dahlia's name. When she opened them again she decided the project could be procrastinated for at least a day.

But then a face caught her eye. She enlarged it to make sure she was seeing what she thought she was, then let out a laugh.

It was Max, pointing to the fish on his plate and plugging

his nose.

"What's funny, Mama?" Hadley scooted closer and peeked over Sutton's shoulder. "That's Max!"

"Yep. And I don't think he liked that fish," Sutton answered, happy to share in Hadley's excitement over seeing an old friend.

"Because fish is gross." Hadley stuck out her tongue and made a gagging noise.

"Manners, baby."

Hadley climbed onto the couch next to Sutton and rested her head on Sutton's shoulder. "Are there more pictures of him?"

"I don't know. Let's see."

Sutton put the pictures on slideshow, and they weren't disappointed. There was Max pulling off a duck face like a boss, and then in a selfie with someone she didn't know. The next picture showed him lying on the grass under the stars, followed by a bunch of shots he'd photobombed.

By the time they got to the picture of Max surrounded by fireflies, Sutton and Hadley were both laughing. Hadley was clearly in love with Max, and Sutton thought she might be a little in love with him too, or at least with his pictures. He had a good eye.

But then she came to the picture that took her breath away.

"I know those numbers, Mama!" Hadley yelled and read off the numbers Max had written on a napkin months before. "What are they?"

"I think it's his phone number."

"We can call him? Can we call him right now?"

Hadley bounced on the sofa, but Sutton didn't answer her. She sat frozen, staring at the man she'd been thinking about for months holding the information she'd been searching for. Just when she'd accepted the idea she'd never find him, she had. And he'd been under her nose the whole time.

Seth walked in the front door then and Hadley hopped up to meet him. "Uncle Seth, we found Max!"

"You found who?" He picked her up and carried her back to the couch.

"No one," Sutton said.

"Max!" Hadley's words ran over her mother's. "My friend from Auntie Dolly's wedding when she didn't get married."

Seth raised an eyebrow and Sutton closed the lap top.

"I think it's time for you to go to bed." Sutton stood and took Hadley by the hand. "Kiss your uncle good night."

Hadley reluctantly followed her mom's orders. Bedtime was still an hour away, but Sutton wanted to avoid Seth's questions. Judging by the look he'd given her after kissing the top of Hadley's head, he knew exactly why she was rushing her daughter to bed.

Half an hour later, Hadley fell asleep, and Sutton couldn't avoid her brother any longer. She made her way back down the hallway, hoping he'd gone to bed, too. He hadn't. He sat on the couch going through the pictures Sutton hadn't closed on her computer.

"Is this him?" Seth held up Sutton's laptop with the picture of Max and his phone number filling the entire screen.

Sutton nodded. She had told Seth a little bit about Max, but Hadley had told him everything, including how they'd all danced together to a slow song.

"Are you going to call him? He obviously wants you to." Seth put the computer back on his lap and studied Max.

Sutton wondered if he'd try to stop her like he'd tried to stop her from marrying Brett. "He was so great with Hadley," she answered, without really answering. "I think he's a good guy."

"Maybe." Seth set the laptop aside and stood. "I'm not going to be able to stop you, am I?"

She considered his question, then shook her head.

"Be careful." He hugged her tight before walking out of the front room, and down the hall to his bedroom.

Sutton took the fact Seth didn't freak out as a good sign but still waited twenty minutes. When she heard his first snore, she picked up her phone. Another five minutes passed before she worked up the courage to dial Max's number.

Two rings and thirty nervous seconds later, a long beep and a robot voice informed her the number had been disconnected.

Sutton hadn't known how much she wanted Max to answer her call until the moment the line went dead, and she realized the number she'd seen in his picture wasn't good. He'd obviously wanted her to call him, so why would he give her a bad number? His picture had really only been good for one thing: the area code confirmed he lived in North Carolina.

That should have been enough to convince her to forget about him. For a while, it did.

She threw herself into her work and used her spare time to edit the pictures Dahlia wanted in the book for Deacon. The project took all of January. There were just so many pictures—

and a surprising number of them were of Deacon and Lily together. He was even smiling in some of them.

She kept hoping there would be more of Max, but he must have done a good job of convincing people to take a lot of pictures because they'd done exactly that. Other than the dozen selfies he'd taken and another dozen he'd photobombed, he wasn't in most of the pictures.

Until she got to the last batch. They were all him.

Max with a bike. Max on a bridge with a bike. Max in front of a statue—no, on a statue. Max feeding ducks. Max with a hot dog. She looked at them all, then scrolled through them again more slowly making sure she was seeing what she thought she was seeing.

Max in front of a brownstone similar to the one she lived in. Max on a foot bridge like the one in Central Park. Max sitting next to the Hans Christian Anderson statue in Central Park, feeding the duck in it, and then another of him feeding real ducks on the boat pond. Max watching a puppet show at the little theater Hadley loved. Max eating a hot dog from the stand in front of the Met that was *her* favorite.

Had Max been visiting New York? Or, did he live here? All the pictures looked like he knew his way around the city. No tourist would know which hot dog stand was the best one. Her heart beat faster as she scrolled through them. He would have had to take them within two weeks of the un-wedding when the app was still open.

She looked at the date of each picture, especially the ones in Central Park. Her breath caught when she saw the numbers. She remembered the date because it was the same day she'd called Deacon looking for Max, and he'd blamed her for Dahlia leaving. The same day she and Hadley had been in Central Park and Sutton had promised her she'd find Max.

And she could have if she'd looked a little closer to home. All she had to do was look up, because she and Hadley had been feeding the same ducks that day.

She had a renewed sense of excitement knowing Max might be somewhere in New York, but also a new sense of dread. Finding Max still meant looking for a needle in a haystack.

She could email Dahlia and ask her about Max again, but Dahlia had taken three months to answer Sutton's first message. How much longer would she take a second time around? Hopefully not as long because she had to try.

Sutton kept the pictures of Max open and opened another window to email Dahlia.

Dear Dahlia, she typed.

Does Max live in New York? Can you find out?

Namaste

The likelihood Dahlia knew where Max lived was somewhere in the Easter Bunny is Real range, especially considering Dahlia currently lived on an ashram in Bali. But Sutton didn't have any other ideas.

Her one real hope was her original one: Deacon. She had to finish the book for him and include a note begging for his forgiveness and Max's contact info.

She took a last look at the pictures of Max, studying the one in front of the brownstone in particular. Could that be where he lived? She could see the number seven on the front, but no street names. Max had basically left her one square of a thousand-piece puzzle.

But she'd always liked puzzles, and she was determined to solve this one. A man who loved Alexander Hamilton and puppet shows was a man worth puzzling over.

With renewed motivation, she finished Deacon's photo book over the next week and dropped it in the mail in time to arrive by his birthday on February fourteenth. She chose to ignore the irony of the bride who jilted him sending him a present to open on Valentine's Day. She hoped he'd ignore the irony too and not the package itself. The book was important for healing his relationship with Dahlia, but the note asking for forgiveness and Max's number was what really mattered to Sutton.

While she waited, prayed and crossed her fingers that Deacon would reply, she studied Max's pictures. He obviously loved Central Park, and she wondered if he lived in one of the nearby neighborhoods. That could be a place to start her search.

Central Park was three miles around, so searching for him would still be looking for a needle, but in a much smaller haystack. She had no idea what she'd do if she actually found the building. That would be a whole new pile of hay, but she'd cross that farmyard when she came to it.

She started by narrowing down neighborhoods surrounding the park to the ones he most likely lived in. Park Avenue was unlikely, although not impossible, and so she started there. Why not assume her dream guy lived on the priciest street in Manhattan?

Google Maps and satellite imaging helped her zero in on the buildings within a three-block radius of Park Avenue. Her eye for detail had made her one of the most requested wedding photographers in Charleston, and that same eye helped her eliminate the buildings in the first block of the grid she'd created to keep track of all the streets to check. She scanned streets for two hours and crossed off Park, Madison and 5th Avenues. All streets she had been ninety percent sure Max couldn't afford to live on anyway.

She decided to be smarter about her search after that and skipped zooming in on the pricey apartments on the Upper East Side. Even with an entire neighborhood out of the running, she still had a Herculean task ahead of her searching a city of six million for one Max. But she'd promised Hadley she'd find him, and the pictures he'd left for them convinced Sutton she needed to keep that promise. For herself as much as for her daughter.

The problem was, she didn't have the two extra hours a day required to search through ten blocks out of thousands. More galleries were asking for her work which kept her busy during the hours Hadley was at school. The hours with Hadley at home were filled with art lessons, homework, and playdates. Sutton barely had time to warm up frozen dinners, let alone search the whole city for a man who'd probably forgotten her in the six months since they'd met.

Still, Sutton kept searching. She recruited Seth to help her. He agreed only after she'd shown him the pictures and he'd stared at each one for at least ten minutes before deciding Max probably wasn't a perv. But Seth had even less time for the Max search than she did, so neither one of them made very much progress.

As the weather turned and flowers started blooming in Central Park, she and Hadley spent so much time there that even Hadley started asking if they had to go again when Sutton suggested it. But she couldn't stop going and looking, hoping to see Max in one of the spots from his photos.

In the end, she should have asked Fate to do its job since a twisted version of it—or was it Irony?—was what ultimately helped Sutton find Max. On a night when her thoughts were focused on something besides her search for him, she saw him standing on a subway car going the opposite direction from her train, his arm wrapped around a tiny blonde with a lot of curls.

Fate would have been kinder than Irony. They were less than ten feet apart but moving away from each other, one of them obviously with someone else.

Chapter Eight

The compound fracture in Max's left leg and his broken pelvis took three months to heal. The doctors kept telling him he was lucky to be alive. He didn't feel so lucky stuck in bed with screws, plates and rods inside and outside of his body. He knew more about internal and external fixation than he'd ever, *ever* wanted to know.

The view of the skyline from his hospital bed helped for the first few days before the sky changed from a crisp autumn blue to dreary winter gray. As the holidays approached and he returned to his apartment, depression set in.

He couldn't travel back to North Carolina for Christmas, so he'd spent the holiday alone, skyping with his family, drinking too much egg nog, and watching really terrible Hallmark Christmas movies. He'd never tell anyone, but he *may* have cried during the one with that chick from *Full House*. Actually, she may have been in more than one. They all kind of ran together after a while.

His phone had been destroyed when the taxi hit him, and a month passed before he got a new one—being sedated eighteen hours out of the day made the easiest tasks seem overwhelming. Along with the new phone, he'd finally traded in his North Carolina number for a New York one. He'd meant to do it months before he gave Sutton his number but waiting for her to call had given him an excuse to put off the chore.

Then the taxi had forced his hand.

Letting go of his last hope of finding Sutton only made the skies grayer and his life drearier. His twice a week physical therapy appointments didn't help either. They left his whole body aching and his spirit yearning to be well enough to do all the things he used to do. He usually biked everywhere, even in winter, if the bike paths were clear of snow. Being inert was *not* in his DNA.

The only thing that made physical therapy bearable was his therapist, Monica. She was cute and bubbly with crazy blonde curls that made her round face look rounder. He hadn't asked, but if he had to guess he'd bet she'd been a cheerleader in high school. She never lost confidence in him, but she also didn't let him off easy. When he wanted to give up, she made him do one more rep.

By April, Max's body was almost back to his pre-accident condition. By that time, he and Monica had become friends. They might have been more if Max could forget about the spark he'd felt with Sutton or if Monica had been at all interested in him— or men in general. What she was interested in was the story of him and Sutton. Once she heard it, she was convinced Max and Sutton were meant to be together and determined not to let him give up his quest to find her.

"Your story would be the perfect Hallmark movie!" she'd exclaimed more than once. She was a big fan of everything Hallmark. Which also meant she was the perfect friend to keep Max's biggest secret: his Christmas binge had led to an addiction. He couldn't stop watching them. He'd even ordered the Hallmark app for his Roku. He wouldn't admit that to anyone but Monica.

On a typical Friday night, she'd come over and they'd choose the one with the cheesiest trailer—no easy choice—then try to guess what lines the characters where going to say. Every time they got one right they'd take a drink, but only of Dr. Pepper because Monica didn't drink anything stronger than that. When they called a plot hole they got a Red Vine.

Watching cheeseball movies and eating junk food wasn't a bad way to spend a weekend, but it wasn't doing much for either of their love lives. Monica had pointed that out on a number of Friday nights before finally insisting one night that Max get out his laptop.

"We're going to find that girl," she said with the same determination she'd used to get him walking again without a limp.

"Good luck. I've tried," Max said.

In a much deeper voice he said, "I did it for you," at the same time Dean Cain said the phrase to the "spicy Latina" onscreen. Monica was too enthralled in her research to notice, but he took a drink of his Dr. Pepper anyway.

"I've emailed and given her my number. I think if she wanted to see me again she would have found me." His ego had taken a pretty hard hit over the last few months. He'd expected to hear from Sutton and hadn't and he'd lost his mobility. And his six pack. He looked down at his gut and set the Dr. Pepper back on the coffee table.

"Tell me her name again," Monica demanded, ignoring his whining just like she had in physical therapy.

"Sutton Bradley."

Monica found the same website Max had found months before and clicked through Sutton's photo gallery. "She's really good."

He leaned over and looked at the pictures even though he'd seen them before. "Yeah, she is."

"Oh, and pretty!" Monica turned the screen to him, so he could better see the picture of Sutton he'd looked at more times than he'd ever, *ever* admit. He couldn't find her through the seemingly-abandoned website, but he could remember what she looked like. He could remember her dark hair and the eyes that almost matched it until the light hit them to reveal a Blue Ridge Mountains shade of blue.

"You said you think she's divorced?" Monica asked, and Max nodded. "Is Bradley her maiden name?"

He had no idea because he had no idea how long she'd been divorced, assuming she was divorced. Deacon hadn't been a lot of help in that department, and he hadn't wanted to ask him again. In fact, with the accident, he really hadn't been in touch with Deacon at all. Very few people knew Max had been in the hospital. He hated the thought of people feeling sorry for him or feeling obligated to check in on him.

"I think so. I really don't know anything about her except that she's a photographer and she has a daughter named Hadley." Max kept his attention on the movie, not wanting to get his hopes up that Monica would actually be able to find something he couldn't.

"That's the key!" Her fingers flew over the keys as she typed something. "If we can find a record of her birth, it will have Sutton's name on it too, including her maiden name."

Max shifted in his seat, working hard to keep his eyes from wandering to the computer screen as Monica continued tapping away. Her idea was a good one, but she'd definitely crossed the line between curiosity and flat out stalking. He didn't stop her, but he couldn't have any part of her cyber stalking without feeling like a creeper.

"This could take a while, but I'm going to find her." Her eyebrows creased as she ran her finger over the screen, scrolling through whatever she'd found. Max forced himself not to ask.

"Honestly, don't put too much time into it. With my luck, you'll find her, we'll actually connect, and she'll turn out to be a total nightmare." He flinched using the word to describe Sutton.

"She won't." She went back to typing. "That's not how this works. Have you learned nothing from these stories?" She waved her hand toward the TV where Dean Cain and the painfully stereotyped Spicy Latina were staring deeply into each other's eyes.

"Maybe not, but I know enough to know what she's going to say next," he answered.

"None of that matters now," Monica said along with him. "Nothing matters but you."

"And now the kiss." He bowed his head in deference to the traditional final scene of every Hallmark movie he'd ever watched: the fade out shot of the kiss with the sun setting in the background of whatever old inn/summer camp/rehabbed house the happy couple had spent the first hour-and-a-half fighting over.

"And scene," Monica said as the scene ended, and the credits rolled. "Which is my cue to get out of here before my train quits running for the night."

"I'll walk you to the station." Max stood and held out a hand to help her stand.

"Yes, you will. You need to get that leg moving after sitting for so long." She was right, as usual. He could already feel his knee stiffening where he now had three screws holding the bones together.

The station was only a couple blocks away, and Monica talked about the finer plot holes of their movie while they walked. Max listened and laughed, but his mind was on Sutton. What if Monica really could find her? Six months had passed since he'd met her. Would she remember him? As much as he still wanted to see Sutton again, enough time had gone by that he wasn't sure he'd have the courage to call her if Monica did find her.

He could have left Monica at the entrance to the station, but it was after midnight and he wanted to make sure she got on the train safely, so he walked her all the way to the turnstile. When he saw the three guys on the other side and the way they looked at her, Max knew he'd made the right decision by not leaving her at the top of the stairs. He also wasn't letting her ride the train by herself.

"I think I could use a little more exercise. I'll ride with you." He pulled out his subway card and slid it through the scanner before she could argue.

"You don't have to," she said, but then glanced at the three guys. Each one had a face tattoo that looked more prison than parlor done. "But thank you."

She followed him through the turnstile, then put her arm through his as they walked to the platform. "Don't flatter yourself into thinking this means anything besides making me feel safer," she whispered.

He nodded but kept his eye on the men who didn't have any problem checking Monica out even with her attached to his arm. They spent a long ten minutes waiting for the train. No other passengers showed up, and the men got ruder and more obnoxious the longer they had the platform to themselves. Monica moved closer to him, and Max positioned himself, so he could keep an eye on the men.

Their train pulled in at the same time a train coming from the other direction screeched to a stop. Max waited a few seconds to see where the men would get on, but when they didn't make a move, he put an arm around Monica and stepped on the empty car. The ex-cons followed. Max didn't know how he'd take on all three of them if he had to, but he had a much better chance than Monica would have had alone.

Probably. She was tough. With his weak leg, if anything went down she might have to protect him.

Rather than sitting down, she grabbed the pole in the middle of the aisle. Max held it too and put a hand on her shoulder as the doors closed behind him. He looked out the windows into the train across from them but kept his senses alert to the men sitting at the other end of the car.

A woman in a dark blue dress only a few shades lighter than her black hair stepped into the opposite train. Something about her caught his attention as she took hold of a handle. When she looked through the windows directly at him, he knew what that something was. He knew those eyes. He knew that face. He'd thought about the woman they belonged to every day for the last six months.

Their eyes locked and, he could see that she remembered him. The train jerked forward, and Max stumbled with the motion. The other train moved in the opposite direction and in a matter of seconds she was gone.

Monica looked over her shoulder at him, but his eyes were still pointed forward, trying to make the face he'd just seen reappear.

"Do you know that woman?" Monica asked.

"That was Sutton," he answered, and for the first time in months, the possibility of finding her became real again.

Chapter Nine

Sutton slid out of the dress she'd bought especially for the opening she'd been at, leaving it crumpled on the closet floor. She put on her comfiest pajamas and curled up in her bed next to Hadley.

The little girl stirred awake and stretched her arm across Sutton's neck. "I was waiting for you, Mama," she murmured before falling back asleep.

Sutton kissed her forehead, then closed her eyes to keep tears from spilling. She was grateful she hadn't told Hadley about her search for Max. Hadley still talked about him, but not nearly as much as she used to. She knew Hadley would keep growing and little by little the memory of Max would be replaced by other memories. The thought made her sad but also relieved. She hoped she'd be able to do the same. Seeing Max on the train with another woman had convinced her she had to forget him.

That was easier said than done.

By July, Sutton still hadn't completely forgotten him, but she'd also stopped looking for him on sidewalks and in subway stations. Definitely not in subway cars. That hadn't worked out at all the first time around. The muggy weather gave her the perfect excuse to avoid Central Park, even though Hadley had started begging to go again.

But of course, Dahlia, being Dahlia, decided to reappear at exactly the wrong time with the info Sutton had asked for months before. She even called instead of emailing, now that she was back in the States. Sutton hadn't even known she'd returned from Bali.

"Hey, girlfriend, I've got good news for you," she said, as soon as Sutton answered the call, not bothering to ask how she'd been or if anything new had happened in the nine months since she'd been gone.

Sutton was fine, and nothing exciting had happened—other than a fruitless search for a potentially perfect man. Still, Dahlia could have asked.

"I've found Jacob—I mean Max—"

"—It's okay, Dahlia. I'm not—"

"—He does live in New York. I don't have his number, but you could totally find him." She was so pleased with herself, Sutton didn't even bother interrupting again.

"That's great, Dolly. I'll try."

"Now that I'm thinking about it, I don't know why I never set you two up. You'd be perfect for each other—"

"—How was Bali?" Sutton interrupted. If Dahlia said anything else about how she should have done the thing Sutton had asked her to do and act like it was an original idea, Sutton would lose her mind.

Dahlia took a deep breath, and Sutton could almost picture her in lotus position, meditating. "Sooo incredible. Bali changed me, Sutton. I'm not your same Dolly. I'm a new woman. An enlightened woman. I've worked hard to become more aware of my surroundings and the people in them."

"That's great. I'm really happy for you." She wasn't lying. Sutton loved Dahlia, even when she was self-centered and clueless. There had always been a part of Dahlia willing to do anything for anybody.

"That's actually why I'm calling you. I need a huge favor—"

Of course, she did. She hadn't completely changed.

"Do I even want to ask what it is?" Sutton doubted it. The last favor she'd done for Dahlia took a month of work. Deacon had sent her a thank you note for the photo book, but he hadn't given her Max's number.

"You'll like it, and I pay well."

Sutton stayed silent, waiting for Dahlia to explain.

"Deacon and Lily are getting married—"

"—What? How did that happen?" As soon as Sutton asked the question, the pictures of Deacon and Lily flashed in her mind. It made total sense they were getting married. More sense than Deacon and Dahlia walking down the aisle. "How do you feel about that?"

"I wish I would have thought of setting them up years ago, before I made the mistake of saying yes when Deacon asked me to marry him. Biggest mistake of my life and biggest near-miss of Deacon's."

Dahlia sounded genuinely happy, and Sutton hoped she wasn't misreading her tone. If Dahlia really was happy for them, then maybe she *had* become more enlightened.

"I want to do something for them, and that's where you come in," Dahlia went on, and Sutton got a sinking feeling in her stomach. She knew what was coming. There was only one reason why Dahlia would need Sutton for a wedding present.

"I don't do weddings anymore." Sutton steeled herself for the protests she knew were coming.

"I know, but listen. The wedding is in two weeks and the photographer they booked needs a new kidney or something. They can't find anyone else on such short notice."

Sutton wasn't sure why that should concern her, even if Deacon had forgiven her. But Dahlia's powers of persuasion hadn't diminished in the whole enlightening process she'd gone through. Sutton had a refusal on the tip of her tongue, but she didn't have a chance to get it out.

"Jacob will be there."

"You mean Max?"

"Yeah, him."

Sutton thought back to the night she'd seen him on the train with the woman. They'd definitely been together, but maybe they'd broken up.

It was stupid to book a flight to Charleston based on that hope. But it was stupider to keep thinking about him, wondering if she'd missed the best chance for love she'd ever have because she hadn't given him her number.

"All right, I'll do it," she said to Dahlia.

As soon as Sutton ended the call she pulled up the pictures

of Max she hadn't looked at since April. Maybe there was still a chance for them, after all.

Chapter Ten

Max's phone dinged, pulling him out of his stupor. For the past fifteen minutes he'd been staring at the same document he was supposed to be reviewing. Muggy air hung over the city like a wet beach towel, sapping his motivation to do anything other than think about Sutton.

Even with Monica's help, he still hadn't found her, and they'd tried. If Max hadn't seen Sutton on the train that day, he probably would have given up; they weren't meant to be.

But he *had* seen Sutton and the look on her face. A look that registered surprise followed quickly by hurt. He could only imagine what Sutton thought when she saw him with his arm resting on Monica's shoulder. He'd wanted to give the impression to the three potential threats on the train that he and Monica were together. He was pretty sure it had worked a little too well.

He picked up his phone and read the text.

Getting married 10/10. Small wedding on the beach. Can you be there? This one's for real.

Even though Deacon's name was very clearly, and boldly, at the top of the text, Max had to read the name and the text again to make sure he'd read it right. Deacon was getting married again? Well, not again, since the first time didn't actually happen.

What???? To who? Max texted back, not even caring about his grammatical error.

Lily.

Max could have guessed Lily almost a year ago when he'd seen Deacon with her at the reception. He just couldn't have guessed they'd end up together so soon.

I'll be there.

He was happy for Deacon. He liked Lily. They would be great together, and Deacon sounded like he was in a good place again. Maybe in a good enough place that Max could talk to him about Sutton.

Max started to type a new message to Deacon when a text came in from Monica.

I found her!!!!! She's in New York.

Max stared at the words. Ever since seeing Sutton on the subway he'd wondered if she lived in New York. She hadn't been dressed like a tourist. When he thought about it, even when he'd met her in Charleston she'd looked like a New Yorker; he'd just been thrown by her accent.

Before he could answer Monica, she sent him another message.

Her last name is Harris. Google her. Her photos

are in a bunch of galleries in Soho.

He read the text again.

And again.

Then one more time.

There was only one *her* Monica could mean.

Harris? He texted back.

No wonder he hadn't been able to find her. He'd been looking with the wrong name in the wrong place. "Sutton Harris." He said the words aloud, liking the way the letters felt in his mouth. The hard syllables of her first name followed by the soothing sounds of her last name. Strength followed by softness. The name fit her.

How did you find her? Max typed.

As an attorney, it's better you don't know. Plausible deniability and all that.

Max laughed, then glanced around his office even though he knew the door was closed and no one without x-ray vision could see his phone.

Thanks. For everything. Looking her up now, he wrote.

You. Must. Tell. Me. Everything. Already working on my Hallmark script.

He laughed again, but then took a deep breath and opened a new window on his computer. With renewed hope in Google's omniscience, he typed *Sutton Harris* in the search bar.

The Truitt Gallery popped up first with a link to a page of her photos and information about the opening scheduled for that night.

He stood and walked the length of his office, adrenaline

burning through his veins. That's how he would see her. He'd go to her show. This was happening. The thing he'd been imagining for months. Thanks to Monica, he might actually see Sutton again. And not just on a train moving away from him. She was within his reach.

But ten square feet was about a hundred feet short of what he needed to calm himself down. He sat back at his desk, pulled up Facebook and typed in Sutton's name. Nothing. He tried Instagram with the same result. He had no way of finding out if she was single or not, other than going to her opening.

Somehow, he survived the day without crawling out of his skin. His bike ride home helped settle his nerves, but by the time he'd showered, changed and walked to the subway station, his entire body hummed with a nervous energy born of excitement and too many cups of coffee. He didn't worry that she'd forgotten him, but he wondered if they'd feel the same chemistry they had the night they met. He hoped they would. He knew he would.

His biggest fear, the one he pushed to the back of his mind every time it crept out of the shadows, was that she'd found someone else. Why wouldn't she? Any guy would be crazy not to fall for her. *He* hadn't been able to get her out of his head for almost a year, and they'd only spent a few hours together.

He wiped his sweating palms on his pants and stood as the train reached his stop. The doors slid open and he stepped into the bustling crowd whose energy heightened his own and pushed him up the stairs onto the sidewalk. The air smelled musty with impending rain, and he'd only walked a block when he felt the first drop.

The sky started with a sprinkle but didn't wait long before letting go with heavy drops. The sudden storm reminded Max of the afternoon showers so common on summer days in North Carolina, and he was glad he'd forgotten his umbrella. He loved the rain.

However, he didn't want to be soaking wet by the time he got to the Sutton's show, so he pulled his jacket over his head and ran underneath store awnings to shield himself. Despite his best efforts, he was still drenched when he stepped in the door of the gallery.

He shook the water out of his hair, then scanned the room looking for Sutton. People were gathered in pockets talking and looking at Sutton's photos, but he didn't see her. Max followed a path around half walls displaying her work, taking time to look at a few pictures, but too nervous to really study them. He kept searching for her, expecting to see her around every corner.

Until finally, he did.

Even with her back to him he recognized her. She was wearing the same black dress she'd worn to Deacon's un-wedding. At least, he thought it was the same dress. It fit her like the dress at the wedding had, emphasizing all her strengths, from her posture to the toned curve of her arms.

She was standing in front of a photo large enough he could see part of it. A tree partially blocking a skyscraper. Not groundbreaking, except for the angle from which she'd taken the picture. She'd found something in plain sight and made people see it again.

If Max hadn't been sure the woman in black was Sutton, the little girl twirling next to her would have given her away. A smile crept to his lips.

He opened his mouth to say Sutton's name at the same time the man standing next to her took Hadley's hand. Max closed his mouth as the man moved close enough to Sutton to wrap his arm around her waist. She did the same to him, then laid her head on his shoulder.

Max froze. If he moved she would see him, and suddenly he didn't want to be part of this picture. Not as an observer, and definitely not as the stalker he suddenly felt like. Shrinking, hiding or running. Those were his options. Saying her name, being seen. Those were not.

Sutton had moved on.

Moved on wasn't really the right term. There'd never been anything to move on from. They barely knew each other. They'd had one night of talking and dancing, and he'd built it up in his mind to be something amazing.

Max tore his eyes away from Sutton and Hadley and turned to leave, keeping his head down to avoid looking at Sutton's photos. He wound his way around corners back to the entrance. The rain came down harder as he stepped onto the sidewalk, but he didn't pull his jacket over his head again.

Before he reached the subway station, rivulets of water ran from his hair down his neck and under his shirt. His leg ached from the damp and the exertion it took to push past the people on the sidewalk. The rain should have cooled him, but the air was too wet to leave him anything but sticky, and the humidity grew more oppressive the further underground he walked.

Things didn't get better on the crowded train, and he got off a stop early. As soon as he got to street level, his phone pinged, and he ducked under an awning to read the message. Even without seeing it, he knew it would be from Monica.

How's it going??? He tucked his phone back in his

pocket.

He didn't answer her until after he was home and had showered. The shower helped wash away the stickiness but did nothing for his conflicting emotions. Rehashing everything with Monica sounded about as enjoyable as seeing Sutton with someone else again, but she'd be able to talk him through the embarrassment fixing to set up shop in his chest. Plus, she wouldn't stop texting until he responded. She'd already sent two more messages just since he'd been home.

Max slumped to the couch and typed, **She was with another guy**.

A string of texts followed.

After all the work I did to help you find Sutton, you couldn't even say hello to her? (That beef was legitimate.) ***Did she have a ring on her finger?*** (He hadn't stayed long enough to check.) ***Maybe that guy was just a friend or a relative.*** (Maybe . . .) ***Looking at someone's back doesn't tell you anything about a person.*** (He could tell Monica a lot about Sutton's back—the curve of it, the way she bent in every direction to get the best shot—Max could study Sutton's back all day.)

He didn't answer them, or her phone calls. He sat on his couch feeling small and stupid for spending the better part of a year looking for a woman he'd spent a few hours with and knew next to nothing about.

Except that she had a daughter, and they were both incredible, and meeting them had been the highlight of his year. The highlight of a lot of years. And if he'd asked for her number, maybe he could have been the guy standing next to Sutton, his arm around her, celebrating her talent.

Max didn't normally dwell on his mistakes, but he kept company with a lot of regret over the following weeks. He tried taking out a couple women from work who'd been sending him some pretty strong signals, but all he could think of was Sutton. He went home both times feeling even worse because he'd ruined their nights along with his.

Finally, on the morning he was leaving town for Deacon's wedding, he couldn't take it anymore. He dialed Monica's number and didn't have to wait long for her to answer.

"I'm not giving up on her," he said as soon as she answered.

"Thatta boy!" she cheered. "I knew you'd come around!"

He hadn't planned on starting his search at Deacon's wedding. Sutton was a friend of Dahlia's, and Deacon didn't like her. Why would she be there? But Dahlia would be, and if anyone would know the deal with Sutton, it was her. Maybe the guy at the gallery really *was* a relative.

Half an hour before the service was scheduled to start, Max heard music coming from the beach. He recognized Emmett's voice—they must have been warming up—and decided he had to congratulate him on his single that was getting a lot of buzz. Tucking his hands in his pockets, he walked the path to the beach paying more attention to the landscape than the woman walking toward him.

"Jacob!" she said as he passed her. It took him a second to realize that she was talking to him. When he looked up, he recognized her right away.

"Hi Dahlia." He didn't bother telling her his name was Jake, but that she should call him Max. He'd told her that. Told her at least a thousand times.

"I'm so happy to see you," she squealed and wrapped her arms around him, squeezing him tight.

She'd never hugged him before. Ever. But before he could get over his shock, she grabbed his hand and pulled him toward the beach. "I know someone else who's going to be even happier to see you!"

Her long skirt billowed in the wind, and he had a hard time keeping up with her. "She's been asking about you for months."

Max slowed their pace. "Dahlia, wait." He had a feeling he knew who Dahlia was talking about. If he was going to face Sutton, he had to know just how excited he was allowed to be. "I saw Sutton with someone. At her gallery show. A man."

Dahlia stopped. Her eyebrows knit together, then slowly unwound as her lips spread into a smile. "You mean Seth? That's her brother!"

Her brother? He'd spent the last six weeks agonizing over seeing Sutton with another man, and it was her brother? He felt equal parts stupid and relieved. Before he could say or feel anything else, Dahlia yanked his hand, and they practically ran the last hundred yards to where the path opened up to the beach.

Chairs lined an aisle leading to a simple wedding arch surrounded by palm trees. Emmett was singing a song Max hadn't heard before while a cellist accompanied him, but he and Dahlia ran past them. He could see where they were going now.

He could see who they were going *to.*

Deacon and Lily were on the beach just past the wedding set-up, posing for pictures. Max's eyes moved from the couple to the photographer, but his view was blocked by palm trees. His feet, in the meantime, threatened to stop, like they wanted to keep him from running into disappointment. He stumbled in the sand, almost falling, at the same time the photographer stepped from behind the tree.

Sutton.

He should have known from his first search that he'd find her in the place he least expected, but he still didn't trust he was seeing who he'd really, *really* hoped to see the moment Dahlia grabbed his hand.

"Is that—" Max started to ask, but Dahlia was two steps ahead.

"—Sutton!" she called to the photographer whose irritation at being interrupted quickly turned to surprise, followed by the smile Max had been waiting almost a year to see again.

It sent the same lightning-strike level charge through him he'd felt the first time he'd seen it. Seen *her*. She waited for him and Dahlia to reach her, grinning and biting the corner of her lip in a way that made it unlikely he'd ever forgive himself for sneaking out of the gallery six weeks before. He should have listened to Monica, and if, by some miracle, he and Sutton ended up together, it'd be worth all the "I told you so's" Monica would send his way.

"Sutton," Dahlia said as she planted Max in front of her, "meet Max."

She'd finally gotten his name right, and he didn't care. He looked in Sutton's eyes and forgot about Dahlia and everything else that wasn't Sutton.

"I finally found you," he said, breathless.

Sutton handed her camera to Dahlia and stepped toward

Max. She glanced at his hand, then latched one finger around his pinky.

He stepped closer.

When she didn't pull away, he took her entire hand in his, and she wrapped their hands around her waist. With his other arm, he drew her even closer. Close enough he could feel her breath hitch.

She let go of his hand and her arms went around his neck, her fingers resting lightly on his hairline, and her lips found his.

Their first kiss was tentative and gentle, a toe-dip in the ocean to test the temperature. The second kiss waded into deeper water, exploring new territory, leaving Max with the feeling of trying to stay upright in the Atlantic with waves shifting sand under his feet.

The third kiss was a dive into those sand-shifting waves, a letting go of any attempt to fight the force that had pulled them together, despite everything that had kept them apart.

Sutton paused long enough to press her forehead to his and whispered words he'd never forget.

You don't know how happy I am to be found.

About the Authors
Brittany Larsen

Brittany Larsen has written, four contemporary novels based Jane Austen classics. The first was self-published, while Pride & Politics and Sense & Second Chances were both released by Covenant Communications. Her fourth, and last, Jane Austen retelling (unless she can't resist doing another) will be released by Covenant in July 2018. She hopes someday to be the first author ever to come up with a totally original idea. Until then, she'll be culling the classics for her next story. To learn more about Brittany, find her online at brittanylarsen.net.

Becca Wilhite

Becca Wilhite loves books - reading and writing them. By day, she teaches high school English. By night, she's a wife and a mom. In between, she squeezes in wordplay. To learn more about Becca, visit her online at beccawilhite.com.

Jenny Proctor

Jenny Proctor was born in the mountains of Western North Carolina, a place she still considers one of the loveliest on earth. She and her husband currently reside in the Charleston, SC area and stay busy keeping up with six children and a growing assortment of pets. She loves to hike with her family and spend time outdoors, but she also adores lounging around her home, reading great books or watching great movies and, when she's lucky, eating delicious food she doesn't have to prepare herself. Jenny has four published novels and several novellas. Her clean Romantic Comedy LOVE AT FIRST NOTE was a 2016 Whitney Award Winner in the Contemporary Romance category. To learn more about Jenny, visit her online at jennyproctor.com.

Melanie Jacobson

Melanie Bennett Jacobson is an avid reader, amateur cook, and champion shopper. She consumes astonishing amounts of chocolate, chick flicks, and romance novels. She grew up in Louisiana and now lives in Southern California with her family and a series of doomed houseplants. She holds an MFA in Writing for Children and Young Adults from the Vermont College of Fine Arts and is the author of nine romantic comedies and several novellas. Find Melanie online at melaniejacobson.net.

Made in the USA
San Bernardino, CA
05 November 2018